HUMANITY'S DESPERATE BID FOR A NEW HOME

The immense arkship *Odyssey* and its ten thousand hibernating settlers have left behind a dying Earth—journeying for fifty years to the nearest star and its lone habitable planet, Proxima b.

This new home for humanity is perpetually bombarded by deadly solar flares on its dayside, while the icy wasteland on its opposite hemisphere freezes in endless darkness.

When the battered *Odyssey* arrives, its crew discovers the automated radiation shield has failed. Something appears to have damaged or perhaps even sabotaged their technology on a world where humans have yet to set foot.

Astronaut Darcy Clarke, a young pilot born aboard the *Odyssey*, teams up with recently awakened engineer Tanya Baxter to repair the failing shield in hopes of allowing the colonists to land before their vessel falls apart.

Waiting for the two explorers on the surface of Proxima b is the geoglyph—a continent-sized landform that resembles a giant metallic work of art.

Is it a massive ore deposit, an alien message, or something far stranger and vastly more dangerous? Or perhaps even sabotage for their technology on a world where humans have yet to set foot?

PERSEPHONE

PERSEPHONE

KEVIN J. ANDERSON

JEFFREY MORRIS

WFP
WordFire Press

EBook ISBN: 978-1-68057-620-7
Trade Paperback ISBN: 978-1-68057-621-4
Dust Jacket Hardcover ISBN: 978-1-68057-622-1
Special Edition Leatherette Hardcover ISBN: 978-1-68057-623-8
Audiobook ISBN: 978-1-68057-624-5
Cover art by Dylan Hansen
Art Director, Jeffrey Morris
Cover design by Frederick Haugen
Vellum layout by CJ Anaya
Published by
WordFire Press, LLC
PO Box 1840
Monument CO 80132
Kevin J. Anderson & Rebecca Moesta, Publishers
WordFire Press eBook 2024

Printed in the USA
Join our WordFire Press Readers Group for
sneak previews, updates, new projects, and giveaways.
Sign up at wordfirepress.com

This novel is inspired by the original screenplay for the forthcoming motion picture *Persephone*, written (and to be directed) by Jeffrey Morris.

To Jorge Heredia, who is always there to provide vision, support, encouragement, and even a good laugh exactly when needed. We couldn't have made this interstellar journey without you.

—Kevin J. Anderson and Jeffrey Morris

CHAPTER 1

The giant arkship hurtled into the Alpha Centauri system, carrying ten thousand hibernating colonists. The *only* colonists—the last survivors of the human race.

A pair of nearby bright stars, still more than a tenth of a light-year away, each looked like Earth's almost forgotten Sun. Closer still hung the small red dwarf, Proxima Centauri, and its lone habitable planet, Proxima b—their destination.

Damaged and pockmarked by numerous meteor hits over the decades, the *Odyssey* was at the end of its fifty-year journey, more than four light-years from Earth.

Home sweet home, Darcy Clarke thought. *At last.*

If these last survivors could not establish a sustainable presence here, then the human race was toast. Darcy and her companions, fellow mission specialists, had a job to do before the rest of the colonists awakened.

She had never seen Earth, had not set foot on any planet in her entire life. She'd been born on the *Odyssey* just after the halfway point, twenty-five years ago, but she knew full well what was at stake. Captain Faraday had spent untold hours making sure that Darcy remembered the importance of Earth and all that had been lost in the environmental catastrophe. When they were young, Darcy, Kyle, and Corey had watched videos of the roiling, dying planet as the arkship sailed off to a new hope, and the captain even played the horrific transmissions of the unexpected nuclear exchange, the swift mortal wound....

Darcy's own father had also hammered the memory of Earth into her in an even more personal way, showing pictures of places he'd lived, where he'd met her mother, the restaurant where they'd gotten married. He and the captain made sure that Darcy, Kyle, and Corey understood the desperate Hail Mary this mission represented.

A century earlier, a fast probe called the *Breakthrough Starshot* had been sent to the Proxima star system for a quick look, and the results had shown a planet capable of supporting terrestrial life. The *Starshot*'s readings showed that Proxima b was tidally locked, the same hemisphere always facing the red sun, but it did have a breathable atmosphere and liquid water, despite heavy radiation from frequent stellar flares.

Conditions would be difficult, but better than any other planet in the old solar system—and certainly more hospitable than Earth would be in a few decades as it spiraled into irreversible ecological catastrophe. Based on that survey, humanity had decided to take this chance, to hope the new planet would sustain them.

On the strength of that hope, the *Odyssey* and two planned sister colony ships had been built. That desperate gamble had taken place long before Darcy was born, back when her parents were young. Now, after the fifty-year journey, it was her part to help get the new colony on Proxima b ready before the thousands of hibernating colonists were thawed.

And timing was tight.

The pre-fab colony should have been ready and waiting for a ship full of colonists. But it wasn't.

A half century earlier, before the *Odyssey* departed from Earth, a separate automated mission—*Forerunner*—had been launched at high acceleration toward the Alpha Centauri system. *Forerunner* arrived years before *Odyssey*, and its limited AI systems had deployed countless habitation modules across the dayside continent, as well as nutritional algae farms, a power grid, and most importantly a widespread network of shield-generator nodes that would project a protective field, like a safe zone, to keep humans alive under the constant wash of radiation. The automated settlement was supposed to be ready and waiting for the colonists when the *Odyssey* came into the system at full deceleration.

But as the arkship approached, Captain Faraday and the skeleton crew had discovered that numerous nodes had gone offline and the extensive energy shield was failing.

Four members of the crew would have to make all necessary fixes while the *Odyssey* shot past the planet and went through an extreme braking maneuver around the red dwarf.

Darcy sat at the piloting controls in the scout ship AeroFox Two—tense, nervous, excited, and absolutely ready to detach from the *Odyssey* and launch for the planet. She, Kyle Dyson, and Jim Corey had spent a year in simulators training for this.

In a nearby docking clamp, inside the larger workhorse AstroBug, Jim Corey was also ready to launch with a reawakened engineer, an expert in the shield network.

Darcy clicked her comm and glanced sideways at the countdown clock. "Hey Corey, you ready to go?"

"I was born for this, Darce." His handsome face grinned at her on the AeroFox's comm screen.

"I thought you were an accident."

"I made up for it with rigorous training."

She smiled back at him as she scanned the system checks on her pilot panels. "Kyle and I still have the nicer ship."

Her AeroFox was an angular reconnaissance craft designed to fly in space as well as in an atmosphere, while Corey's AstroBug was larger and more powerful, but clunkier, in her opinion. Both ships looked like tiny toys stuck on the hull of the enormous arkship, ready to be deployed as the *Odyssey* streaked past the planet.

"You ready, Kyle?" She looked over at gangly Kyle Dyson, the third of the three misfit children who had been born during the *Odyssey*'s voyage. Strapped in at the AeroFox's science station, the dark-skinned young man seemed even more nervous than she was. Darcy had known Kyle all his life—literally. She knew how he thought, how he reacted. He was smart, eccentric, and awkward, and sometimes needed reassurance.

"Sure. What could go wrong?" he asked, then chuckled at his own joke.

She tried to boost his confidence. "Don't worry—we got this."

Fidgeting in his chair, the young man played with a small gyroscope, a precious antique that someone had brought along on the *Odyssey*. He spun the toy in the air, trying to distract himself, but he gave up. "Yes, we got this. Don't we, O?"

He took more comfort from the yellow infinity symbol glowing on his main screen, the avatar of his AI companion.

Omni spoke in a warm, familiar voice. "Have no fear, Kyle. We have all trained for more than two hundred hours in the simulator. I am watching over all AeroFox systems for you. We will accomplish our goals and repair the shield network in time."

"I know we will, O." He fiddled with the toy gyroscope again. "But it's only natural to feel a little anxiety when the whole human race is depending on you."

Darcy and Kyle both wore gold-and-black flight suits. She was fit, attractive (Jim Corey said so, though he didn't have a lot of points of comparison), with close-cropped dark hair, large brown eyes, a small chin, a hard smile ... or a soft one, depending on her mood.

Kyle and Corey were both a year younger than Darcy—born before Captain Faraday had cracked down on any new births. The arkship's resources were limited, especially after all the disastrous breakdowns in the last decade. But once they settled on Proxima b, there would be plenty of room and resources—provided Darcy and her team could fix the solar-flare shield.

The countdown continued. One minute left.

For her own reassurance, she glanced at the photo she had affixed to the control panel—her mother and father, beaming with pride and possibilities, next to four-year-old Darcy in the *Odyssey*'s hibernation section. They were laughing over something that nobody remembered anymore. It was one of the only images she had of the three of them together. She touched the photo, then turned back to the controls.

"Showtime, guys. You ready to go, Corey? Should we race to the planet?"

The young man's image appeared on the comm screen. "It's not a race—it's a mission." Corey was easy, calm, but he knew how to tease her. "But you bet I'm ready to go. AstroBug checks out."

His face was lean and strong, with high cheekbones. Corey's heritage was called "Native American" in the ship records, although that had lost any meaning once they'd left the remnants of America, and the remnants of Earth. She had been looking at Jim Corey ever since he'd been born, and she still hadn't grown tired of his face.

"We have to time this right," Corey said. "The *Odyssey* is still going way too fast."

As the countdown for deployment reached zero, she returned her focus to where it belonged. As the *Odyssey* raced past the planet, they had to launch at just the right moment. Even if all the systems were automated and each ship had its own independent Omni AI, Darcy liked to stay in the loop. "Here we go. Captain Faraday says this is like jumping from a moving train."

"Whatever that means," Kyle joked from the science station.

The clamps disengaged with a loud, resonating thump, and then the AeroFox was loose from the arkship's hull. The AstroBug also dropped away, heading out as the giant dumbbell-shaped ship continued toward the red star, still decelerating.

From here, mottled Proxima b was a crescent, showing mostly its night side, veiled with an atmosphere and adorned with dancing greenish aurora lights at the poles. Its orbit was in the red dwarf's life zone, with liquid water on its surface and an atmosphere that people could almost breathe. But one side—the colony side—perpetually faced the angry sun, while the night side remained cold and dark, facing the stars from which the humans had come.

Even after twenty-five years of deceleration, the giant arkship had not shed enough velocity to safely enter planetary orbit. So, the *Odyssey* would have to swing around Proxima and use its gravity to slow down, then lumber back to the planet, slow and exhausted.

In the meantime, Darcy, Corey, and Kyle, along with Engineer Tanya Baxter, would have only a few days to fix the shield network and any other glitches, prepare the hab modules, deploy more comm satellites, and roll out the welcome mat for the last survivors of the human race. The automated colony needed some TLC before it was ready to receive permanent residents.

As Darcy watched the *Odyssey* dwindle in the distance, she felt more alone and isolated than she'd been her entire life....

First things first. She had been dreaming about this planet ever since she could remember. Darcy was in the right place, on the right mission, doing what she was supposed to do. Adrenaline pumped through her veins, and she realized she was grinning like a fool.

Kyle flashed her a mischievous smile. "Time to make it official. If this is going to be our new home, 'Proxima b' just won't do for a name. I think we should call it *Persephone*."

Though she had to concentrate on her controls, she spared him a glance. "Persephone?"

Kyle seemed proud of himself ... or full of himself. "The name sounds better, and you know it. O and I talked about it a lot."

"I agree with Kyle," said Omni's simulated voice. "If my opinion matters."

Darcy snorted. "You talk too much to your AI."

The two spacecraft separated, each heading off to different missions. As Corey guided the saucer-shaped AstroBug down toward the planet, Darcy placed the Fox in a high synchronous orbit above the mysterious night side. Her job was to deploy three new communication satellites.

An incoming transmission appeared on her main screen, flagged with the *Odyssey*'s mission patch, the long dumbbell-shaped vessel riding a pillar of fire on a field of stars. By now, the colony ship had dwindled to a bright dot among the stars, but Captain Gwen Faraday's image appeared on the cockpit screens. The old woman had been like a den mother to them all their lives. Faraday was in her early seventies with dark skin, intelligent eyes, and a warm, maternal smile. But she also carried a sense of weariness—which was not surprising, since she had just crossed more than four light-years of empty space, and she had never expected to be on duty most of that time.

Faraday sat at her console on the *Odyssey* bridge, while several members of the skeleton crew worked at stations behind her. "Sorry I wasn't able to see you all off in person. We had another problem down in engineering, but the situation is under control. *Odyssey* will complete our final braking maneuver around Proxima Centauri in about forty-three hours. Because we're passing so close to the star, we won't be able to send or receive transmissions for at least a day and a half. You're on your own for the time being."

Her maternal smile took the place of the worried concern. "Afterward, assuming we haven't been cooked by the star, we'll start thawing the popsicles as soon as we clear the photosphere. We need to begin offloading them as soon as we get into stable planetary orbit, in order to reduce the strain on our systems."

Darcy found the captain's voice soothing, as she always did, but the urgency concerned her.

"We know what's at stake, Captain," Corey transmitted.

Strapped in his seat, Kyle spoke quietly, "I would rather have had a pep talk."

Faraday continued, "I know you know the plan, but humor me while I go over it again. Darcy and Kyle, your job is simple in the

AeroFox. Deploy the three comm satellites, but hang back and observe, provide support to the AstroBug as needed.

"Corey, you and Engineer Baxter fix the malfunctioning shield nodes. Rely on her expertise. She knows more than anyone about the shield—that's why we pulled her out of hibernation. She invented the thing.

"And Engineer Baxter—I know the past few days haven't been easy for you. You were revived much earlier than we planned, but we need you."

Darcy felt the gulf growing every second as the arkship raced away. "We know our jobs, Captain. You can count on us."

The captain continued, "You all trained hard for this mission, and I know what you're capable of. You can handle it on your own. Good luck, guys. Faraday out."

CHAPTER 2

Though relaxed on the AstroBug's flight deck, Jim Corey kept his senses on high alert. This was not a simulation—for the first time in his life. No human had ever been to this untouched planet before.

After Faraday signed off, Corey heard a snort from the other cockpit seat. "They're *colonists*, not popsicles!" Dr. Tanya Baxter frowned. "You know how many times I've been called that since I woke up?"

Corey tried to downplay her irritation. "That nickname's been used by the skeleton crew shifts, up and down, for the past fifty years. We don't mean anything by it. We'll help you fit in soon enough, don't worry."

An unexpected, extravagant yawn deflated Baxter's annoyance. "I know it's nothing personal. I just feel like crap after waking up from hibernation, like a damned hangover." The systems engineer was in her early fifties—old enough to be Corey's own mother, whom he'd never known. Her long dark hair was rumpled, and she had shadows under her eyes from the years-long sleep.

With a sigh, Baxter turned to the secondary panel and called up a display. Corey watched her pluck at the stimsuit unitard that covered most of her lean body, and he could tell it bothered her.

Because she had so recently emerged from the hibernation pod, the stimsuit monitored her vitals, and the network of electrodes stimulated her sluggish muscles and circulatory system. Corey was glad he'd never needed to spend a stint in hibernation.

Baxter cracked her knuckles, and she seemed to want to get down to business. "The captain woke me up for a reason, kid, and that shield network is my baby. Let's see about getting the systems fixed. You can act as my apprentice. Maybe it's as simple as replacing a blown fuse on a few transmitting towers."

As the AstroBug flew high above the planet, Corey raised his eyebrows. "Solutions usually aren't that simple."

"No, they aren't. You just get us over the dayside so I can have a look at what's going on down there."

At her station she called up the most recent shield diagnostic. Proxima b would have been a nice place, except that the red star threw frequent tantrums, cooking the day hemisphere with solar flares. Before a human colony could survive there, the radiation shields had to be in place and functioning.

After being dropped to the surface and set up automatically, the whole system should have been working just fine. Once *Forerunner* had deployed all the components, the shield network had functioned just fine for two years. But now, as the *Odyssey* closed in, it began to fail....

Baxter's brow furrowed as she studied the diagram showing the hundreds of nodes across the sunlit hemisphere. The projected shield interacted with the planet's magnetic field to filter out the harsh solar radiation. The protective bubble should have covered most of the hemisphere, but now dozens of the nodes were dark. By her design, all the towers had to interact to form a large electromagnetic web, or else the place would remain uninhabitable.

That would leave a lot of empty hab modules and far too many disappointed "popsicles."

Baxter clucked her tongue. "Two more towers are down since I woke up—thirty-four total! But nothing in the diagnostics explains why they're malfunctioning." She called up a scrolling column of data, then sighed.

"We'll try to do a remote fix first," Corey said. He knew there was no room for error, after what the captain had confided in him.

Cutting across the shadowed nightside hemisphere, he took the AstroBug down to a lower orbit. High above them, Darcy and Kyle worked on their own mission. From an external camera he could see the first of three trapezoid-shaped communications satellites being released from the AeroFox. The satellite rolled gracefully out of the external cradle on the scout ship's hull, moving into position in synchronous orbit.

Darcy transmitted, "Sat-A is deployed over the night side. One down, two to go. Corey, test the link when ready."

He traced his fingers across the panel's control patterns, sent out a ping, watched the response. "Copy. Sat-A's signal is loud and clear."

A set of solar panels unfurled from the package, then thrusters fired to rotate the communications satellite to face the red star. The sat would maintain its position above the planet's night side as an integral part of the colony's new comm network.

Darcy transmitted, "Kyle and I will deploy the other two satellites, while you and that engineer have all the fun."

"I've got a name, kid," Baxter muttered.

"Fun?" Corey chuckled. "Not sure I'd call this mission fun. What if I have to land and give one of the transmitting towers a swift, hard kick?"

"You better not land without me, Jim Corey," Darcy warned. "I called dibs years ago. First footprint on the new planet!"

"You're cute, Darce. That's why I love you."

"Love you, too. But I still want to be the first person on Proxima b."

"Persephone," Kyle interjected, off screen.

Corey looked down at the dark, mysterious planet as he flew toward the bright sunlit side. "Keep dreaming, babe. I was born for this."

Darcy's dark eyes glittered. "So was I ... and I was born first!"

The AstroBug crossed the terminator into daylight, still in high orbit but descending. The glorious red sun rose in front of them, and the alien panorama spread out, a stark painting of browns and tans, speckled with lakes and larger bodies of water. Though he had seen many images of Earth, Corey didn't know first-hand what a planet was supposed to look like. This one would have to do.

But the "anomaly" was what took his breath away, an amazing, impossible pattern drawn across the barren landscape, like a humongous tattoo.

"The pictures didn't prepare me for that," Baxter blurted out. "Holy shit, that's huge—and amazing!"

"Now I see why Kyle was so fixated on it," Corey muttered. "He wasn't exaggerating."

The enormous geoglyph was a bizarre pattern of semi-straight lines and angles in an incomprehensible design across the sunlit hemisphere. He had heard Kyle's eccentric theories for the past two years, but now even he had to admit that the pattern couldn't possibly be natural.

CHAPTER 3

From the command bridge of the *Odyssey*, Captain Gwen Faraday looked ahead, always looking ahead. That was how she had brought ten thousand hibernating passengers across more than four light-years.

Though Proxima Centauri was only a red dwarf, it looked like a tumultuous cauldron as the arkship approached. The dumbbell-shaped vessel flew straight toward the star in a tight, dangerous braking maneuver. It was the only way she could slow the vessel enough not to overshoot their destination. Faraday and her minimal crew knew how truly dangerous it would be, though, and what damage the aging *Odyssey* might suffer during the closest approach.

Due to scarce resources, only fifteen people were awake during the final months of the voyage. They took care of the hibernating colonists while using band aids, duct tape, chewing gum, and sheer willpower to hold the arkship together and bring it across the finish line.

These crewmembers were among the very few who knew the truly desperate condition of the ship, but they kept mum. Faraday preferred hope and confidence instead of despair. If not for rosy optimism, this entire mission would never have happened in the first place. And the human race would be extinct.

Faraday felt tired and old—likely because she *was* tired and old. Under the heavy deceleration now, each movement felt like more of a chore than it should have been.

Faraday still remembered leaving Earth half a century ago. She had only expected to be awake for about a third of the journey, and by the time the *Odyssey* arrived at its new home, she should have been fresher, stronger, and younger than this. But ... accidents happened. Despite all the planning of Earth's greatest scientists and engineers, not everything turned out as expected. It never did.

Standing at the broad viewing window, she watched flares rising up from the orange-red star, myriad sunspots silhouetted against nuclear fire. She braced herself for the even more extreme deceleration that was soon to come. They would come within grazing distance of hell itself.

Long ago, the *Odyssey* had left Earth with high hopes and determination. Based on what the *Breakthrough Starshot* probe had shown, Proxima b would be a new chance and a new home. Alpha Centauri was the closest star system to Earth, but the enormity of the fifty-year voyage hadn't really sunk in. Most of the colonists would sleep throughout the journey anyway.

The *Odyssey* was not supposed to be the only giant vessel to escape the Earth's climate collapse. As the end drew nearer, the orbital construction yards had been a flurry of activity using materials extracted from the asteroid belt, metals and ceramics, enormous girders, hull plates, all to build a mammoth arkship along an axis: one end with a bank of powerful engines, then a smaller central habitation ring with greenhouses, quarters, and bridge deck rotating in the middle of the ship.

The front section of the dumbbell, though, was the heart of the mission—a heavily shielded disk loaded with ten thousand hibernating colonists. Row after row of pods, sleeping ambassadors for humanity: the best engineers, scientists, architects, biologists, historians, artists, leaders and visionaries—people with every skill needed to build a new home on Proxima b.

But the *Odyssey* was only the first of the three great arkships. Construction was well under way on two other large colony vessels, the *Valkyrie* and the *Phoenix*. With the growing turbulence and disasters on the surface, everyone could see that Earth was in its death throes, and so the nations and corporations worked together.

Faraday remembered looking down on the climate-ravaged planet from the orbital construction site. Recent generations—including her own—had done more damage in mere decades than nature could have caused over millennia. Once the ecosphere reached the tipping point of the greenhouse effect, Earth had spun swiftly out of control: floods, wildfires, dust storms, and continent-sized hurricanes. Before long, the planet would become another Venus, and the human race couldn't outrun the cataclysm. Some of the boldest or wealthiest futurists had tried to create sanctuaries or private redoubts on the Moon, and then a disastrous colonization attempt on Mars had broken the heart of humanity.

The people of Earth had to look elsewhere for a real second home.

The three enormous arks were the largest space construction projects ever attempted. Faraday had been on the new *Odyssey* command deck when she received word that her ship was ready for departure two months ahead of schedule. A remarkable feat. The *Valkyrie* was also nearly finished, undergoing final inspections and shakedowns as thousands of colonists were loaded aboard and placed into hibernation.

From the bridge, Faraday had looked out at the graceful lines and the beautiful *Valkyrie* in spacedock nearby. She felt a wistful pang. The *Valkyrie*'s first-shift captain was also the love of her life, Michio Sakamoto. For years, their relationship was discreet and utterly professional. She and Michio had planned a long future together—but not until they reached their new home.

Once the *Odyssey*'s big fusion engines fired, she had turned her dreams toward Proxima b ...

Faraday was the first of the *Odyssey*'s three shift captains, the one who would stay awake for the initial launch out of the solar system. Just before departure, she went to the hibernation deck to observe her fellow captains, Neil Andolino and Sanjay Premanik, who were already slumbering away in their pods. Faraday would find out for herself what it felt like in five years when she took her shift down.

Right now, she was sure Michio would be thinking of her over on the *Valkyrie.* Two months behind *Odyssey*'s schedule, he had only begun the process of loading thousands of people into their hibernation pods as a constant stream of shuttles came up from Earth....

When all the popsicles were down, leaving only a hundred awake to serve on the crew, the ship had seemed so quiet—until the engines ignited, driving the huge vessel out of Earth orbit, beyond the Moon, crawling toward the edge of the solar system and the great crossing. Both the *Valkyrie* and the *Phoenix* were on schedule and would follow as soon as they were completed.

Faraday barely had time to settle into the routine, though, before disaster struck. Under constant thrust, the *Odyssey* had only just reached the orbit of Neptune when the flashpoint occurred on Earth—and all communications were lost.

Nobody really knew what had happened back there. From what Faraday could tell, a sudden and dramatic nuclear exchange took place, countless warheads bursting in a devastating electromagnetic pulse. And Earth fell completely silent, presumed dead.

No further word came from the *Valkyrie* or the *Phoenix.* Captain Sakamoto never replied to her urgent transmissions. The comm systems offered only the silence of space and despair.

But there could be no turning back. The *Odyssey* was on her way to the Alpha Centauri system. Now every crewmember knew that this ship carried the last survivors of the human race.

Now, after the long voyage, Faraday watched ruddy Proxima Centauri ahead of them and decided she'd had more than enough time for cathartic reminiscing.

The automated Forerunner mission had sent their pre-made colony ahead, countless aeroshell-encased modules that included hab modules, heavy machinery, packaged supplies, and all the equipment a full-fledged colony would need. Everything should have been ready and waiting—but now significant glitches had caused the failure of the shield network. Faraday's "squad" would have to fix it in time.

Tanya Baxter was the best expert for the job. And she was proud of Darcy, Corey, and Kyle. She had watched and raised the three unexpected children throughout their lives, and she had instilled in them the importance of the mission. They had all the skills they would need.

Now staring out the polarized bridge window at the thrashing red dwarf, she could feel the arkship vibrating. Quaking with fear? Proxima's heavy gravity already had them in its grasp.

Faraday looked at the countdown clock. After fifty years it had come to this.

"Hold together for me," she whispered. "Just a little bit longer."

CHAPTER 4

A s the AeroFox moved into position to deploy the next geosynchronous comm satellite over the planet's dayside, Kyle Dyson put away his toy gyroscope in favor of gawking out the window. He and his Omni companion had been waiting years for this. At last he was seeing the mysterious geoglyph with his own eyes.

Ever since the first blurry images had been transmitted from *Forerunner* two years earlier, Kyle had been fascinated by the strange surface patterns, bizarre formations thousands of kilometers in breadth. No matter what the readings said, all those straight lines *couldn't* be some natural occurrence, a freak of nature. Kyle knew it had to be something more. Space graffiti from alien hooligans? Even that suggestion led to unsettling conclusions.

Now he shifted away from the view out the window and turned to the higher-res camera images. "This is a lot better than seeing blurry pictures through a telescope. That was getting old."

"I did enhance those images as much as I could, Kyle," Omni broke in, sounding hurt.

In dim and private places aboard the *Odyssey*, Kyle and his AI friend had spent endless hours speculating with each other, proposing theories about the strange planetary markings. "It wasn't a criticism, O."

At the Fox's controls, Darcy concentrated on deploying the next satellite. "There'll be time for sightseeing later, Kyle."

Then Jim Corey transmitted from the AstroBug. "Kyle, that thing is amazing. Now that you see it for yourself, what do you think, buddy?"

Kyle felt his cheeks grow warm. "Omni and I already shared a bunch of ideas with the crew, but nobody seemed interested."

During the past two years on approach, Kyle had showed the images to the handful of workers out of hibernation, speculating that the markings were vast alien highway networks or canal systems or maybe even a celestial circuit board. Darcy and Corey had always been amused by his crackpot ideas, though Captain Faraday herself had been noncommittal.

Omni was a much more receptive audience, so Kyle and the AI had studied each new picture the *Forerunner* beamed back, and then a year later the arkship was close enough that they could use high-powered telescopes to resolve clear images—and the prominent geoglyph was awe-inspiring. Now, seeing the real thing was beyond his wildest expectations.

He cleared his throat before he answered Corey on the comm. "Could be lots of things. Maybe a gigantic Welcome sign, or maybe it means Keep Out."

"Great," Darcy said. "Whatever it is, they're about to have new neighbors."

For the past two years, in anticipation, he and his Omni had combed through the *Odyssey*'s library files for reports of any similar gigantic markings. Kyle had been amazed to learn of the bizarre patterns across the Nazca Desert in Peru—hundreds of incredibly straight lines, complex representations of spiders, monkeys, jaguars, and hummingbirds that were many kilometers long. Some eccentric theories even suggested that ancient astronauts had visited Earth.

When he looked at the bold circuit-like pattern on

Persephone, he had to wonder if ancient astronauts had come here as well, leaving some secret code for later visitors to unravel?

But as Kyle had grown more convinced of an alien explanation, Omni told a cautionary tale of the astronomer Percival Lowell at the end of the 19th century. Using a large refractor telescope—an instrument vastly inferior to what Kyle used to study Persephone—Lowell had imagined an intricate network of canals built on Mars by an alien civilization. Lowell had published his maps and sketches, developed the poignant story of a dying Martian civilization, and his stories enthralled the public … only to be entirely debunked by higher-resolution telescopes and later probes.

Kyle took the warning from his AI friend and waited to see further proof. But now …

The AstroBug was in a much lower orbit far beneath them. Corey transmitted, "Nature does strange things, Kyle. Those could just be fractures along straight fault lines, filled with upwelling ores."

"Seriously?" Kyle said. "Those metal lines have existed next to volcanoes for eons, with constant seismic activity, and yet the geoglyph markings are still straight and totally free of ash. What would cause that?"

Omni's calm, authoritative voice spoke from behind the infinity symbol on the AeroFox screen. "The initial *Forerunner* landers concluded that the formations were statically charged veins of ore welling up from deep underground. Hence, the lack of dust."

Kyle scoffed. "We'll know as soon as we can see it for ourselves."

Darcy was more focused on deploying the second satellite. The boxy object drifted away from the AeroFox and unfurled its solar arrays. "Satellite-B in position and functioning. Check pingback before I launch the third sat."

Corey sent a test signal from the AstroBug, and Darcy logged the response.

Still focused on the controls, she said to Kyle, "Whatever that geoglyph is, think of all those lines of exposed metal for the taking when we build our colony. There's enough copper in those veins to last us centuries." She traced readings as she prepared to launch the third comm satellite from its cradle. "Who cares what miracle put it there?"

Kyle didn't hide his exasperation. "*We* should care! The geoglyph is so interesting, so ... profound! Why not do a little science before we dig up the place?"

Darcy wasn't bothered at all. "We can snap a few mining surveys to determine the best places to excavate. That's science."

Kyle knew she would never understand. Darcy had tunnel vision.

"We'll have time for discretionary stuff once we get the shield network fixed," Corey said. "First priority. If our colonists can't move into all those hab modules, then nothing else matters."

"It matters to me ..." Kyle muttered. "The geoglyph might not have as much time as you think. The patterns diminished dramatically since *Forerunner* installed the shield network." From successive images over the past two years, Kyle had watched the geoglyph change visibly. Its coloration grew duller and its extent contracted, leaving scars instead of bold lines.

Kyle was firm as he said, "Just look at it. You can't tell me you don't see planet-sized artwork down there! Some kind of message that we need to understand."

"Alien writing, plain as day." Darcy cracked her knuckles at her own controls. "It says *KILROY WAS HERE*."

Frowning, Kyle fidgeted with his gyroscope, trying to quell his annoyance. No matter what he said, Darcy never would take his theories seriously.

CHAPTER 5

W orking at her AstroBug station, Dr. Tanya Baxter tried to concentrate on the malfunctioning shield network, but she found herself fuming about things she shouldn't worry about. None of these three kids had ever experienced a hibernation hangover.

"Popsicles," she muttered out loud, to make sure Commander Corey heard her. After sleeping for decades, she was justified in being grumpy. "Don't be surprised if I come up with a nickname for you three kids, too—and I guarantee mine won't be as cute."

Corey smiled, unflappable. He was handsome, fresh, energetic, and half her age. "Fair enough."

Baxter stretched her limbs and cracked her neck. "Ugh, I feel like shit. I need rest, not that I haven't had enough already." She plucked at her clingy stimsuit, and the fabric snapped back, molding itself to her skin. She could feel the fiber mesh pulse and constrict as it worked on her body. "This thing isn't helping either. Constantly grabbing and squeezing."

The Bug's main Omni AI manifested as a blue infinity symbol on her screen as it spoke in a formal, computerized voice. "The stimsuit can be taxing as it rebuilds your muscles, Engineer Baxter. Do you need an adjustment to your medication to decrease your sensitivity? I can authorize it from the auto-dispensary."

"I just need more coffee, Omni." She levered herself out of her seat, went to the sleek wall panel, and snagged a disc-shaped decanter device connected by a thin tether. Detaching the Autobrew, she pressed the button, selected her beverage, and sipped from the mouthpiece. She closed her eyes as the strong, bitter liquid filled her mouth and her senses. "Ahhh, waking up from hibernation is always better after a cup of coffee. All right, Corey, let's figure out what's wrong with those shield transmitters so the new colony is ready when the ... popsicles arrive."

Corey flipped switches. "Realigning our trajectory so we can access the network and track down those glitches."

Omni chimed in, "My interface can tap into the primary shield node on the surface. I can communicate directly with the system."

Baxter called up the pattern of self-erected towers that she and her team had designed back on Earth. "Let's see what's going on. Omni, take it from the top."

The AI was persistent in its attempts to help. "Do you want me to summarize the automated Forerunner mission and describe the components that were delivered and set up by the caretaker AI? Once each of the two hundred shield-node packages struck the surface, the protective aeroshell folded back so the towers could erect themselves. And then—"

She cut off the Omni. "You're being too literal. I need you to review the current shield situation." She took another sip of the fresh coffee. Each swallow seemed to bring her more back to life.

"Sorry, Engineer Baxter. As the systems engineer, you are of course completely familiar with the design and setup of the shield network." The simulated voice sounded contrite. "This is a more recent recap. Once in place, the transmitters created the protective electromagnetic shield to block Proxima Centauri's flares. For twenty-four months, all elements functioned nominally, but then the nodes began to fail. At present, thirty-four of the towers are offline. Therefore, the shield barrier is only ten percent effective at protecting human life."

"In other words, useless—right when everybody is going to show up," Baxter grumbled. "The *Odyssey* is only a few days away. Rad-levels on the dayside are damn near off the scale. I guess the ship can remain in orbit until we can figure this out, and the hibernating colonists will just have to sleep a while longer."

In the nearby pilot seat, Corey looked at her with a strange expression. "That might not be an option."

"We didn't come this far to frantically cut corners when it matters most," she said. "I'm confident in my shield, but there must be fallback options in the overall mission plan." On the projected diagram, large red gaps stood out, a seemingly random spray of shield-node malfunctions. Baxter shook her head. "Because my whole design is interlinked with Proxima b's own magnetic field, when a node goes offline, it doesn't just create a gap in coverage—it affects the entire protective bubble."

Corey seemed determined. "We'll fix it."

Baxter rubbed her eyes as if that would dislodge the hibernation fuzz. She turned back to Omni's blue avatar. "What about the caretaker AI running the network down there? It's supposed to be independent and self-sufficient. Why didn't it activate the diagnostic-and-repair protocols?"

"It tried and failed, Engineer Baxter." The infinity symbol throbbed faintly on the screen. "I am not sure why."

It still seemed like a solvable engineering problem. "Isn't the caretaker AI another Omni? Can't you just connect with it and get all the data you need? Teamwork."

"My counterpart on the surface is a much more limited system than I am. That is why Captain Faraday sent us for real-time access and manual repairs if necessary."

Corey looked eager. "Ha! That means we're going to have to put footprints on the ground. My first time ever on a real planet!"

Baxter could not summon the same enthusiasm. "I hope we

don't have to land and poke around just yet. The ship's gravity was bad enough on my tired old muscles."

"Your body hasn't adjusted yet—especially not to one-point-two Gs. It's not the Earth gravity you're used to."

Baxter smirked. "It's been fifty years, kid. I'm not 'used to' anything. But I'm not a weakling either." As if to contradict her determination, the older woman rubbed her eyes and yawned again. "I'll put up with whatever, so long as we fix the shield network. Engineers are used to getting our hands dirty. But let's see what we can do remotely first. Omni, what are you waiting for?"

The blue infinity symbol glowed. "Excuse me, Engineer Baxter? Waiting for what?"

She pointed impatiently at the screen. "Run a full diagnostic! Connect with the other AI system and tell me what the problem is."

Omni brightened. "Oh! Yes, I am already on it, and also collaborating with Kyle Dyson and my counterpart on the AeroFox for additional input and analysis."

Baxter drained the rest of the coffee serving as she waited. "And I woke up for this ..." It was not at all when she had expected to find when she emerged from the hibernation pod....

She remembered the day, still groggy. The dreams in her head were a blank blur of memories and confusing thoughts, not surprising since she had kept her brain in a freezer for fifty years. Lying in the pod, she had blinked to clear her vision, and heard droning voices. It took her another few minutes to remember where she was.

Like so many nights in her previous life, especially toward the end after the bitter split with her husband, she had closed her eyes and wished it would all just go away, hoping she would wake up to a better day.

As she had finally focused on Captain Faraday's grim expression, Baxter instantly realized that this might not be the better day she had hoped for. The captain's face wore extra decades—hard decades, from the looks of it—and Baxter realized that a lot of time must have passed. The *Odyssey*'s three captains were supposed to take equal hibernation shifts, so that none of them stayed awake for more than a third of the voyage. Why had Faraday put on so many years?

"Are we there yet?" she had asked.

That brought a smile to Faraday's face. "Almost there." Then she grew more serious. "We had to wake you up a little early, Tanya, because we need your help. There are problems with the shield network on Proxima b, and we've got to fix it before we can revive the colonists. There isn't much time."

That cleared some of Baxter's residual daze. "How much time? How far are we?" She struggled to climb out of the confining pod, but everything around her started to swirl as if going down a drain.

Faraday placed a hand on her shoulder, eased her back down. "It's not a complete emergency yet, Tanya. Take a breath."

She'd gone through the waking process one step at a time. She sat on the edge of the pod with aching muscles, not yet ready to take her first step. After Faraday brought her an Autobrew and dispensed a fresh, hot coffee, Baxter thought she had reached paradise after all. She let out a long sigh, took another sip. "First coffee in half a century, and it tastes damn good."

After that, with the assistance of some *Odyssey* crew members, she made her way to temporary quarters in the habitation ring. She was shocked to learn that there were only fifteen people awake instead of the hundred who were supposed to be on shift. Baxter took her first shower in half a century, and she certainly loved the feel of warm water. Slowly, one millimeter and one minute at a time, she began to feel human again.

When the fog had cleared, she met with the captain and several on-call engineers, who briefed her on their imminent arrival in the Proxima system—and the unexpected failures in the protective shield vital to the colony.

The Forerunner mission had delivered the self-erecting

components on schedule, some assembly required. Unfortunately, as had happened with many "simple, out-of-the-box kits" that Baxter had purchased in her previous life, the pieces didn't always fit together as planned.

She nodded, seizing on the problem. "You were right to wake me up. I'll start analyzing with the information on hand and begin developing a plan." As the shield system's original designer, Baxter was the one who was supposed to fix everything.

Then she learned about the *Odyssey*'s numerous environmental breakdowns and the dwindling resources. The patches of airmoss on the ceiling and walls were now blotchy and pale instead of thriving green. Their air production was running out.

"You are just full of good news, aren't you?" she had said.

"There's more," Faraday said, then told her what had happened to the other two captains, and also about the three unexpected children born en route.

Captain Faraday insisted that the kids—who were now grown, in their twenties—were fully trained with the simulators and equipment, and they were the personnel best qualified to fly the first mission to the planet. And Baxter would go along with them to fix the shield network.

When she got to her feet from the briefing, she felt her wobbly legs. Seasick from the long hibernation and barely able to stand, Baxter did not feel ready to take on saving a colony.

In high orbit, Darcy acknowledged that the second comm satellite was deployed and functioning over the dayside. She contacted Corey and shared her satisfied smile on the screen. "Two of three comm sats in place and functioning. AeroFox is getting into position to deploy the last one. We're right overhead—I'm waving at you." She paused. "Don't forget ... I love you."

On the screen, she saw the embarrassed flush on his face, and he glanced away. "Love you too, Darce. AstroBug out." Even though they'd already spent their entire lives together, he remained shy about public displays of affection.

Instead, Darcy glanced at the old family photo by her piloting controls, the little girl standing between her parents, her barely remembered mother and her dear father, whom she had not seen in years. He'd gone back into hibernation when Darcy was sixteen.

Feeling wistful, she spoke aloud for the benefit of Kyle, who was engrossed in a high-res survey of the geoglyph. "The captain will start waking the popsicles right after the braking maneuver on the other side of the sun. My dad will be one of the first to wake up. Can't wait to see him." She thought of the plans she and Corey had made while her father was sleeping; the two of them had been just teenagers when he'd gone back into the pod. She allowed herself a smile. "I wonder if he'll be upset that Corey and I are a couple."

Kyle absently played with his toy gyroscope. "I'm pretty sure he could see that coming. You two have been joined at the hip since we were kids. A match made in heaven ... or at least in interstellar space."

He teasingly pointed his finger to his mouth, pretending to gag.

"Oh, go play with your Omni," Darcy said, but she was smiling as she got back to business.

CHAPTER 6

After an entire life spent studying the data and images from Proxima b, Corey was aware of what the new planet would be like. He wasn't prone to wishful thinking. Not really. But he wasn't sure about the stark landscape below.

"It certainly doesn't look like Earth," Baxter mused from the console next to him, "but beggars can't be choosers."

As the AstroBug descended, Corey gazed wistfully at the terrain lit by the red sunlight. "I've never actually seen a planet before, not with my own eyes."

Baxter pulled a streak of dark hair away from her face. "Considering what Earth looked like in its last days, you weren't missing much. And by now Earth is far worse than what you see down there."

Corey set his jaw. "I still wish I could have seen it. It would have been even better if people hadn't ruined it for future generations."

"You'll get no argument from me, kid. We better take care of this new world. It's our second chance ... and our last chance." Baxter's expression was tightly focused. "Let's see what it'll take to reboot the whole shield network, so our people can live down there. The nearest tower is a couple hundred kilometers from the terminator line." She pursed her lips, scanning her screens. "I can't fix the thing until I figure out what's gone wrong."

Corey glanced at the AI avatar on the screen as he took the ship lower. "Omni, start doing your thing."

"What specifically is 'doing my thing,' Commander Corey?"

He was patient with the ship's AI, having grown up interacting with it on the *Odyssey*. Kyle's separate Omni clone, which he treated like an imaginary friend, had a quirkier personality than this one. "Please ping the automated network below and make contact with the caretaker AI that controls the shield web."

"It has been unresponsive so far, Commander Corey."

Baxter let out a salty laugh. "Sometimes people need to be shaken hard to wake up—just like I did when I came out of hibernation." Her voice grew more impatient. "If you can't link with the shield network, then we'll need to land and do some hands-on tweaking."

Corey began descending through the stratosphere. "I am a Go for that. I've already practiced my speech."

Baxter fought back a persistent yawn. "I thought Darcy Clarke wanted to be the first one."

"I usually let Darcy have her way, but ..." He playfully shrugged. "If mission parameters require it, what can I do?"

Omni's voice broke in, "Still attempting to establish contact with the caretaker AI. No response so far."

"Then use a more aggressive protocol to jumpstart it," Baxter said. "Overwrite if you have to."

"Agreed, Omni," Corey said, feeling the urgency. Nobody else knew how bad the situation really was. "Highest priority. Kick the doors down if you have to."

As they flew down toward the nearest faulty shield node, which was not far beyond the line of terminator storms and the night side, Corey gazed at the bright metallic lines of the geoglyph far below. They were like inverted canyons of metal that had seeped up through cracks. He could see why Kyle was so fascinated with the thing.

Baxter continued to study the diagram showing the blank areas where the shield coverage had failed.

The AI responded, sounding sheepish. "I sent stronger pulses, used a backdoor subroutine, and triggered some pattern responses in the caretaker AI. My signals are aligning, but the handshake routines are difficult. I am reimposing a template. I expect to break through very soon."

"Good. We'll be over the first shield node in just a few minutes." Corey kept the pilot controls steady.

"Link established, Commander Corey!" Omni's voice held clear satisfaction. "Now that I am inside the shield network, with a full diagnostic routine I will be able to—"

The artificial voice stuttered to a halt.

After a pause, Corey pressed, "Omni, what is it, buddy?"

The AI sounded ragged. "Something is not right. Attempting to disengage from the secondary network ... power surge! Significant danger! Commander Corey, you must—"

A shower of sparks erupted from the control panel, throwing Corey backward. At her station, Baxter was flung to the side as the AstroBug's engines suddenly fired up and the AI guidance systems sent them spinning.

At full thrust, the ship reeled out of control.

CHAPTER 7

The red dwarf churned like a demon's eye in front of the arkship. Captain Faraday wondered if later generations of colonists would ever look on their new home star with the same fondness that she had viewed Earth's golden sun.

Looking through the bridge's filtered window, she said aloud, "We'll just have to get used to sunspots and flares from now on." The blotchy photosphere was compelling, even hypnotic, as flares stretched out like desperate signal fires.

"It looks angry," said Commander Mia Kleve, the skeleton crew's first officer.

Faraday nodded. "In another day, we'll reach the critical stress point. Double check all vital systems, then triple check, because we don't get a do-over if we screw this up."

It was a balancing act. The *Odyssey* had to fly close enough so that the star's gravity would help them skid to a stop, but not enough to break the arkship into pieces. If their course calculations were off by the slightest degree, the *Odyssey* could plunge down into the star.

She wasn't going to let that happen.

Faraday felt a pang of worry for the emergency mission, the AeroFox and AstroBug dropping away like birds leaving the nest. If the braking maneuver turned into a disaster and the *Odyssey* didn't survive, then those four would be stranded alone on an alien world.

She reminded herself that as the arkship's only remaining captain, she was responsible for every single person, whether they were awake or in hibernation. She forced a smile and turned to her first officer. "We can do this. I've got a couple of bottles of Earth scotch sealed away, and we'll crack them open after this braking maneuver."

Though nervous, the bridge crew let out a cheer from their stations.

"Understood, Captain," said Kleve. "But no celebrating until after we get around the star, intact."

"You'll get us through it, Captain," said David Hamelin from the helm. "You always have. Above and beyond."

"That's me, Captain Above and Beyond." Faraday sighed. "I thought all my stress would end after flying away from Earth. I'm supposed to be in hibernation right now."

"You can retire as soon as we get to the planet, Captain," said Kleve. "Kick back on the veranda with your feet up, looking out at the sun."

As she gazed at the churning Proxima Centauri, Faraday didn't find it relaxing at all. She looked down at the flight path and the countdown, bracing herself. "I wasn't even expecting to be awake for this...."

Over the course of the long voyage, the three designated captains were scheduled to take shifts, five years awake, then ten years down in hibernation. A hundred crew members would also cycle up and down, the minimum needed to monitor the *Odyssey*'s fusion engines, greenhouse farms, life support, air filtration, and thousands of hibernation pods.

Faraday had drawn the first shift, on duty during the departure from Earth. According to the mission plan, she would stay in contact with the home governments and the other two arkships. She knew how grim and heartbreaking that duty would be as the Earth fell into its final death behind her. Monster hurricanes would wreck every city within a hundred miles of the coast, and wildfires would rage across entire states, burning all year long and filling the air with unbreathable smoke, while horrific droughts would parch the grain belt that had once produced so much of the world's food supply.

She had secretly hoped the human race could hold on for at least five years, because then she would be in hibernation, sleeping through the worst part. But Faraday was on the bridge when the *Odyssey* received the distant garbled signals, the flood of nuclear warheads and the planetwide EMP that fried the communication network and any technology that would have helped the last humans survive the climate ravages.

Afterward, her hundred crew members had lived in despair, unable to raise any communication from Earth or—even more devastating—from the *Phoenix* or the *Valkyrie*. The other two arkships should have been completed and ready to depart by now.

She had always imagined the *Valkyrie* would be keeping her company during the voyage, flying a few years behind the *Odyssey*. She had thought she'd be able to send messages back and forth to Michio Sakamoto. Their transmissions didn't have to be love letters, because she and Michio could express their emotions just by looking at each other on screen.

But he had also vanished into the empty silence of Earth. She would never hear from him again. The *Odyssey* was the only ship left, with the only humans left—in the universe.

And so Faraday was the one who had to deliver the news to the second-shift captain, Sanjay Premanik, when they woke him after five years of blissfully unaware hibernation. He was devastated, but vowed to carry on. When it was her turn to sleep, Faraday had gone into her own hibernation pod, praying that when they revived her a decade later, she'd awaken to good news....

But when she'd blinked her eyes open from the groggy cold sleep, she hadn't seen the expected face of Neil Andolino, the third-shift captain. As a courtesy, each captain was there for the handoff to give the replacement a thorough briefing. As Faraday shook off her "popsicle" grogginess, ready to learn the arkship's current situation, she saw only grim-looking medical techs and deeply disturbed officers in front of her. One man even had tear streaks down his face.

"What happened? What time is it?" She rubbed her eyes. "Are we in year fifteen?" She forced a dry chuckle. "I set my alarm clock."

"Year thirteen," said one of the medical techs.

"Only thirteen? I should have two more—"

The tear-streaked officer blurted out, "Captain Andolino is dead. You were next in line."

Faraday slumped back into her pod as if all her muscles had turned to water. "Tell me what happened?"

Four people tried to explain at once, and she managed to extract the story from the overlapping chatter. The *Odyssey* was passing through the Oort Cloud, the scattered shell of dark cometary debris at the far fringes of the solar system. The cloud was so diffuse that it was not considered a hazard, and the enormous arkship couldn't have maneuvered even if sensors picked up debris ahead.

By bad fortune, the *Odyssey* had plowed through a particularly dense knot of debris, which turned into a shooting gallery. The communications array was damaged. Even though they had already lost all contact with Earth, Captain Andolino took it upon himself to climb inside a bottle suit rigged with repair waldoes for external work. Although the skeleton crew had several space construction experts, Andolino insisted on going out himself. He had initially worked on the array, and he was perfectly qualified for the job.

Then a tiny chunk of debris had struck Andolino's bottle suit like a sniper's bullet, and the decompression killed him before he could get back inside.

Thus, Captain Faraday was awakened two years early. Stoic and duty bound, she resolved to get back on the usual clock, so she stayed on shift for seven more years, until year twenty, when it was time to pull Captain Premanik out of hibernation for his second shift. She did not look forward to telling him another round of horrific news. Explaining that Earth was dead had been bad enough the first time.

But there were worse things than simply delivering bad news.

When Sanjay Premanik awakened, Faraday was there to greet him with a forced smile. They were the only two captains left. At first, looking down at his lean, tan face, she didn't see anything wrong. His eyes blinked slowly. His mouth opened, and he tried to speak words, but they came out as gibberish. Premanik's face distorted into a grimace, and he went into seizures. The medical techs swarmed around him, strapping him down, resuscitating him.

"Freezer burn!" one of them called—an odd and terrible side effect of hibernation, extremely rare and considered a minimal risk compared with all the other hazards the *Odyssey* faced.

Premanik remained wild and delirious. His gaze flicked back and forth, and he uttered wails of agony instead of words. The med techs tried every known treatment, but Premanik died within two weeks.

Leaving her as the only surviving original captain.

Faraday lived with a weariness that weighed on her heart and soul. She'd already been sickened by the nuclear exchange on Earth, but from the start everyone had known that those left behind were doomed. She had not, however, prepared for the fact that two of the three captains would perish before the *Odyssey* was even halfway to its destination.

Faraday trained a few junior officers and prepared them, but she decided that she would just stay awake for the duration. She vowed to get the arkship to the Proxima Centauri system, and she settled in for a long flight across the gulf of space.

Though she could not stop dreading, Faraday imposed a sense of calm even in a cascade of malfunctions. "One disaster at a time," she said. "One disaster at a time."

She had no spare captain, and her beloved Michio was gone with whatever had happened to the *Valkyrie*. This was going to be a much longer voyage than she had expected.

Now, as the *Odyssey* hurtled toward the red dwarf, she stared at the flares and muttered, "One disaster at a time ..."

CHAPTER 8

The AeroFox reached the orbital position to deploy the third and final communications satellite. Time for Darcy and Kyle to finish their part of the job while Corey and Baxter fixed the shield nodes.

Jumbled in his seat at the science console, Kyle finally took a break from staring at the geoglyph and verified her readings. Absently, he toyed with the gyroscope as he ran checks. "First two primary comm satellites are synched now. Persephone will have a communications network whenever anybody down there wants to make calls."

Darcy activated the comm. "Hey Corey, how's it going down there? Shield network fixed yet? You better not be leaving footprints on the surface without me. Kyle and I still have one more sat to deploy—"

Omni's voice sounded more alarmed than any AI was supposed to. "Astronaut Clarke, we may have a problem!"

"You're supposed to solve problems. Explain."

Kyle suddenly perked up. "What is it, O?"

"I was linked to my counterpart Omni on the AstroBug so we could analyze the malfunctioning nodes. He forced an interface with the local caretaker AI—and then he projected an outburst of extreme distress. I have lost contact!"

Kyle sat bolt upright in his chair. "Extreme distress? What are you talking about, O?"

Not waiting for an explanation, Darcy hit the comm again and raised her voice. "AstroBug, come in. Corey, do you read me?"

Kyle responded in a rush, commandeering the telescope so he could zoom down to pick up the other ship. "Tracking the AstroBug, zeroing in—Darcy, look!"

The atmosphere distorted the enlarged image, but she could see the big saucer-shaped ship careening out of control as if flown by some suicidal prankster. The Bug plummeted sharply toward the surface.

"Corey! Get your engines under control!"

The AstroBug spun and looped in the air, then reversed course and hurtled toward the shadow of the night side. It dwindled to a speck and disappeared into the turbulent terminator-line storms.

Kyle tried to track it. "Whoa, they're nearly over the horizon! We'll lose contact."

"We've already lost contact." Darcy looked to their own AI. "Omni, can you reach your counterpart?"

"No response, Astronaut Clarke. Something severe occurred when he linked with the shield network. The caretaker AI may be corrupted."

Darcy did not doubt Corey's abilities as a pilot. They had run through hundreds of simulations together, surviving the worst scenarios. Maybe this was one of those terrible situations. "Omni, can you project where they're headed so we can follow?"

The increasingly grainy telescopic image split in half to accommodate a wire-frame of the planet's globe showing a flight-path projection that arced over to the night side.

Omni said, "Based on the current trajectory, the AstroBug will intersect with the surface just beyond the terminator on the night side."

Darcy's throat went dry. *Intersect with the surface?*

Kyle blurted out, "You mean they're going to crash!"

"Shit. What are the odds of survival? Best guess, Omni."

The AI tried to sound reassuring. "Jim Corey is a skilled pilot. However, based upon their velocity and the erratic flight path, he does not appear to be in control of his craft."

Darcy breathed hard, concentrating. The AeroFox was stuck up in very high geosynchronous orbit. She needed to make a decision, black or white. She reached for the piloting controls. "We're going after them, but it's going to take some very hard burns."

Kyle nearly fell out of his seat, snatching his toy gyroscope before it fell to the deck. "Darcy, we're up in high orbit! It'll take hours to get down there."

Working intensely, she began plotting a course on her navigation computer. "Better than waiting up here for hours. I'll take the direct route—atmospheric express. We'll be down there in a jiffy."

"Yeah, like a meteor," Kyle said. "That's insane."

"But not impossible. Check the math."

Omni fell noticeably silent, as if an AI could hold its breath.

The nav computer projected a clear plot on the screen, complete with error bars and danger zones. "Omni, plot a series of burns. First one to drop us from synchronous orbit, second one to increase our descent velocity, then a final braking thrust to slow us enough for atmospheric entry."

"Damn, *very* hard burns." Kyle stared at the course plot, then severe inflection points, then turned to the glowing yellow AI symbol for reassurance. "Can we do it, O?"

After a beat, Omni said in a cautious voice, "While I would not advise this course of action, my calculations indicate the approach is possible, with a reasonable probability of the AeroFox's survival."

"The g-forces will put us through the wringer," Kyle said.

Darcy drew strength from the photo with her parents, that bright-eyed girl with a whole future ahead of her. "Sorry, Kyle, but that's Corey down there—and Baxter."

The young man's face was ashen as he reviewed the extreme maneuvers that would drop them down on what seemed to be a suicide plunge. "But what if we all end up crashing? We never trained for anything like this."

Darcy was intent on the panel in front of her, trying to ignore him. At this moment, the AstroBug was reeling out of control, heading toward a crash! "I trained in plenty of extreme simulations."

"And how many of them did you survive?"

"This is the only one that counts." She buckled her straps, getting ready for a wild ride. "Omni, warm up the main drive system." She flashed a glance at her crewmate. "Kyle, prep our ship for landing—this could turn into a rescue mission. Every second counts."

He swallowed hard, drew a deep breath. "Right ... it's Corey, after all."

Darcy even heard a tinge of excitement in Omni's voice. "Plasma drive online and ready."

Through the Fox's front windowscreen, she saw the strange geoglyph patterns across the bright dayside, but it was the dark shadow of the terminator line that held her attention now. The careening AstroBug had already vanished into the night, out of contact. Her heart ached. She needed to find him. She didn't know what she would do without him....

Kyle struggled to clip his restraints in place, but fumbled his little gyroscope. It fell to the floor with a *clink*. "Ah, no!"

"Initiating the first burn." Darcy closed her eyes and gave her faith to the AI, this AeroFox, and any gods who were listening. She touched a flashing red button. Point of no return

"Wait a sec!" Kyle unclipped so he could grab his toy.

Positional jets flipped the AeroFox 180 degrees in space. Darcy didn't even have a chance to get disoriented before the main engine fired. The exhaust plume was a blinding blue beacon that killed the ship's orbital motion. The extreme deceleration caused the AeroFox to drop toward the planet below.

Caught off guard by the lurch, Kyle was thrown out of his seat. He tumbled like a piece of loose debris against the bulkhead and smashed against a console. His gyroscope ricocheted and clattered across the deck like a projectile. He yelped in pain, managed to grab onto the stem of his chair as the burn continued.

"Get strapped back in and hold on!" Darcy said through gritted teeth. The cabin vibrated as the whole ship shook with the violent deceleration. Her neck muscles tightened as she strained to breathe as the g-forces increased.

Kyle wrapped an arm around his side, wincing, as he struggled to pull himself back into his seat. He grabbed one of the loose restraint straps, sweating and straining in real pain. "How ... how many gees are we pulling, O?"

As Darcy fought with the rattling deceleration, Omni's voice sounded maddeningly calm. "Currently approaching nine gees. You are not in a safe position, Kyle."

The young man's face dropped into a grimace. "Great, and this is the *first* maneuver. I'm going to break into—"

Though her vision was blurry from the vibration and the strain, Darcy saw that the burn was about to end. "Engine cut off in three ... two ..."

The bright thruster flare abruptly ceased, leaving the ship poised in deceptive silence. Then it began to drop like a stone toward the planet.

CHAPTER 9

The AstroBug was going down—piloting controls unresponsive, Omni offline—but Jim Corey knew every system and subroutine. As the ship plunged through the terminator storms caused by the temperature variance on the day-night line, he shut down the main controls, rebooted, and rerouted, but he could get no response. It was damned hard to concentrate while the engines fired at random.

The AstroBug was tossed about and thrown into the air, despite another last burst from the thrusters. Fortunately, the saucer-shaped vessel had enough velocity to plow through the storm's worst turbulence like a tossed brick. Corey couldn't steer worth a damn.

Finally, by diverting the damaged AI controls, he managed to cross-connect the safety overrides and restore some semblance of manual control. "Got it! I have attitude-control thrusters."

Strapped in and white with tension, Baxter gripped the arms of her chair. "If there's anything I can do, let me know. Otherwise, I'll shut up and let you fly."

Glitchy readouts appeared on his screen, including a vital radar scan of the night-dark terrain below. He saw rugged upheavals, a volcanic dome, ice sheets, everything shrouded in perpetual cold night—no good options at all.

"The Bug's main engines are dead, but I do have attitude jets. I can aim us—a little bit." His breathing was fast and hard, his eyes hyper-focused on the radar image below, the altitude readings and their estimated point of impact. "Omni? Omni, you there, buddy?"

No response. He had never counted on doing this alone. "The Bug is like a cross between a glider and a rock."

They soared just above a prominent volcano that spewed lava and ash into the night, and Corey scanned his options for a landing area, which were rapidly decreasing. "I wanted to leave the first footprints on Proxima b—not a big smoking crater." He made a decision, fired the starboard thrusters. "There—radar image reads as desert ... flattest spot I can find. We're going down either way."

Baxter didn't second guess him. "Sounds perfect. Bring us in."

As the Bug plunged toward the ground, the terrain lines matched the radar projection. In the space of a heartbeat, they rushed over the flat area—which was not a desert after all, but a wide ice sheet, a vast frozen lake.

No choice now.

The AstroBug struck the surface, skidding and careening. The hot engines still coughed, burned, then flickered out. Ice melted into curtains of steam all around them, and the pilot deck lurched, tilted. Metal groaned and roared, scraping on ice, and the AstroBug spun like a hockey puck until it finally came to a halt.

CHAPTER 10

I n between the hard engine burns, the AeroFox's pilot deck became weightless. Darcy exhaled and felt lightheaded.

Beside her, Kyle let out a low moan, wincing as he dropped away from his seat. "That felt like a big, heavy boot stomping on my chest." He crawled across the deck to where the gyroscope had settled under the comm panel and seized it.

Darcy fought down her frantic concern. All she could think about was the crashed AstroBug. "Every nanosecond counts, Kyle. Get yourself strapped in and suck it up!"

The young man retrieved his stupid toy and pulled himself back into his seat. "Sorry. I wasn't thinking—"

Darcy yelled, "Get ready, here we go again."

Kyle grabbed the straps, but tangled his arm in them as he tried to clip himself in.

The AeroFox flipped 180 degrees for the second burn, and Darcy held on, adjusting her orientation. "Omni, how are we doing?"

"First burn maneuver successful. We are on trajectory to reach the AstroBug's projected point of impact. I am still unable to raise my counterpart Omni."

The ship soared toward the darkened hemisphere. "Kyle, use the high-magnification scopes. Can you see anything over there?"

She dreaded finding the fiery plume from an explosion—or strewn debris from a wrecked ship.

Kyle struggled to call up images. "We're not going to see anything through that turbulence." His voice was ragged, and he wiped unexpected blood from the side of his mouth. "We have to get through it before we see calmer air on the dark, cold side."

She could see flashes on the horizon, a murk of ominous lightning that skittered around the clouds and shadows. She had only one priority. "If the Bug made it through, then so can we. Prepare for our last burn."

Kyle gripped the arms of his chair and groaned. "Great ... I think I broke something."

"Tank pressurization complete, Astronaut Clarke. Our timing is critical."

She gritted her teeth. "Get ready for more pain, Kyle. This one will be worse than the first—"

The ship abruptly fired its main engine, and the heavy acceleration flung the AeroFox toward the looming planet below.

Kyle cried out in pain, but Darcy concentrated on breathing, on enduring ... on Corey. He needed her! They'd always had each other's backs, every adventure they cooked up together while exploring the *Odyssey*, every training session, side by side.

Please, be alive!

The tremendous acceleration pushed her back into her seat, much worse this time, and when she turned her head toward Kyle, it felt like wrenching away from a vice. He was like a wadded-up ball, his eyes closed, his expression full of agony. He had fallen unconscious.

She couldn't unstrap and check on him. The AeroFox controls demanded her full focus, even with the AI's assistance. The air buffeted and roared past the hull, as the ship streaked like a bullet straight toward the storm line. The surface loomed right in front of her eyes, and it looked suddenly, startlingly *real*.

Was this what Corey had thought just before he crashed?

With a jolt, the thrusting engine cut off again, leaving her shaking like a rag doll. She had barely a second to brace herself before the AeroFox automatically flipped over for the third time and aligned for the final approach. Kyle looked crumpled and broken in his seat, and the incredible g-forces were taking their toll on her, too.

She whispered to herself, following protocol. "Velocity five thousand meters per second. Prepare for braking thrust." She heard no response from her companion. He was still sprawled in his chair, passed out. "You with me, Kyle? Omni, can you wake him up?"

The AI displayed a diagnostic image of Kyle Dyson in a separate window from the trajectory path, projections of turbulence ahead, and the radar scan of the planet's dark surface. "Astronaut Clarke, Kyle is unconscious. Something appears to be wrong." The artificial voice sounded shaky, worried. "I'm reading internal bleeding and some tissue damage."

Darcy could see how grave his injuries were. "The first burn threw him around like a rag doll."

Omni said, "You both experienced several minutes at nearly ten Earth gravities. It is remarkable that you didn't black out as well."

"This was the only way to get to the crash site in time." She didn't want to admit that she had no idea what "in time" meant.

"Even so, I have grave concerns about the stress of our upcoming final burn. Kyle's injuries require medical attention."

The terminator storm and the night side of Proxima b was just ahead. She could only think of the AstroBug crashed, damaged, cut off ... "We're on a rescue mission, Omni. We don't have much choice." The planet was coming up fast, and she had to make a decision. "There's no going back. We'll use the X-Doc on Kyle as soon we land, but our priority is to find the crash site."

Omni hesitated for just a second. "Very well. I will monitor Kyle as best I can."

The timer display rolled down to zero. "Hang on!" Darcy said, mostly for herself.

The main engine roared to life one more time, slowing the craft's meteoric descent and pushing up hard. The ship trailed a line of superheated gas in its wake as it crossed over into the dark.

Behind them, Proxima Centauri created a crimson sunset on the horizon.

CHAPTER 11

After the AstroBug came to a jerky stop on the expanse of ice, the sudden lack of movement was disorienting. For a long moment Corey didn't know what to do, what to say. Baxter stared out the window at the alien darkness outside. They both caught their breath in shock and disbelief.

Finally, he said, "Yeah, I'm the best damned pilot on this whole planet."

"Well, we landed in one piece ... mostly," Baxter said. "I'll take that as a win."

Red emergency lights illuminated the cabin. Corey checked the few systems that were still working and tried to assess their situation, but he didn't get much of the outside view. "I aimed for the flattest spot I could. With radar, an ice floe looks an awful lot like a landing field."

Baxter climbed out of her seat and retrieved an emergency tool kit. "I prefer that to slamming into the side of the volcano."

The AstroBug tilted as it settled into the cracked ice, then the angle alarmingly shifted by several degrees. Outside, surrounded by slush, the saucer-shaped vessel began sinking. "The lake's surface has a thick layer of ice, but it's liquid underneath!"

Through the windowscreen, a flashing strobe light looked like lightning, and Corey knew the craft's emergency beacon had initiated, regular pulses calling out for help.

He looked at the dead comm controls. He knew Darcy and Kyle were up in synchronous orbit, and no doubt they would come swooping in. That gave him a great sense of relief, but also dread. He had to contact Darcy before she did something reckless. "We need comms working! I've got to talk to the AeroFox."

Baxter swiped hair away from her face. "We're stuck, Corey. You think we can rescue ourselves?"

"Of course," he said without thinking.

The AstroBug settled more as the ice shifted and started to swallow them up. How deep was this lake?

Corey ran another diagnostic, trying to reroute more of the ship's integrated systems from the nonresponsive AI. Something unknown had fried it. "I hate to do this to you, Omni, but if you're not there, we have to figure it out without you."

With a screwdriver, Baxter opened an access panel beneath the main communications console. Pulling it free, she set the panel plate aside—and watched in dismay as it slid down the tilted deck. "Remind me not to let go of any loose screws."

Corey shook his head, looking at the blank gray AI screen. "Where did that pulse come from? All of our controls went haywire. The skies were clear, no lightning on the dayside—"

"It came from the shield grid." Baxter stowed the screwdriver in the kit and pulled out a test sensor, which she jabbed into the wiring. "When our AI broke into the caretaker network and awakened one of the offline nodes, the surge response knocked everything out. Like a malignant computer virus."

Corey asked, "Do you think it was the same thing that scrambled the shield network?"

Baxter raised her eyebrows. "I'll let you know when we get over to one of the corrupted transmitting towers on the dayside. But we can't fix the network until we get ourselves out of this mess."

He didn't ask the most important question out loud—how

would they get the shield fixed and ready to go by the time the *Odyssey* returned? Ten thousand people were at stake—and right now.

Baxter poked around inside the circuits and shook her head. "Sorry, kid. We're not going to send or receive any messages. That pulse knocked out the comms as well as the AI."

Corey swallowed hard. "Darcy's got to be freaking out up there." He rotated his chair from Flight position to its Surface configuration, locked it in place, fuming. "I know the EMP came from the shield grid, but how could it generate a burst that powerful? Was it using the grid's energy source? Was it just a short circuit, or was the EMP directed *at* us, like an attack?"

She shrugged. "As the systems engineer, the best I can say is— I have no idea."

As if in response, the AstroBug's cabin shuddered, and Corey grabbed his pilot chair to stabilize himself. The toolkit slid away down the deck, but Baxter managed to grab it in time.

Outside, with a grinding sound, chunks of ice shifted as the Bug settled farther into the broken ice and the empty water below.

Walking off balance on the slanted deck, Corey went to the nearest windowport. "Well, I might not have crashed us into a volcano, but a big ice-covered lake isn't ideal either."

A new automated alarm blared. "Now what?" Corey pulled himself over to scan the readings. "Great ... we're leaking fuel."

"How bad?"

"Bad." He punched the control panel, but the alarms didn't stop. "How did I end up crashing on my first real mission?"

Baxter unplugged and replaced a burned component, twisting it in place. "You got us down alive—an important first step."

Corey went to the AI base controls, restoring power, still hoping to hear a response from the ubiquitous friendly voice. "We better see about Omni. I can't do this all myself." A flicker of amber lights winked, then stabilized into a dull green. "Omni, buddy, can you hear me?"

After a long silence, the AI's voice responded weakly. "I am here, Jim Corey ... at least part of me is."

He felt a wash of relief. "Are you okay? What happened?"

Omni paused, either running a silent diagnostic or just trying to remember. "I was assessing the malfunctions on the shield grid, attempting to link and download information from the caretaker AI. When I accessed the primary node, an energy surge jumped into our ship's systems. After that ... my records are faulty." The normally calm voice sounded deeply sad. "I sincerely apologize for any inconvenience I may have caused."

Baxter snickered at Omni's comment, but Corey felt bad for the computer. He had grown up with that voice, that helpful presence, that infinite source of knowledge. "It's not your fault, buddy."

Baxter leaned closer to the AI console, where the blue infinity symbol flickered on the screen. "What do you mean 'part of you' is here? What's missing? And how can we supplement it?" The scraping groan of shifting ice increased outside. "We're not in a very good situation here."

The AI voice responded, "I can speak and share information, although my systems remain compromised. The unexpected EMP surge caused significant damage. It came through the shield node from an unknown, external source."

Though he worked through the problems one step at a time, trying to remain cool, Corey felt a growing sense of urgency. As more of the AstroBug's diagnostics came back online, he could see how precarious the ship was. "You better get yourself uncompromised, Omni. Comms are out, and I need you to send status updates to the AeroFox, wherever it is. And the *Odyssey*, too, just in case they can still receive."

The AI sounded crisp and professional again. "Understood, Commander Corey." When the ship listed another few degrees, Omni reacted as if it had just realized its situation. "Oh, it appears we have landed on Proxima b! I am sorry I missed it."

Baxter snorted. "Ya think? Use whatever sensors are still

working and tell us more about our surroundings—we can't see much through the damned windows."

"I am still getting my bearings, Engineer Baxter. Resetting external sensors." The screens flickered again, and a more detailed graphic showed the AstroBug's position on the broken lake ice, as well as approximations of the surrounding terrain and the rugged shore not far away. "The AstroBug is on a frozen body of water, and our impact fractured and melted the ice."

"I call it a *landing*, not an impact." Corey felt defensive.

"The frozen surface is two meters thick and currently supporting the AstroBug, but the integrity of the ice is questionable. The weight of this vessel makes our position highly unstable."

The simulation showed the AstroBug teetering, and then the ice crumbled, letting the heavy vessel break through and plunge down.

"Out of curiosity, how deep is this lake, Omni?" Baxter asked.

"The water extends one point five kilometers beneath us. Once the ice breaks, we will sink to the bottom."

CHAPTER 12

The AeroFox rocked in the buffeting wind as it hurtled like a meteor through the wall of the terminator storm. Trying to ignore the roar outside, Darcy stared at the wireframe grid of the projected landscape on her monitor. A blip marked the expected crash site dead ahead. "We're right on the line!"

Above and behind them, streaks of lightning danced wildly through the turbulence. The glow of the heat shield diminished around the AeroFox, and at last Darcy could see more clearly. Barely visible through the storm, an ominous wall of mountains rose just ahead, like hell's gate.

As they pushed through the thickening terminator storm, she let her instincts kick in, a lifetime of training and simulations. The altimeter and the wire-frame screen in front of her showed their steep and rapid descent.

The Fox spun in the roiling atmosphere. Lightning discharges whipped across the windowport, skirling along the hull. A severe lurch knocked them sideways, and Darcy wrestled to keep the craft on course, firing attitude jets. Almost through!

Just as Darcy managed to stabilize the craft, a malevolent whip of lightning hammered them like a nuclear explosion. The worst blast they had experienced. As the AeroFox reeled, even more lightning struck, like a malicious electrical hammer.

Arcs of blue fire jumped around the pilot deck, and a brilliant flash surged from the AI core. Darcy lurched back and flung her hands away as sparks showered out of the control modules.

Omni's yellow avatar flickered and faded out, then all of the ship's internal power failed, plunging the deck into shadow, but the flashing madness outside was like a strobe light. Wisps of acrid smoke curled up from Omni's primary control unit.

Finishing their automated sequence, the Fox's retro-rockets ceased firing, and now the AeroFox dropped without guidance. Darcy yelped as the scout craft skipped over the ridge that suddenly filled their view, and she heard a loud and sickening scrape as part of the lower hull caromed off an outcropping.

Blessedly, the main power came back online, and the reactivated retros kicked in, adding a last vital boost. The AeroFox broke through the worst part of the storm wall.

Darcy scrambled with sluggish controls to align their course. It certainly wouldn't help Corey if she crashed the rescue ship, too. Now that they were on the night side, she peered into the dark sky ahead with both fear and awe.

Alarm klaxons resounded in the cabin. The adjacent console module burst into flame after the lightning surge. Thick, oily smoke coughed upward.

"Omni, activate the fire-suppression system!" The AI didn't respond, and Darcy felt another chill ripple down her back. "Omni?"

Flickering flames emerged from the console that housed the AI core. She couldn't release the controls now to grab the extinguisher. "Kyle! Can you get that?"

At the science station, Kyle Dyson remained strapped in, but unconscious. He'd really been knocked around.

On her piloting panel, the projection showed the planet's rugged surface—and where they were going down. "Fine, I'll just do this myself. That's what a crack pilot is for." She hoped Kyle was all right. The smoke kept flickering up into the cockpit.

She worked the landing controls, and panels opened in the

ship's lower hull, despite the damage from the grazing impact. Landing struts extended and locked into place.

The surface rose up, and she searched for a smooth patch. Everything happened in a blur. Darcy went through the landing sequence she had done a hundred times before in simulations. The AeroFox's thrusters blasted away dirt, clearing thousands of years of debris. She was sweating from every pore in her body. "Come on, come on!"

Supported by a cushion of gasping jets, the ship crunched down onto the cracked, alien surface.

Landed.

On Proxima b.

CHAPTER 13

The consequences of even small mistakes aboard the giant arkship could be significant, and accidents happened. The first ones had started twenty-five years into the voyage.

Reaching the halfway point in the *Odyssey's* journey was cause for celebration. In the habitation ring's main hall, Captain Faraday had called together the hundred operational crewmembers. She wasn't much for giving speeches, but this was an exception. Twenty-five years.

She raised her glass and smiled at the familiar faces, seeing their hopeful expressions, their joy. "Halfway!"

"Halfway!" they all shouted.

"On the longest journey humanity ever attempted." She smiled, just letting the idea sink in.

"So it's all downhill from here, Captain?" called out a handsome, broad-shouldered engineer, Sebastian Clarke, who had arranged his hibernation shift to be awake for the same five-year stint as his wife Denise. They'd been a couple before leaving Earth, married for three years, although they had both been in hibernation for the last two decades. Now they were awake again and working together. Denise stood beside her husband, grinning at his joke.

A chuckle ran through the audience as they lifted glasses of the best wine that the captains had loaded aboard, along with special bottles of brandy, vodka, rum.

Faraday chuckled. "Downhill? I prefer to call it the home stretch." A hundred glasses were raised again. "To the home stretch, and to our new home on Proxima b!"

For twenty-five years, the *Odyssey* had accelerated away from Earth, endlessly pushing, picking up speed until by now they'd reached a sizeable fraction of the speed of light. Upon reaching the halfway point, Faraday oversaw the most complex maneuver the *Odyssey* had undertaken. Time to turn the ship around and use the big engines for deceleration.

The massive fusion thrusters had shut off, letting the great arkship coast along in the empty void. Then maneuvering thrusters fired from opposite sides of the enormous dumbbell, rotating the *Odyssey* like a pinwheel until the front faced back toward Earth's yellow sun, which was now just a bright star behind them. Then the big engines had fired up again, adding reverse thrust. The floor became "down" as gravity was restored, and the great arkship started a quarter century of steady, constant deceleration.

Burning their remaining fuel, the thrust would cancel most of the *Odyssey*'s velocity by the time they arrived in the Proxima Centauri system, although they'd still need a severe braking maneuver to slow them enough for orbital insertion around their new home.

Once the *Odyssey* completed its reversal, Faraday had announced this celebration. But she felt weary deep in her bones. She had been scheduled to sleep through the halfway event while Captain Premanik led the crew. She had been awake for seventeen years already, with twenty-five more to go.

All downhill from here ...

"To the home stretch," she said again and savored the red wine, an Oklahoma cabernet sauvignon. She remembered when she'd bought the case of bottles. The ravages of climate change had ruined most of Earth's traditional wine-growing areas, but the weather shifts had created remarkable new vineyards in unexpected places. Silver linings ... very small silver linings.

A long time ago, she and Michio had taken a tour of the new Oklahoma wine country, spending three glorious days tasting vintages, looking out at the lines of dusty grapevines, pretending that everything was normal. At their favorite winery, the chief vintner, a tall and gangly man named Ken "Dig-Dug" Duggan with a cowboy hat as big as his grin, explained how his team had set aside a portion of the best wine in seasoned barrels. Duggan waxed poetic about how the barrels would impart the subtlest, richest flavors over the next ten years. Impressed, she and Michio had invested in a case from the Duggan Cellars, to be delivered when it was ready.

But it was all a fantasy. She and Michio, as well as Dig-Dug Duggan, knew that Earth didn't have ten years left. So, they had bought a case of a recent, available vintage as well, which was what she sipped now. As Faraday rolled the flavor around in her mouth, the taste made her think of Michio, the *Valkyrie*, and all that she had lost.

The captain felt generous during the celebration. In the greenhouse domes and chemistry labs, the maintenance crew had crafted a variety of alcoholic beverages, fruit wines, beer, moonshine, even some concoctions that she had not known before. Colonist innovation and imagination!

For the turnaround party, they were also drinking real Earth booze, and likely no one would ever taste wine like this again. Although hope was a necessary survival trait for these remnants of humanity, it was also painful.

If she and Michio hadn't waited to get married, have children ...

Even so, she found the celebration liberating. In a few years, half of these people would go back into hibernation again until the ship reached Proxima b, while a new work crew was awakened. The laughter and conversation grew louder as the people became tipsy, feeling excitement instead of tension for a change. Other attendees turned gloomy, drifting away to be by themselves.

Faraday let herself just feel satisfied as she drank a second glass of the rich wine. The whole dream of saving part of the human race, building three incredible arkships, flying off to the nearest star ... it had seemed impossible, the most desperate of last chances. "At least we made it this far," she said to herself.

Sebastian Clarke came up to her, smiling. "Captain, I'm proud of the job you've done. The *Odyssey* faced terrible adversity, and you met the challenge." His words were slurred just a little, but his meaning was sincere. "We are proud to serve under you."

Snuggling against him, Denise, a communications engineer, smiled in that giddy warm way that contented couples had. "Thank you for letting us both stay awake at the same time."

Sebastian kissed the top of Denise's head. "I promised you we'd have a honeymoon unlike any other."

"You kept your promise."

They left the party together, arm-in-arm, no doubt heading toward their quarters. Faraday just stood with a thin smile on her face. "At least we made it this far ..."

When the captain next saw Sebastian and Denise, they wore entirely different expressions. Concerned and embarrassed, they wouldn't meet her eyes when they entered the captain's private office.

Faraday tried to lighten the mood. "You look like you just realized you forgot something back on Earth. Too late to go back for it." The joke fell flat, and she knew it.

Sebastian flushed. "Accidents happen, Captain."

Denise lifted her chin and was more defiant. "And so do miracles."

Faraday answered in a cautious tone, "In my experience, accidents occur a lot more often than miracles do."

"I assure you it wasn't intentional, Captain," Sebastian said in a rush of words. "We took all the precautions ... or we thought we did."

Denise added, "But even the best birth control isn't one hundred percent effective."

Faraday caught her breath as she put the pieces together. She looked at Denise. "You're pregnant."

"I've suspected for more than a week," Denise said, "and I took the test twice. We'll go to the doctor and run another full round, but I'm convinced."

The captain felt a chill. "Our mandated policy is that we can't have any births during the voyage. The *Odyssey* doesn't have the spare resources. We can't increase the population on board. That's why there's only a hundred crew awake at a time." She rattled off words that Sebastian and Denise both knew already, but the couple listened in silence. "We can't run a nursery on the ship. What kind of life would it be for children to grow up here, with twenty-five years left in the voyage?"

Faraday blinked as another idea occurred to her. "Before the fetus develops further, maybe we should put you down into hibernation. Once we arrive at Proxima and set up the colony, it can be the first baby born on our new world. That's when we truly need to start increasing our population."

Sebastian's heavy eyebrows drew together. "I won't agree to that, Captain. I can show you all the records, the case studies. Every instance of a pregnant woman entering hibernation resulted in a miscarriage. You may as well just abort the fetus now."

Denise looked angry. "And we won't do that! We're the last survivors of the human race. It would be foolish to terminate a spark of hope."

Sebastian was also angry. "We won't allow it, Captain. I refuse. It's my wife's body, and she—"

Faraday held up her hand. "I wasn't suggesting that. I didn't know about the medical evidence regarding pregnant subjects. It wasn't ... it wasn't on my radar." She thought of all the questions and risks of hibernation, and she could never forget Captain Premanik waking up from his sleep pod, his mind destroyed by freezer burn. "I agree that's not an option, but this will certainly be a challenge." She considered how she would explain it to the rest of the skeleton crew, but realized that news of Denise's pregnancy would likely be greeted with joy, a sign of hope.

"Even after the baby's born, we can't put it in a pod," Sebastian said. "The studies show that children do not tolerate hibernation well. Our baby will have to stay awake at least until they're sixteen or seventeen."

Faraday knew that full well. That was why there were no children at all among the ten thousand popsicles.

Denise interjected, "Our little boy or girl would be twenty-four when the *Odyssey* arrives."

Faraday closed her eyes. "I'm trying to get my head around the idea of a baby aboard the *Odyssey*, much less a kid or a teenager. But we'll make the best of it. Heaven knows we've been through enough disasters. I insist we treat this as a good thing."

Now the thoughts and ideas started to fall into place. "Omni is already set up with countless educational and simulation programs, parental assistance and readiness routines for new children once we settle into the colony." She sighed. "We may as well consider this a test run, although your son or daughter is going to feel awfully lonely as the only kid aboard the *Odyssey*."

CHAPTER 14

Though Darcy had managed to land the AeroFox on the alien planet, she didn't have time to celebrate. Somewhere out on the dark landscape, Corey and the AstroBug had gone down and needed rescuing.

But first, she had to rescue herself.

As soon as the scout ship came to rest, she scrambled into action. With a rapid-fire flicking of switches, she shut down the engines, disconnected her safety restraints, and jumped out of her piloting seat. Keep moving. No dithering. She knew what to do.

She snatched a compact fire extinguisher from its wall clamp and sprayed the flames crackling out of the central AI deck. The sparking, spurting fire died in a wash of white vapor. The resounding alarms still grated on her nerves.

She hauled herself over to the science station, where Kyle slumped in his chair. The science console was blank, showing no indication of the AI avatar. The status panel was dark.

"That was a hell of a lightning blast." Darcy raised her voice, "Hey, snap out of it, Omni—I could use a little help here."

She moved close to the unresponsive Kyle so she could work his controls, neutralizing the alarms. When the sudden unsettling silence fell inside the craft, the rattle and moan of eerie wind outside grew much louder. Distant thunder rumbled from the terminator storm wall not far away. Through the Fox's windshield, she considered the dark wilderness outside, distant mountains, a blur of flowing lava from a cracked slope. Heavy snow flurries obscured her view.

Corey and the AstroBug were out there, somewhere.

She leaned against the console, closed her eyes, and counted to five as she pulled herself together. A flash of nearby lightning was so bright it penetrated even her closed eyelids. She blinked, straightened. Back to business.

"Kyle, can you hear me?" She looked at his closed eyes, his slack expression, a small trickle of blood at the corner of his mouth. She lowered her companion's seat to bring him closer. Darcy's extreme flight maneuvers had beaten him up and thrown him around, but he was still alive. If only he hadn't dropped his stupid gyroscope at the wrong moment ... "Kyle, we made it! We're on the surface. Welcome to Prox—uh, Persephone."

With a deep groan, he clutched his stomach and side. "This gravity sucks. It feels like you parked a shuttle on top of me."

Suddenly Darcy felt the difference. "Yeah, it's definitely different from the *Odyssey*. I'm just glad you're awake and all right."

He wiped away the blood at the side of his mouth. "Well, 'all right' may be an exaggeration, but I'm awake enough to know that I feel like crap. I've never been bounced around like that before. Something might be broken inside me." He looked up. "O, are you there?" He waited for the AI to answer, but heard nothing. He looked back at Darcy. "What happened to us?"

"You were unconscious through the worst of it. The AeroFox got blasted by lightning—more than once—and I'm pretty sure we clipped a mountain range on the way down. This ship is as beaten up as you are."

Kyle started to move, winced, thought better of it. "Mountains and lightning? Didn't your training teach you to avoid those things?"

"I must have missed that part." She stood up, satisfied that he seemed to be recovering. "We need to reestablish communication with the Bug. They're over here somewhere, and they've got to be all right." She lowered her voice to a whisper. "He has to be all right." She gestured to the smoke stains and the fire-extinguisher residue around the main AI console. "Omni's out. The lightning strike was bad, hit his core systems."

Concerned, Kyle tried to get to his feet. "I'll see if I can reboot —" Before he took a step, though, he crumpled, wracked with pain, and collapsed back into his seat. He took a succession of quick, ragged breaths. "I think you squashed a few things inside me."

"Sorry." She put a gentle hand on his shoulder. "We'll get you fixed up." She adjusted him into a more comfortable position. "When we were flying the heavy maneuvers, Omni said the high gee-load might've hurt you."

Kyle's face looked gray. "O is always over-protective. But this time I think he may be right ..."

Even without the blaring klaxons, alarms continued to sound in her head. She needed to suit up and go find the AstroBug, save Corey—but Kyle was right here, also badly hurt. "Let's give you a once-over with the X-Doc." She could set the automated medical device to work on him and fix whatever his body needed.

Then she spotted the black mark from an electrical fire across the medical station. Darcy extracted the X-Doc case from the wall unit—but it was little more than a smoke-stained husk. When she pried it open, it was obvious the smoldering unit was beyond repair. "I guess we should have brought a spare."

Kyle squirmed, but put on a stoic expression. "I'll grit my teeth and take a painkiller. We need to get my Omni rebooted. He could be a big help." He coughed a single time, and his eyes widened in surprise at the burst of pain. He touched his stomach again. "Have you located the AstroBug yet? How far away is it?"

Darcy could tell he was covering up how much he was hurting. She rebooted the science station systems and started scanning the vicinity for the AstroBug, dreading she would find only debris. The projection screen compiled a map of the surrounding area, highlighting the position of the AstroBug. She sighed with relief. "Looks like I got us to within two klicks. Best I could do under the circumstances."

Kyle forced a weak smile. "Not bad, considering that you slammed into a mountain and all ..."

"Very funny." She enlarged the map, imagining the obstacle course between here and the Bug. "But I need to get going. Corey and Baxter might be in trouble."

With very slow, careful movements, Kyle leaned forward, straining to see the screen. "See the radar echo? Looks like the AstroBug is sitting in the middle of a frozen lake. I hope the top layer is thick ..."

Darcy reset the comm system, checked the readings. She needed to hear Corey's voice. "AstroBug, come in. Do you read?"

No response. She tried three more times.

Kyle said, "If our transmitter was damaged, you could talk all you want without getting an answer."

"Or his own comms could be down. I shouldn't focus on the worst-case scenario." Resolved, she looked down at her battered companion. "I'm going outside to have a look."

Kyle squirmed against the side of his seat with one shaky arm. "I'm going with you—just this once."

She looked at him in surprise. "Not a good idea. Stay here and get Omni working again."

A flash of anger crossed his face. "No, Darcy. I've been waiting to set foot on this rock all my life. It's not just you and Corey. I've been watching through the *Odyssey* telescopes for the past two years. I'm not going to let a few bruises stop me now." His eyes gleamed with a thin sheen of tears. "Please."

She gave him a solemn nod. "All right, we go together. Just to have a look."

The AeroFox's side hatch hissed and disengaged, and the airlock deployed like an accordion. A ladder extended to the ground.

Darcy and Kyle wore form-fitting envirosuits, protective garments that included a half-mask respirator over their mouths and noses, an oxygen backpack, and sleek Augmented Reality goggles over their eyes. Persephone was supposed to be survivable, though the cold night side presented a lot more challenges. All the rest of the colony infrastructure was on the dayside for good reason.

Exhausted and deferential behind her in the airlock vestibule, Kyle waited while Darcy moved to the ladder. She worked her way down with ponderous caution despite her excitement. Kyle's voice came through her comm implant. "Move it, Neil. Buzz is itching to get down there."

Darcy jumped the last meter to the ground, and alien soil crunched under her feet. *Persephone* soil. She stood still for a moment and laughed to herself. She felt giddy as she absorbed the enormity of the moment. "That's one small step for a woman ..."

Kyle laboriously descended behind her, trying to hurry in the heavy gravity but clumsy due to his injuries. He lost his grip and fell the last few rungs, slamming hard onto the ground. "And one giant face-plant for me." She could see his sheepish expression behind the half-facemask and the goggles. "Glad no one's recording this."

Darcy helped him up. "You all right? Did you hurt yourself?"

"Right now a lot of things are hurting, but I wouldn't miss this for the world."

She supported him as the two stepped away from the AeroFox, looking around in awe. Her exposed skin felt very cold, but the air was warm in her facemask.

She scanned the horizon. In the far distance, a rugged volcano spewed lava and smoke into the black sky. Kyle pointed to it. "Is that the mountain you hit?"

"Not sure. I was a little busy at the time."

The rocky ground was studded with patches of ice that looked like hard, dull metal. Darcy held out her gloved hand, tried to catch the flurries around them. "This stuff in the air ..."

"I think it's snow," Kyle said. "You've seen pictures."

Above, through a hole in the clouds, she could see a bright band of green aurorae created by the solar flares and radiation storms. The nearby double star, Alpha Centauri A and B, was bright enough to cast shadows.

Kyle swayed a little, and Darcy reached out to steady him, worried about his injuries. "Just give me a sec." He crouched down and scooped up a handful of dust. "We're the first humans to set foot on a world outside our solar system."

"And I'm never going to forget it." She activated the flash-scanner on her wrist and used it to take an image of her foot on the dusty ground. She had to hope Corey was still alive, that she could share this triumph with him.

Kyle let the handful of dirt fall back onto the ground.

Her heart skipped a beat as she saw a pulsating light in the distance, a blinking beacon like a searchlight. "There they are!"

She snatched the laser ranger from her utility belt and pressed the high-res binoculars against her goggles. As the scope focused, she tracked until she aligned with the beacon, increased magnification—and the AstroBug jumped out at her. The large ship had landed on the frozen lake and was now embedded in the ice.

"It's intact, as far as I can tell."

Kyle extended his hand. "Can I see?" Though she just wanted to keep staring, she handed him the laser ranger. He said, "It looks like they soft-landed, but their rockets partially melted the ice, which refroze around the base."

"Soft landed." She repeated his words, just to reassure herself. "Maybe they're alive."

"Yeah, but it'll be a hell of a job getting them out of there." He handed the laser ranger back to her. "But what made them crash in the first place? Why did they suddenly reel out of control? As soon as their Omni connected with the shield network, everything went haywire—like something was wrong with the AI. Was it some kind of virus? An external pulse?"

She clipped the laser ranger back to her utility belt. "We can stand here making up questions all day, but I'd rather have answers. I'm going over there to find out—even if I have to walk."

Kyle leaned against the metal ladder. "While we're out here, Darcy, we should take a minute to inspect our own ship. We didn't exactly land like a ballerina either."

Impatient to get moving, Darcy joined him as they made a quick but thorough circuit of the AeroFox, checking the hull, the landing struts, the engines. The third comm satellite remained in its launch cradle, intact but never deployed. When they reached the lower hull that had scraped the ridge, she was relieved to see only superficial damage on the exterior.

Kyle snorted in his facemask. "It's barely even scratched."

"It sure didn't feel like a scratch." Facing the hull, Darcy activated her AR display, and diagnostic information scrolled up, indicator lines overlaying the wrecked portion of the craft. "The damage is mostly internal." She opened a panel and yanked out a line-replaceable unit, which showed clear singe marks.

Kyle said, "We need to print replacement parts before we'll ever get airborne again—but we can do it."

Darcy felt her urgency increase. "Later. I have to get to Corey first."

They both knew Kyle was not in good enough shape to make the two-kilometer trek. He said, "You go get Corey and Engineer Baxter. I'll keep working here to get my AI pal back online."

She couldn't agree quickly enough and helped Kyle to the ladder and airlock. In the distance, more lightning flashed, like evil electrical laughter.

CHAPTER 15

As he worked his way along the AstroBug's central corridor toward the exit airlock, Corey imagined a sinking ship on the seas of Earth. Too apt a metaphor.

The metal deck was slanted and slippery as he reached the egress hatch, and the ship shuddered as it listed a few more degrees. He had hoped the lake ice would refreeze and stabilize them like a clenched fist, but no such luck. He had to go outside and figure out how to get the ship free before they sank to the bottom of the deep lake. He didn't like that fuel leak, either....

He could stay in direct touch with Baxter through his implant, but external comms were still down. Corey really wanted to signal the AeroFox to let Darcy know they were still alive before she did anything crazy.

The thought of her brought a smile to his face as he stood at the airlock. Balancing himself against a tilted wall, he pulled out an oxygen mask from a locker, donned it, and adjusted the seal over the lower half of his face. As he inhaled the cold, dry air, he slapped a flash-scanner around his wrist.

As he cycled through the airlock, his own excitement increased. He was about to look out on the new world where the human race would make a home. Finally, the heavy external door swung open into a gust of wind and a swirl of snowflakes and ash.

The last gasps of ship air escaped past him into the darkness as he muttered, "Fifty years in space for this?"

He looked down at the ice slabs piled up against the Bug's hull. He wouldn't need a ladder at all. He jumped out and landed on the hard surface. "Ha!" He extended his wrist and snapped an image of his booted foot on the ice of Proxima b. That would be good enough to show Darcy. "I should have thought of some profound words to say."

He turned back to look at the ship. The AstroBug had cracked through the frozen lake, and cracks radiated outward. Blocks of ice had uplifted, grinding together around the hull. The saucer-shaped vessel was now precariously balanced, embedded but tilting.

When the slabs shifted, Corey nearly lost his balance again. The AstroBug made a scraping, screeching sound as it sank another half meter into the slush. This was worse than he had feared. Grim, he climbed back into the airlock chamber and held onto the hatch rim, taking one more look at the alien surface before he cycled through.

When he returned to the pilot deck, he could feel the entire vessel shaking. At her station, Baxter was studying schematics of the Bug's plasma engines and maneuvering thrusters—both showed prominent red warning zones. The engineer looked up at him, her brow deeply furrowed. "Did you just set foot out there?"

"Yes, left a scuffed footprint and everything—but history won't remember it, if we don't get out of here alive."

She studied the screens again. "I've been trying to transmit a distress call, if anybody's listening. I think our external antenna is damaged. Or underwater."

Corey said, "Sometimes you don't get an answer, no matter how often you try." The thought struck him, as he remembered how much he had longed for an answer, any kind of answer, from Earth all his life. "When I was a kid, I spent years sending messages, hailing Earth, and waiting to hear any kind of response. But nobody was home."

Baxter looked at him, stricken. "I still haven't gotten my head around it yet, everybody on Earth just ... dead."

He had been nine years old when he first sneaked into the arkship's abandoned comm center. The *Odyssey* had heard only utter silence for over thirty years.

Using Omni, he studied up on the tight-beam transmitting array and the pickup grids mounted on the front and rear sections of the ship. The comm hub had been cold and empty when he entered it, lit only by emergency lights, but according to the diagnostics, which Corey ran again and again, the transmitting setup was functional.

The receiving array showed a fair amount of damage from the old impacts in the Oort Cloud. That could have been repaired with spare parts and a team of mechanics working in bottle suits, but Captain Faraday hadn't allowed it after the tragic losses of Captain Andolino and Darcy's mother.

But nine-year-old Corey needed to know. Without authorization, he sat inside the comm hub looking out at the infinite starfield. He transmitted a welcome, just a kid in a crew uniform, dark hair cut short and serviceable. His message was like waving a flag, trying to get someone's attention. "Hello? Hello, is there anyone back on Earth? This is the *Odyssey*. My name is Jim Corey. I was born here on the ship. I ... we think about you a lot, Earth. Please respond and tell us about what's left there. We're still a long way from Proxima b yet."

It would be two years before his signal even reached Earth and another two years before he could expect a response—he'd be thirteen. Even so, Corey returned to the comm hub and sent out more messages every month, then every six months, then every year on his birthday. Darcy had joined him each year, adding her voice to his, her hope to his.

Corey remembered his tension four years later when they

might possibly receive a response. He and Darcy had sat together in the dim communication hub, listening. They returned day after day, hoping for some kind of acknowledgement. Nothing.

He felt heavy with disappointment. "You'd think they could at least say hello."

"Either they can't respond, or they don't want to respond," Darcy said.

Young Corey narrowed his eyes. "Or maybe our comm array is messed up, and we can't send or receive after all."

Darcy's mother had been trying to fix it when …

Year after year, Corey had dispatched his "message in a bottle." Eventually, though, he gave up and devoted his attention to the planet in front of him, not the planet behind. After all, the only home he had ever known was the *Odyssey*. Now, he had his own job to do, his own ship to fix.

Baxter zoomed in on the engine diagrams, rotated the view of the AstroBug. "I'm calculating how much thrust we can manage with the fuel we have left. These readings don't look good, plenty of instabilities—and that leak is significant. What did you see out there?"

Corey let out a quick sigh. "We might have thirty minutes to an hour tops before we sink. It wasn't part of our mission to explore the bottom of an alien sea." Then, excited by a new idea, he went to the pilot control, called up another set of screens. "Part of why we flew this big-ass ship down here was so we could access its rover. We were going to drive around to the shield nodes."

Baxter quickly realized what he meant. "So, we'd better get the rover out before we both go swimming." The ship rumbled, slid, settled further. She looked even more queasy. "I'd feel much better on solid ground."

Corey typed a sequence into his flight terminal, then his shoulders slumped. The display showed the AstroBug's profile, the layer of water and ancient ice—and the lower hatch was completely inaccessible.

He groaned. "The vehicle hangar is submerged and surrounded by ice. We're not getting the TerraCat out."

"So, how do we expose the hatch?" Sweat glistened on Baxter's forehead. "You can feel us sinking."

Corey hunched forward, concentrating. "All right, we just need a shove in the right direction. Once I prep the rover, I can fire the Bug's engines long enough to tweak our angle, raise the access hatch above the ice line, and then we can drive the TerraCat out."

Baxter looked alarmed. "If we fire the AstroBug's engines, won't that shift the ice and let us sink like a stone?"

He didn't take his eyes from the diagram. "Unless we do something, we're going to sink anyway—and soon. But if we get the rover clear, we can roll off the lake ice to the shore. While I'm at it, there should be enough fuel left in the AstroBug for me to blast us out of the ice, make a short hop, and land on solid ground. Piece of cake."

"Piece of something ..." Baxter said. "You're planning to fly this thing with a fuel leak?"

He jabbed a finger on the screen. "The fuel levels are sufficient for the Bug to fly a few hundred meters. We don't have a choice, unless you want this to become a submarine instead of a spaceship."

Baxter grumbled. "I liked it better when I was sleeping in the hibernation pod."

Corey had made up his mind. He enhanced the affected areas on the schematic. "Look, the leak is isolated, and I'll only need to be airborne for a minute or so. We're not trying to get back into space."

Baxter snorted. "We're stuck on the surface for good, and that rover will be vital. Let's just hope we meet up with Clarke and Dyson somehow. Remember why we're here—we've got a lot of work to do on those shields before the *Odyssey* swings back around."

Corey felt a chill. "Damn right." Now that the plan was set, he got moving. "It'll take about fifteen minutes for me to warm up the thrusters." He watched the energy levels rise, calculated the thrust and angle necessary. First, he'd just do a repositioning nudge, then a big push.

Baxter spoke to the AI avatar. "Omni, are your systems rebooted?"

"I have rerouted and restored, Engineer Baxter."

She visibly steeled herself. "While Corey gets ready, let's continue the shield-network analysis so we're ready to go."

The AI sounded eager. "I will study the patterns from the shield node anomalies, using the data I obtained from my counterpart before the corruption occurred. That will allow me to establish a baseline and determine the best protocol for repairing the transmitter network once we get back to the dayside."

With Baxter's attention focused on her primary job, Corey hoped she wouldn't notice his own uneasiness. Growing fractures in the ice made the Bug's situation increasingly precarious. He doubted they actually had the thirty minutes he had guessed. Much less, in fact.

Baxter worked on the schematic of shield nodes spread across the opposite hemisphere, with far too many of them glowing red and offline. "I didn't travel four light-years just to get cooked by solar flares in my new back yard. This shield network is going to work." She looked up at him. "Meanwhile, kid, you go start the car."

Lightning flickered across the dark sky through the windowport. Despite the cold, the blowing snow, and the distant volcanoes, Corey knew that this place was *survivable*. "If all else fails, we could always live here on the night side for a while."

Baxter grimaced. "Hiding in the dark for the rest of my life? No thanks. I was promised a tropical paradise."

"Never believe those kinds of promises." Corey headed for the access ladder. "I'll get the rover ready to roll. You better switch into an envirosuit."

Baxter plucked at the mesh-reinforced stimsuit that covered her body. "I am more than happy to ditch this torture device. Time to be a colonist instead of a popsicle."

CHAPTER 16

During Denise Clarke's pregnancy aboard the *Odyssey*, Captain Faraday noticed a shift in the crew's mood. The hundred workers completed the endless maintenance and monitoring duties, but now there was a palpable spark of hope.

Sebastian was a doting father, and Denise was a beaming mother-to-be. The on-call medical personnel ran frequent, almost obsessive, prenatal checks and announced that the baby would be a girl. No one worried about the complications of having an infant on board the vast ship or what the consequences would be for the child growing up all alone between the stars.

When little Darcy was born, the skeleton crew celebrated. Captain Faraday made up her mind to stay distant and objective, but she found that impossible. She spent a lot of time admiring— the better word was "adoring"—the baby, as did two other young women: Lucy Dyson, a water reclamation and filtration engineer, and Miranda Corey, an agricultural specialist and greenhouse technician. The two were young and vivacious, the type who would have been socially popular on Earth. Miranda dominated the friendship, with Lucy following whatever her companion suggested. They seemed excessively interested in the baby girl.

Faraday should have seen the problem sooner.

Miranda and Lucy were clingy and overly attentive. Although

Sebastian and Denise arranged for opposite work shifts so that one parent could always watch their little girl, the other two young women insisted on taking babysitting stints. Miranda was enchanted with the darling little infant, and Lucy echoed her words and feelings.

Baby Darcy was a sharp reminder of everything that had been lost back on Earth. They talked with their friends, drank too much of the ship-distilled moonshine. Miranda grew maudlin over her desire to become a mother, too, because Denise Clarke was such a fine example. Lucy repeated how much she wished she could have a baby of her own.

Faraday was keenly aware of the drawbacks of an entire colony ship with ten thousand human popsicles and not a single child or teenager. Proxima b would be a difficult place to live until the solar-flare shield was verified, the hab modules established, and the first crops harvested. It was too difficult a place to have babies running around.

The United Nations had issued a very hard mandate during the selection process when the thousands of candidates were chosen: the best and most qualified scientists and engineers, the teachers, the farmers, the narrow slice of the human race most likely to succeed. No children or teens were included because their immature physiology did not tolerate the hibernation process. All those young people had to be left behind, doomed on Earth.

But starry-eyed Miranda's longing increased, and her fantasies were fed and reinforced by Lucy's ready agreement. Where one person might have been ruled by common sense, two people could talk each other into great stupidity. Miranda made up her mind to get pregnant, and so did Lucy. They vowed to have their own babies.

The overworked skeleton crew could not watch every member every minute. The young women accessed the ship's sperm bank, the countless samples preserved for genetic diversity in the new colony. Miranda and Lucy were not particularly selective, but took any samples. They monitored their hormonal cycles to chart their ovulation, and they inseminated themselves repeatedly, until within a week of each other, Lucy and Miranda both discovered that they were pregnant. Grinning and triumphant, they issued a statement to the entire crew, without even telling the captain first.

As the story came out about what those two had actually done, the crew greeted the news with uneasiness instead of unqualified joy. The young women became bitter at the reaction. Faraday reprimanded them both, but there was little she could do. It was too late, and soon there would be three babies aboard the *Odyssey*.

Worse, though, Lucy and Miranda proved to be less than ideal expectant mothers. Faraday received regular reports from the medical personnel that Lucy drank heavily, and Faraday had to impose careful monitoring to ensure her sobriety during the term. Miranda was incensed by the restrictions on her own life, and Faraday lost her temper, railing at the two women. "You each made yourselves responsible for another new colonist, another representative of the human race, and you're damn well going to take the matter seriously."

As captain, she issued a harsh new policy that every member of the awake crew receive mandatory birth control. The *Odyssey* simply did not have the resources for more births. The new rule was completely rational, fully understood by the skeleton crew, yet it was still received with a sour gloom.

When the two babies were born, both boys—Kyle and Jim— the mothers were surprised and unsettled. Miranda Corey and Lucy Dyson were both light haired, fair complected women, but the sperm samples they had chosen at random gave the boys non-white fathers, a Black man for Kyle and a Native American for Jim Corey. Since the young women had inseminated themselves multiple times with multiple samples, they couldn't even specifically identify the name of either father.

The whole crew accepted these new members, while recognizing the challenges the children would face for the rest of the voyage. Faraday spoke to advisors and specialists, and they developed a long-term rearing plan for the children. The babies were healthy and passed all the tests, but the captain was not so sure about the suitability of the two mothers.

Kyle's mother suffered from immediate and extreme postpartum depression. She was listless and miserable, didn't take care of herself or her baby. Of the hundred personnel awake, one man served as ship's counselor, but he was not prepared for anything like this.

In a few months, fifty members of the skeleton crew were scheduled to go back down into hibernation, and another fifty would be brought up to overlap with the rest of the personnel. Both Lucy and Miranda were due for hibernation, while Sebastian and Denise Clarke still had another five years in their stint. The rotation schedule forced Faraday to consider what she needed to accomplish with the people available.

Now that Miranda and Lucy were mothers with newborn babies, could Faraday just put the women back into hibernation pods and let someone else raise their children? Lucy and Miranda were only mediocre workers who did not have critical jobs, but if she kept them awake for the babies, then Faraday could not awaken more qualified replacements.

Then Lucy Dyson tried to kill herself and her baby son, and that was the tipping point for the captain. Lucy was put in restraints, sedated, and given care to ensure that she was healthy enough to go down into hibernation. After Lucy was sealed away in her pod, Captain Faraday—and the rest of the skeleton crew—promised to raise baby Kyle.

Meanwhile, Miranda Corey soured on being a mother, since the reality proved less compelling than the idea of it. She abdicated her responsibility almost immediately. At first she used her baby as an excuse to cancel her greenhouse shifts, asserting that she didn't dare leave her precious infant alone and therefore couldn't work. But when she was allowed to bring the child with her, Miranda instead locked the little boy in her quarters, unmonitored for the entire day. When Faraday discovered this, she reprimanded Miranda Corey in front of all the crew members.

Miranda, though, was sarcastic and aloof. "You want the baby so bad, then why don't you take it?"

It. She couldn't even bring herself to use Jim's name, or think of the child as a person.

So furious she could barely speak, Faraday made a prompt decision to send Miranda into her scheduled hibernation cycle. "Sebastian and Denise Clarke will help raise the boy. You don't deserve the honor."

The *Odyssey* needed two other specialists awake, and Faraday carefully reviewed the personnel records to select the best replacements. She herself had always wanted to be a mother. During the construction of the *Odyssey*, she and Michio had planned to get married and start a family, but since no children could be taken aboard, they had held off. They had denied themselves a family, promising to make up for lost time once the arkships arrived at Proxima b.

Now Earth was gone, Michio was gone, and so was her only chance at being a mother. But Faraday changed her way of thinking. No one had ever promised that being captain would be easy, nor had anyone warned her it would be impossible.

Gwen Faraday didn't believe in the impossible.

And now she had three kids, and they were hers in their own way. As the *Odyssey* crossed the stars, she decided that was enough.

CHAPTER 17

A s alien snow swirled in the dark air, Darcy set off from the AeroFox. No looking back. The Bug's flashing beacon called to her. Her breath echoed in the half facemask, and the AR goggles helped illuminate her path ahead.

"OK, Kyle, I'm on my way," she transmitted.

By now he was back inside the scout ship. His reply sounded ragged. "Say hi for me when you get there. Still working on getting my Omni back online."

She picked her way across the rugged terrain. She wanted to run as fast as she could, but the planet's gravity was already wearing her down, and she had never walked across uneven ground. Two kilometers—that distance simply didn't exist on the *Odyssey*.

"If you can hear me, Corey, I'm coming," she said into the voice pickup. When she didn't hear a response, she grumbled, "And get your damned comms fixed!"

The snow thickened, little pellets of ice that swirled in a dancing fog. A brilliant bolt of lightning lanced across the sky and struck one of the nearby mountain peaks. She kept plodding along, picking her way.

Ahead, the beacon's light remained clear enough.

Kyle hailed her in the comm implant. "Still doing OK, Darcy?"

"Yeah, but this weather is crazy. I'm not used to it."

"You're not used to any kind of weather—or being on a planet at all, for that matter."

Her goggles enhanced the terrain. During her life, she and her two friends had explored every square centimeter of the *Odyssey*, even the hard-to-reach maintenance spots and the cramped circulation shafts. That giant ship had been her whole world; now she found it hard to grasp that no one had ever walked where she was now.

No one. Ever.

They had trained for the dayside, with all of the colony components in place. True, the refugees had always intended to explore the night side, but only after the colony was set up. She muttered to herself, "I hate doing things out of order."

A distant rumble filled the air, and the pebbles at her feet trembled and jittered. The nearby volcano cracked, and scarlet lava spouted into the air. Darcy only had a second to brace herself before the shockwave hit. She stumbled and dropped to her knee.

"Darcy, what happened?" Kyle's voice was loud in her implant.

"Oh, just another volcano." She picked herself up, but the ground was still shaking. "This area is unstable. Corey can't have much time." She tried to pick up her pace, staggering forward.

"Be careful!" Kyle said. "I'm not in any shape to rescue anybody."

Kyle finally found himself alone in the AeroFox. Fighting against the pain of his injuries, he removed his facemask and breathed the ship air. He was glad he'd insisted on going outside with Darcy, although the simple effort of donning the envirosuit had nearly done him in. But Darcy had been so fixated on rescuing the AstroBug that she had not noticed just how hurt he really was.

Now that she wasn't watching him, Kyle could admit to himself that something was really wrong inside of him. He didn't blame Darcy, knowing she had done what was necessary to get to the crash site as fast as humanly possible. He had known to expect the extreme deceleration, but he had still unbuckled his straps at exactly the wrong moment.

Captain Faraday had once told the three of them, "Sometimes when you have no good options, you just have to make a decision and live with it."

This was not at all how he had imagined their first day on Persephone. He wanted to be out there on the virgin world, side by side with Darcy and Corey, planting the *Odyssey*'s mission flag, heroes of humanity! But nothing goes as planned—that was one of the most fundamental lessons he had learned in his educational sessions and simulations while growing up.

Forlorn, he ran a palm over the dark surface of the AI core module. "Things certainly have gone wrong now, O."

He swallowed down the wet metallic taste of blood in his mouth. The X-Doc was ruined, but maybe he didn't want a diagnosis just yet. It would distract him from this work.

Once he had his Omni back, his real friend, he'd feel whole again. Over the years, he had kept his personal copy of the AI separate from the *Odyssey*'s main AI, not synchronizing or homogenizing it, which had allowed his companion to develop its own personality that mirrored his own. O was an actual friend, and the two of them could share ideas, use each other as sounding boards. It was fun.

At the console, he talked to himself as he went through a diagnostic routine to reboot the AI. "We'll get you jumpstarted, O. I promise. There's too much work to do here—you can't just snooze while us humans do everything."

He expected a wry response, a quick retort, but Omni remained silent. He looked above the console, expecting to see the avatar symbol, but he saw only red lights on the diagnostics. Some of the readouts were blank, and that was worse than a failure. He ran the test again, but got the same results.

He removed the access plate to open Omni's central core. He had installed his friend into the AeroFox so they could be together on this mission, but now he felt complete dismay as he exposed the quantum core, the protected matrix that contained the AI's specialized memories, conversations, and experiences—Omni's personality.

The X-Doc wasn't the only system that had been damaged by the major lightning strikes that blasted the ship. The AI's quantum matrix was also charred and broken.

"No, no, no, no, no." Tears welled in his eyes. "No!"

His Omni was dead.

As a child, Kyle had grown up with the wise and ever-present voice of Omni. The ship's AI was everywhere and knew everything.

Captain Faraday was always there, too, always awake, and the members of the skeleton crew considered Kyle, Darcy, and Corey to be the children of humanity. It took a cooperative community to make these three the best possible new colonists.

Omni was a vital part of that. According to the plan, once the Proxima b colony was established, the settlers would begin to reproduce. The first wave of children should have been born by the time the *Valkyrie* and *Phoenix* arrived, bringing even more people. As such, the AI library database contained rigorous educational simulations and routines.

Fascinated by everything, Kyle was an exceptional student. While Darcy and Corey ran off on their own adventures in the giant ship, he immersed himself in the instructional routines. On his own personal device, he cloned the AI so he always had a separate copy of Omni as his own companion.

Kyle would curl up on the bed in his quarters and talk to the module for hours. At one point, he stopped updating the AI clone because he wanted a friend of his own, and the longer he kept his copy separate from the ubiquitous *Odyssey* network—the more conversations they had, the more dreams they shared—the more Kyle's friend became unique.

Once, when a computer engineer named Anderson Wilder discovered what Kyle had done, he demanded that the AI clone be synchronized and updated again. Kyle refused, not wanting to lose his unique AI, and the situation grew inflamed to the point where the young man, clutching his portable Omni, ran crying to Captain Faraday. Wilder was just as adamant, laying out the reasons against having conflicting AIs.

Kyle suspected that the computer engineer's arguments might have been more persuasive if he hadn't been so mean about it, but Faraday had not been swayed by him. She saw no real disadvantage to letting Kyle have a divergent Omni as an odd companion. Afterward, Wilder was cold and aloof for the rest of his awake shift until he went down again in hibernation, not to be revived until they reached the planet.

Kyle had his personal Omni for years. He was always a bit of an oddball, self-absorbed, interested in eccentric subjects. Captain Faraday indulged him, but O knew how to encourage him, how to relate the information in ways the young man could understand. They were the best of friends.

Now, Kyle stared at the charred quantum core. All the stored data that had made up the totality of his Omni had been obliterated. The complete structure of the personality, all the memories and experiences, were wiped.

Kyle forgot the pain of his own injuries and just stared at the blank readouts, the red warning lights, the error messages—looking at nothing, drowning in memories.

At last, he activated the comm and spoke in a hoarse voice. "Uh, Darcy?" The words petrified in his throat.

Her reply was tinged with static. "I'm halfway there, Kyle. No problems so far."

"Uh, there's a problem ... big problem." He squeezed his eyes shut, feeling the warm tears pour down his cheeks. "It's ... O."

He heard the hesitation in her response. "Is he up and running again? If anybody can fix Omni, you can."

His voice hitched as he fought back the emotions. "I can't fix him. The lightning strike destroyed his quantum matrix. All of his data, all our memories and experiences ... not retrievable."

She was a long time answering. "Sorry, Kyle. I know he was your friend."

Alone in the control deck—really alone, without even the glowing AI avatar—he straightened. "Yes, O was definitely ... unique. He knew me better than anyone."

"Are you going to be OK?"

He hoped his voice was strong enough that she would believe his lie, but Darcy knew him too well. "I'll be fine. If it's all right with you, I'm just going to chill for bit. Keep sending me regular updates. You're the cavalry. The AstroBug is counting on you."

Kyle switched off, slumped in the chair and let himself experience myriad forms of pain. The grief was the worst.

CHAPTER 18

Darcy made good time across the windswept barrens, following the AstroBug's beacon. Even under the heavy gravity, she bounded across the terrain, then slowed to plodding again, careful to watch her footing. She didn't dare trip and fall flat on her facemask or twist her ankle in a cranny between boulders.

On the *Odyssey*, every deck was a smooth, hard surface, but each step here brought home the sheer *rawness* of Proxima b. Once the colony was established and the popsicles were thawed, then they would start making roads, taming the place.

For now, nothing was going to keep her from Jim Corey. She would cross even this night-side obstacle course to get to him.

When she reached the fringe of the great frozen lake, the ground was more ice than rock. The AstroBug's beacon flickered, not far away now. For the hundredth time, she sent a signal, but received no response. Their comms must be damaged, because she couldn't accept the alternative explanation that Corey and Baxter had been killed in the crash.

She hopped over an icy boulder, but misjudged the gravity and fell to her knees. She caught herself, but clumsily enough that she was glad Corey couldn't see her.

Ahead, she could see the AstroBug embedded like a fossil on

the frozen lake, surrounded by uplifted white slabs. A volcanic tremor shook the ground, creating a crack through the expanse of ice. Darcy paused, waiting for the shocks to subside, then she picked up her pace now that she had reached the flatter frozen surface. Lit by the flickering beacon, she saw the angled top section of the Bug protruding from the surface, but the rest of the saucer was slowly sinking in the frozen quicksand.

"You got yourself into some trouble, Corey. I should have brought a shovel." As she approached, she could see the glimmer of illumination in the Bug's windowports. "Lights are on. You better be home."

She tried to reach him again. Nothing. Darcy would have to do this the old-fashioned way. She would go up to the front door and knock.

Corey dropped down the last few rungs of the central ladder to the circular garage hangar. In front of him, the all-terrain rover—the TerraCat—sat ready to go, held in place by anchor cables even after the crash.

Working his way across the slanted deck, Corey pulled a charging cable out of the vehicle's socket and entered a sequence on the access keypad. A flush of awakening lights signaled its readiness.

The turntable deck rotated so that the TerraCat faced the egress hatch—which Corey knew had sunk beneath the ice. The vehicle's hatch opened to reveal the interior with spacious seats and driving controls. The rugged machine was exactly what the colonists would need on a potentially hostile world. First, though, he had to get the vehicle out of the bay and onto the surface.

One problem at a time.

Dropping into the driver's seat, he accessed the systems, felt the thrum of the engines. "I know how to make a TerraCat purr." He triggered the release, and the restraint cables reeled back into the wall units. He was ready to go freewheeling, if only he could get it out the door. In a big gamble, he would have to use the AstroBug's engines to shift the sinking vessel and raise the hatch above the level of the ice.

A big if ...

Suddenly, inside the garage hangar, he heard a sharp resounding bang of metal on metal—totally unexpected and out of place. He froze, wondering if some other component had broken or collapsed, but as the succession of bangs continued, rhythmic and urgent, he knew it wasn't a natural sound.

Confused, Corey tapped his comm implant. "Baxter, are you hearing that sound?"

The engineer answered in surprise, "The regular pounding? You mean that's not you?"

Corey felt his skin crawl. "Sounds like it's coming from above."

Omni's voice cut in. "Commander Corey, my sensors indicate that someone is outside Egress Two above the ice layer. I believe you should go to the airlock and answer."

"Someone's outside? Who the hell?" He climbed hand-over-hand out of the garage hangar to the mid-deck, just in time to see the inner airlock hatch swing open.

Darcy Clarke stood there, looking worse for wear ... and utterly beautiful.

He bounded toward her. "Darce! How did you get here?"

Pulling off her half-mask, she gave him a relieved smile. "You didn't answer about a million calls, so I had to come see what sort of mess you got yourself into."

Corey wrapped his arms around her waist and swung her up, even in the heavier gravity. He cut off her further questions with a passionate kiss.

After he released her, Darcy laughed. "Glad to know you missed me!" She glanced away, flushing. "All right, I admit I missed you, too."

"Our external comms were burned out in a surge. We couldn't

send or receive." He stared at her with bright eyes. "I can't believe it! The AeroFox was all the way up in synchronous orbit—how could you possibly pull this off?"

She chuckled. "Isn't it obvious? I'm a better pilot than you."

He gave her a teasing nudge and couldn't help but laugh with her. "You might be a better pilot, but ..." He called up the image from his flash-scanner, showing his boots on the surface. "First footprints on Proxima b."

"Sorry, pal." Darcy pulled up her own flash-scanner to show a similar image of her footprint on the dusty, shadowed ground. "Look at the time stamp. Beat you by thirty minutes."

"Good for you, Neil Armstrong." He graciously accepted defeat. "Come on, you can help. We're in the middle of an emergency." He explained their situation as they hurried along the access corridor. "Physically, Baxter and I are fine. Our Omni was damaged by contact with an unexpected power surge in the shield network, but he's putting himself back together. The surge came from outside the caretaker AI, though—like some malicious virus."

Darcy looked exhausted, as if the situation was finally catching up with her. "There's not good news on our front, either. Kyle's Omni was completely wiped out in a lightning strike. Fried. Kyle says it can't be repaired."

Corey paused. "Aww, I know how much that AI meant to him —they were best buds." He rapped his knuckles on the metal bulkhead. "But is the Fox intact? This ship isn't going to last much longer."

"Mostly intact, but that's not the worst of it," Darcy said. "Kyle was badly injured, thrown around in the wild flight. Our X-Doc is toast, and he needs serious medical attention. When I get you two out of here, we have to bring your spare med unit back to the AeroFox so we can fix him up."

Corey groaned. "Here I thought that fixing the shield network and saving the colony was enough of a challenge for one day." He grew serious. "We have to get those shields up and running, Darce, or else all of this is for nothing."

The big vessel suddenly shuddered and lurched, and Corey met her gaze as the quake subsided. "We don't have much time. I'm surprised the Bug hasn't sunk already with all these tremors. I was trying to get the TerraCat out. How far away is your ship?"

"About two klicks. I just walked it—and would rather not do that again. The TerraCat would be much faster. But have you seen how much ice is piled around your ship? How are you going to get the rover out?"

"I always have a plan." He raised his eyebrows. "I'll use our main thrusters to raise the AstroBug enough to expose the main hatch. Once I do, you can drive the Cat away. Then, once you and Baxter are away, I'll keep using the thrusters to push this ship out of the ice and onto solid ground. We can't just let it sink."

"Sure, piece of cake," Darcy said, scrambling down the ladder behind him. "Easy as pie. Choose your dessert."

When Baxter dove into an engineering problem, the rest of the world went away. Hyper-focus was an advantage in her profession. Absently sipping strong coffee from her Autobrew, she stared at Omni's analysis of the failing shield grid. She had designed it a lifetime ago on Earth, and now she imagined herself in a locked-room brainstorming session with a colleague.

"Why aren't these nodes working?" She focused on the nodes that flashed red. "It makes the whole network ineffective."

Omni said, "Fusion reactors are feeding power to the grid, as designed, but these particular nodes are offline. I was unable to get complete answers when I connected to the caretaker AI that controls the system."

Baxter took another sip, savored the bitterness. "That was one hell of an EMP scramble you received. It sent us into a tailspin."

"I am sorry, Engineer Baxter."

"Not blaming you. Just trying to understand. There's enough energy running through the shield to block deadly radiation over an entire continent—but that glitch seemed almost targeted to block you out."

Omni said, "Now that I have isolated the damage in my circuits and the shield, I can speculate that the pulse came from outside our automated system. It was not part of the caretaker AI."

Baxter looked at the blue infinity-symbol as if it were a face on a screen. "What do you mean, outside our system? How is that possible?"

"It should not be possible, Engineer Baxter. There is no identifiable external source for such a pulse."

Baxter let out a sigh as she slumped into her seat. "Should not be possible—story of my life. God, I'm tired. I was supposed to have another few weeks of sleep."

CHAPTER 19

Thirty years into the voyage, the *Odyssey's* sustainability engineer, a gloomy and abrupt woman named Grace Stoops-Bopp, called it a "cascade effect." She took samples throughout the habitation ring and issued increasingly dire warnings to Faraday.

"Once the airmoss starts dying, it's going to get worse, Captain. Our whole arkship is a closed system with little margin for error. One tiny failure leads to another, then another, and soon there's no stopping it." Stoops-Bopp crossed her arms over her narrow chest. "And the worst failures will come from left field. You'll never be able to predict it."

"Then we have to stop the first one from happening," Faraday said.

"Too late for that," Stoops-Bopp retorted. "The blight is spreading. You can already see it on multiple airmoss patches." She went off to continue her inspection tour.

For three decades the *Odyssey's* environment systems were reliable enough that Faraday had stopped worrying about them. To recycle the air and refresh the oxygen content, the ceilings and walls were carpeted with trapezoidal patches of vibrant green airmoss, a hardy genetically engineered variety that needed virtually no maintenance, could draw moisture out of the humidified ship air, and needed only minimal nitrogen-based compounds that were extracted from the human waste produced by the skeleton crew.

Then the first dark blots appeared on the airmoss patches, initially blamed on some flaw in the fertilizer systems or insufficient moisture. But the blight spread quickly enough that entire sections of moss turned gray and had to be ripped up and destroyed. The two botanists on shift turned their time and effort to finding a way to protect against the blight.

Faraday immediately sealed off the contaminated moss sections, but it was too late. Whatever the original cause, the blight had already circulated throughout the ship. Airmoss began dying off in waves, and with it the ability to produce enough oxygen for the hundred maintenance crewmembers.

Sebastian and Denise Clarke, both of them still awake with their four-year-old daughter Darcy, had called up engineering schematics and considered all the stored equipment that had been loaded for the colony. Sebastian was able to increase the efficiency of the CO_2 scrubbers by several percent, but the *Odyssey's* habitation ring relied on biological replenishment. Even his improvements could not sustain them for more than a few years.

Exactly as Grace Stoops-Bopp had predicted, that was only the start of the cascade effect. Another failure struck when the artificial grids that illuminated the greenhouse domes began to flicker out and fail. Some long-term chemical contaminant in the illumination rods decreased the intensity of light to less than the threshold needed for plants to survive. The crops began to shrivel up.

"We're doomed," Stoops-Bopp said in a deadpan voice. "By the time the *Odyssey* gets to Proxima b, none of us will be alive."

Some crewmembers fell into deep despair, but Faraday just grew angry. "That's an unacceptable answer. Find me another one."

An extreme but obvious possibility would be just to place everyone into hibernation pods and let the arkship fly on its automated course until they reached Proxima Centauri. But those odds weren't good enough for Faraday.

The *Odyssey* was a complex behemoth, and the captain was responsible not just for the maintenance crew, but also for the ten thousand popsicles—as well as the library databases, the cultural artifacts, the seed and embryo banks. All that remained of Earth was here on this one ship.

Even without unexpected crises, the crew had their hands full replacing worn components, fixing leaks, tightening seals. Without anyone awake to handle the million small daily duties, the arkship likely would not be intact by the time it arrived in the next star system.

Sebastian and Denise Clarke looked terrified by the implications, and Faraday knew what was foremost on their minds. Their daughter and the two little boys would not survive a hibernation cycle. There had to be a different way.

Stoops-Bopp ran projections and grimly reported that it would be difficult enough to keep the ship going with the current failures. "And there's sure to be something else. I just know it'll happen."

"I'm the captain. I'm staying awake," said Faraday.

After running countless simulations, they decided that their failing resources could sustain—just barely—a mere fifteen people awake. That was the bare minimum needed for the base level of maintenance. And at least fifteen crewmembers would be needed for the final braking maneuver around the red dwarf.

Fifteen people instead of a hundred to watch over an entire ship and ten thousand colonists. And three little children.

Because of the extreme need to conserve resources, Sebastian and Denise Clarke decided to split their hibernation shifts, one awake while the other slept frozen for five years. That way at least their daughter and the boys would have one parent to watch over them.

Faraday culled the list, keeping only the most essential personnel on duty. It gave her no small amount of pleasure to send

Stoops-Bopp into the hibernation pod; the woman's last words before drifting into the long sleep were, "I don't know if I'll ever wake up."

After a tearful goodbye, Sebastian hugged his daughter and his wife. He asked Captain Faraday to take a picture of them—Denise, Darcy, and Sebastian all standing together in the hibernation bay, a family, so they could always remember. "I'll take good care of her," Denise had promised him.

"Don't you worry, Sebastian," Faraday said. "I'm the captain, but I can also be a den mother. Darcy, Kyle, and Corey will be in good hands."

Eighty-five people had gone into the pods, and the ship seemed quieter, more cavernous than ever before.

CHAPTER 20

As Corey completed the TerraCat's checklist, Darcy poked into a cylindrical food station between the rear seats. "Lots of room for the three of us to roll away from here. We've got tons of vital work to do over on the dayside before the *Odyssey* arrives. I just wasn't expecting to drive all the way over there."

She let out a heavy sigh, thinking about how much would change once all the popsicles were thawed. "In our entire lives we've never been around more than a hundred people. I can't imagine ten thousand of us all together! I hope the captain takes her time and wakes everybody up in stages, baby steps, so we can get it right."

Corey was reticent, and she could tell something was bothering him. They had always been closely connected. "Darce, I need to talk to you." Lines of concern crossed his forehead. "Something you need to know, and there's no point keeping it from you."

She frowned at him. "You never keep anything from me."

"Not for long. Captain Faraday briefed me before we set off on this mission." He paused. "The *Odyssey*'s in trouble—serious trouble."

Darcy leaned closer, unnecessarily lowering her voice. "But we finally made it to Proxima. What kind of serious trouble?"

Corey turned in the TerraCat's driver's seat. "The ship is barely holding together. More systems are failing than you can imagine. You know we couldn't afford to have more than a small skeleton crew awake, even though the original mission planners said that a hundred crewmembers were the minimum to maintain the vital systems. Fifteen people barely kept the *Odyssey* from catastrophic failure, and certainly not in optimal condition. That braking maneuver is going to be very rough, and the captain hopes she can hold the ship together until she enters planetary orbit."

"She'll make it," Darcy said. "And then we'll have time."

His expression was filled with dismay. "No, not enough time. Life support is glitching every day. Cryo-systems are stressed beyond repair. The *Odyssey*'s ICF drive is toast. After this deceleration burn, the engines will probably never fire again. Even the habitation ring is well beyond its service lifetime, considering the lack of routine checks and maintenance. The popsicles will need to be offloaded immediately and brought down to the planet. The captain is afraid the *Odyssey* will fall apart...."

Darcy couldn't believe what she was hearing. "That's impossible! Our last status briefing—"

"Was a lie," Corey cut her off. "All the reports have been lies for the past year or so. Captain Faraday didn't want you or Kyle to know."

Darcy felt as if the wind had been knocked out of her. "And how do *you* know? Why would the captain do that?" She punched him in the arm. "Why would she tell you?"

"She thought you'd already been hurt enough, I guess. The captain didn't want a panic on her hands so close to our arrival. She swore the command crew to secrecy. They even found a way to keep the worst-case predictions from Omni."

Darcy saw that her hand was trembling. "You said the hibernation units are in danger?" She swallowed hard, thinking of her father.

"Some of them may be, yes. But the section with your father is fine, for now."

"Fine?" Her world had been turned upside-down. "Are you sure? How do I know that's not just another lie?"

He kept his voice confident. "Because I'm telling you the truth. You know you can trust me."

"I thought so until just now! Screw that—my dad's in one of those units. You and I should be able to trust each other!"

"You *can* trust me."

Angry, she leaned close and got in his face. "I'm not so sure anymore. I don't care what the captain ordered you to do. We're a team, Corey—you and me—and *we* should come first. Maybe I could have helped!"

"No. You couldn't. It's that bad. Like I said, the captain only told me right before this mission. I didn't have a chance to tell you, and she made me promise ..." He held up his hands. "But now that it's just us down here on Persephone, you deserve to understand how crucial it is for us to get that shield working. It's not something to keep secret from you."

His brows drew together. "The colonists have to be offloaded as soon as possible, and that means they'll need to move into the hab modules on the dayside. They can't survive the solar-flare radiation without the protective field, and they can't stay on the arkship. We're cutting everything down to the absolute wire, not just for your dad, but for all of us."

On the rover's drive control panel, all the checklist bullets winked green. Corey turned his attention back to the vehicle. "After we get the TerraCat out of this hangar, we'll drive to the AeroFox. Kyle can use our spare X-Doc, and you'll fly us over to the nearest node, and Engineer Baxter can fix that goddamn shield! We *have* to get this done!"

Now Darcy's shoulders slumped. "The AeroFox is grounded, engines damaged from all the high-G maneuvers and hard burns I used—but that's what it took to rescue you."

Corey absorbed the information and regrouped. "If neither ship can fly ..." He tensed as he came to a decision. "Then we'll have to drive the TerraCat over to the nearest shield node. It'll be slower going overland, but we'll get there. Once we fix the tower network, we can camp out in any hab module we choose while we wait for the *Odyssey*. You and I can even pick out the home where we're going to live. Are you with me?"

Still shocked by the revelations, she concentrated on priorities. "Like we have any other choice."

Accepting that as the best answer he would get, Corey climbed out of the rugged vehicle and went back to the hatch. "Good. Let's go get Baxter. I have to fire the Bug's engines and climb above the ice enough for you to drive the TerraCat out of the garage."

CHAPTER 21

When the two reached the pilot deck, Darcy tried to pretend that everything was fine.

Tanya Baxter glanced up as she finished analyzing shield-network data. "This isn't the kind of reunion I expected, kid—but I'm glad you're here. Omni just showed me your projected flight path from synchronous orbit. You kicked some serious ass getting the AeroFox down here."

"It was a rough ride," Darcy said. The AstroBug rumbled again as it shifted with the ice. "And not a moment too soon." After the heavy news Corey had just given her, she did not have time for small talk. "Better get ready to pack up and go. You're riding with me in the TerraCat, while Corey tries to blast the ship free."

He hurried to the piloting controls. "Take our Omni's processor core. AeroFox needs it as a replacement. Kyle can rig it up over there."

The AI's blue infinity symbol brightened on the screen. "Despite my current disarray, I promise to adequately serve in my counterpart's stead."

Corey nodded. "We're going to need you."

The AstroBug listed another few degrees as the ice shifted

again. Darcy grabbed the bulkhead to keep her balance. "Come on, there's no time for long goodbyes."

At the controls, Corey pulled up the schematic of the main engines and maneuvering thrusters, then displayed how much of the hull was already submerged. "Sinking fast. We'll need quite a push to get the lower hatch above the ice."

Baxter disconnected the Omni core from its module. "You're nuts to fly this thing after the EMP and the crash. I don't feel like walking far in this gravity, but if the AeroFox is close enough, why don't we head over there on foot and wait for a rescue team? The *Odyssey* is only a couple days out."

Corey's answer was abrupt and implacable, and now Darcy understood why. "No, we have to fix that shield before Captain Faraday arrives." He gave Baxter a reassuring smile. "Relax, you know I'm the best pilot on this planet." Darcy snorted, but he continued, "I'm going to pull this thing out of the lake and set it down right next to the AeroFox."

He pretended to be intensely interested in the piloting controls. "First step is to blast out of this ice and tilt up the saucer to expose the lower garage hangar. You two be ready to roll out the TerraCat as soon as the hatch is above the ice and haul ass to solid ground. Once I free the ship, I'll be right behind you."

Baxter hurried beside Darcy, handing her the disconnected Omni core. "Need me to drive, Clarke? It's been fifty years, but I used to handle a vehicle just fine."

Darcy shook her head. "The Cat has an auto-drive function."

With an indulgent huff, the engineer began disconnecting the spare X-Doc from its wall unit.

Darcy turned back to Corey at the piloting controls. She spoke in a hushed voice. "I'll get us out in the TerraCat, but Baxter's probably right. You know the Bug is in bad shape. Don't push it— do just enough for us to get the rover clear. We can all head over to the AeroFox."

A warm understanding flashed between them. He said, "No

matter what, get that shield network functional or else everybody dies."

"No matter what," she promised.

Baxter lifted the portable X-Doc in its case. "Got it. What are you two scheming about over there?"

Darcy hurried to join Baxter as they headed to the hangar. "Corey and I always have our oddball schemes. Let's go to the TerraCat."

CHAPTER 22

Darcy strapped herself into the TerraCat's driver seat and checked the power levels of the engines. With shaky movements, Baxter climbed into the padded passenger seat. By now she had changed out of the clinging stimsuit and donned an envirosuit, with oxygen backpack and half-mask respirator at hand. She carried the Omni computer core, as well as the new X-Doc in its case.

Darcy watched the countdown from the pilot deck, ready to go. "Strap in," she said. "We can't waste any time."

Even inside the rover, she could feel the Bug shake as Corey test-fired the engines. Baxter gripped the arm of her seat, but said nothing. The test rumbling stopped after only a few seconds, and Corey said over the comm, "AstroBug's thrusters are prepped. You guys ready?"

"As soon as that door opens, the auto-drive is ready to peel out," Darcy said.

As the engineer wrestled her safety straps into place, Darcy activated the vehicle's auto guidance. "TerraCat, override safety protocols and prepare to get us out of here, best possible speed."

A female voice purred up from the control deck. "Override accepted, Astronaut Clarke. Please secure yourselves for sudden acceleration."

"Duly noted." Darcy knew the auto-guidance system would not recognize sarcasm. She touched her comm implant. "Corey, TerraCat is programmed, comms are working, and I've already told Kyle we're coming. He needs the X-Doc pretty bad. Corey, get the Bug's head out of the water before we sink."

"Ready to go. Kiss for luck?"

"Luck has nothing to do with it." She made a loud smacking sound. "But I'll give you a kiss for other reasons."

Corey kissed two fingers and touched Darcy's image on the screen. "I'll trust my piloting skills, but I won't turn down any extra luck." He gripped the control stick with one hand. "Maneuvering thrusters should break the ice and lift us up. We'll breach like a whale on one of Kyle's old Earth videos." He braced himself as he increased power. "When the saucer's lower half is clear, I'll blow the door and power-deploy the ramp. Prepare to get your butt moving out of there."

He watched the diagnostic column, saw numbers wavering between amber and red. He should have enough to pull this off. "Hang on, here we go." With a hard grimace, he pushed the output, fired the thrusters, and felt the big ship move.

The AstroBug rumbled. Fire and fumes belched out of the thrust nozzles, blasting away slush and boiling the ice. Bright ionized gases spilled across the lake's fractured surface. With a loud crack, the frozen fist splintered, and the big saucer tilted and rolled back to a normal horizontal orientation. The thrusters continued to fire.

Gripping the stick, Corey increased the output as he monitored the warning levels. The Bug began to rise clear of the thick slabs.

On the hangar screen, he saw Darcy and Baxter inside the rover, gripping their seats. He called, "Hang on. I've almost got it, but we're still too deep." He ground his teeth together. He would need to fire the main engines to break them free.

Clearly alarmed, Darcy transmitted, "You're using the main engines? If the fuel leak spreads to the plasma buffer, you'll risk an explosion!"

"Let me worry about that. Your job is to get out of here. If Baxter doesn't fix the shield—"

Darcy cut him off. "You're right. Give it whatever push we need."

Corey fired the main plasma drive system. Bright blue engines flared, adding a shove to the thrust from the maneuvering jets. With a loud, grinding sound, the AstroBug heaved up from the frozen alien quagmire.

Darcy stared through the rover's windshield. "Hang on, Baxter. We're about to—"

"Clear!" Corey shouted over the comm.

Explosive bolts blasted open the hangar door, and a wide landing ramp dropped out to the rough ice below. Darcy yelled, "Now, TerraCat! Maximum speed! Woo hoo!"

The calm female voice answered, "Maximum speed, Astronaut Clarke."

Blazing headlights stabbed out across the frozen lake as the TerraCat plunged forward and down the ramp, skipping the last few feet to the ice. The heavy tires bit into the surface, caught traction as the ice continued to break away.

Baxter gripped her seat as the rover raced over the uneven surface and away from the lumbering ship. Her face had gone white. "Well, that was fun."

Darcy's concentration was nova bright. The auto-drive dodged boulders and upthrust chunks of ice. The secondary panel on the console showed the AstroBug's cockpit screen. Corey fought with the controls, working the main plasma engine. He seemed to be doing a hundred things at once as alarms sounded around him.

The intense blue-white torch lifted the large ship up out of the frozen lake, finally getting it free.

As the TerraCat raced for the shore, Darcy monitored the Bug's engine output on her screen, saw the alarms burn scarlet. "Corey!" She saw his face on the screen, and both of them realized the critical warning at the same instant. Fuel had leaked into a vital section of the ship's fusion engines. "Shut it down! Shut it down!"

As the TerraCat swerved across the lake ice on auto-drive, the AstroBug climbed higher, pushing with all the blazing might of its fusion engines. It cleared the ice at last.

Corey's expression was grim. "I love you, Darce. Sorry."

It exploded before it even got into the sky. A fiery blast of ice and debris sprayed across the dark lake and slammed into the rugged vehicle, making them spin and slew.

Darcy screamed.

CHAPTER 23

It wasn't real. It couldn't be real. Corey couldn't be dead! This couldn't be the new planet they had all hoped for.

It couldn't be real.

Darcy kept screaming deep in her throat as she watched the expanding cloud of fire, smoke, and debris roil into the unwelcoming black sky. The hammering sounds of ice chunks and metal pelting the TerraCat were deafening.

As the TerraCat slewed across the icy surface, Darcy couldn't tear her eyes away from the explosion. "Corey!" she groaned in a low whisper.

Baxter reached over and gripped her arm, but Darcy didn't feel any reassurance. Nothing could have happened to Corey! It just wasn't comprehensible. "No no no no no no no!"

She and Corey and Kyle were the three miracle babies, raised and trained on the *Odyssey*. None of them had ever seen death, except as an abstraction, in historical listings or data, in old dramatizations. People had left her life again and again, her father deep asleep in a hibernation pod, her mother lost out in space. Darcy and Corey were supposed to be together forever, making a home for themselves on Proxima b, the new home for the human race. She had never imagined anything would happen.

But it was foolish to think they were perfectly safe, after so many billions had died on Earth. But she and Jim Corey had always dodged death and danger. They had laughed at difficulties, confident in their skills and prowess. It had never failed before.

Captain Faraday had cautioned them even when they were children, but she and Corey had brushed off the captain's concerns. Now it felt like a hammer blow on Darcy's heart as she recalled one particular incident.

When she was thirteen, Darcy and Corey developed a crazy idea. Having grown up on the *Odyssey*, the three kids were given full-time duties, but they also ran loose and explored. Kyle occupied himself with his AI friend, but she and Corey would spend time at the outer wall of the habitation ring, where the bottle suits were mounted into their sockets, docked to the hull and facing outward. Darcy always looked at the empty spot of one missing bottle suit with a pang of sadness, because that had been her mother's....

The bottle suits were a hybrid of shielded extravehicular suits and human-sized spacecraft, slightly larger than a hibernation pod. With reinforced windows on all sides and maneuvering jets, waldo manipulator arms, and magnetic anchor cables, a standing person could reach all the controls for short jaunts around the arkship.

She and Corey both knew the captain would never allow them to go outside, but Darcy insisted, "We don't have to *ask* about everything! It's been ages since the last stem-to-stern inspection tour. About time, don't you think?"

"We aren't authorized to do it," Corey said, though the gleam in his brown eyes showed how much he really wanted to. "What about one of the adult crew?"

Darcy scoffed. "We have as much experience as any of them. Have you looked at the roster? I checked their specialties. You want Siffredi to fly in a bottle suit? He's the most qualified one, and that's not very qualified. My dad calls him a plumber instead of an engineer." She touched Corey's arm. "You and I have been awake longer than anyone other than the captain. We've been training, working, and living aboard this ship all our lives. No one knows the *Odyssey* better than we do."

Corey nodded toward the suits mounted outside. "Why is this so important to you?"

She put her hands on her hips. "It's for *you*! You keep sending messages to Earth, but nothing's getting through—maybe it's our comm array."

Corey's eyes brightened, but his shoulders sagged. "Your own mother couldn't—"

"I know what my mother did! But fresh eyes might see something. You and I could fly out there. The suits have all the necessary repair equipment. We could run diagnostics, check every component of the transmitter array, just to be sure." She shrugged. "Or maybe it's the receiver. Earth could have been talking to us all along, and we just never heard the answer. Don't you want to know?"

Corey had been intrigued, but still skeptical. She twisted his arm, stringing him along. "Do the first simulation set with me, see how confident we feel in the bottle suits. After that ... we can decide."

So Darcy and Corey had spent hours secretly going through practice sessions, using facsimile controls. Omni did his best to pose difficult scenarios that tested their reactions, and soon they felt confident in their flying abilities. They knew they could slip outside and work on the communications array before anyone even realized where they had gone.

Darcy felt cocky. "If we manage to get the array fixed, why would the captain complain? No risk, no reward!" She laughed. "Isn't that what the entire *Odyssey* mission is about?"

Neither of them told Kyle about their plans, because he would have panicked. Once they were ready, she and Corey went to the outer wall, determined to go explore.

Captain Faraday was there waiting for them, looking genuinely furious. "I forbid it!" The anger in the older woman's voice was like a dagger, but even worse was her deep disappointment. "How could you do this? These bottle suits are too risky, and this maneuver is entirely unnecessary. After what happened to Captain Andolino and—" Her voice cracked.

"We were going to fix the comm array," Corey said. "It was my idea."

Darcy flashed a glare at him. "Don't you take the credit."

"Credit? I was trying—"

"You're both responsible, because I know the two of you," Faraday said. "I'm changing the interlocks on the bottle suits, and I'll instruct Omni to keep them sealed unless there's a double authorization from me and another adult crew member."

"You can't just give up on Earth!" Corey said. "Nobody's looked at our comm array for years, and I think I know how to fix it."

"It can't be fixed," Faraday insisted. "So many things can't be fixed. The Earth is destroyed—I watched it myself, the nuclear barrage, the EMPs." Tears welled up in her eyes. "There's nothing left—not of Earth, not the *Valkyrie* or *Phoenix*, not … not my dear Michio."

It was as if a storm had congealed around the captain's body, and she straightened, set her jaw. "No use looking backward. The *Odyssey* is on a one-way trip. Even if you got the comm array working, and even if you found some squalid Earth survivor with a transmitter, it doesn't matter. *It doesn't matter!* We have to look ahead to Proxima Centauri, our new home and our future. You three kids, and all of these colonists, are our future."

She ushered them away from the bottle-suit hatches. "And I won't let anything happen to you."

The TerraCat delivered Darcy and Baxter to the dark rocky shore, and the calm automated voice announced, as if nothing had happened, "We will pause here."

"We have to get to the AeroFox," Baxter said. "Especially if

Kyle is as injured as you say." Her voice sounded ragged but understanding.

"The X-Doc sure as hell won't help Corey," Darcy snapped, then looked away. She squared her shoulders and swallowed the burning lump in her throat. She could imagine Corey reminding her of their absolute priority. Darcy carried the heavy burden. "And we have to get that shield network up and running ... no matter what else happened here." Her face felt hot with grief and anger, but her gaze was cold. "That's the mission priority above all else. Corey said so."

The survival of ten thousand colonists was at stake. But that wouldn't bring Corey back.

CHAPTER 24

Inside the grounded AeroFox, Kyle Dyson sat alone—really alone, with only the burned lump of his Omni core. He stared out at the night landscape where a skitter of lightning threw the terrain into garish relief.

Kyle felt so far away, so separated, not just by distance but by his own pain.

Through his comm implant, he had followed the disaster of the AstroBug. Even from two kilometers away, the explosion lit the sky like another volcano. He heard Corey's last words, Darcy's scream.

"Darcy, I'm so sorry ..." he said into the comm, but she didn't answer. He wasn't even sure she'd heard him.

Kyle sat by himself, clutching his toy gyroscope. Jim Corey was dead, and his personal Omni companion was gone. In the young man's sheltered, perfectly monitored life, such things did not happen.

He didn't know how to mark the passage of time, or even what he was going to do. The familiar, ever-present AI companion wasn't there to hold a conversation. Kyle just hunched over, felt the twisted ache inside him, a deep-seated *wrongness*. He knew his injuries were bad. He really needed the X-Doc....

Sometime later—maybe it was hours—he saw the bouncing

white headlights approaching, the beams spilling out in front of the TerraCat. It was like a miracle. Someone was still alive! He said automatically, "O, get ready to receive—" But his AI wasn't going to answer.

He worked the controls himself as the rover rolled up to the AeroFox and slowed to a stop. Wincing, Kyle propped himself up in his chair as the airlock cycled. He wanted to rush to Darcy to reassure her, but he could barely get to his feet.

She and Engineer Baxter entered the craft, both of them subdued. Darcy lugged the X-Doc's heavy case, while Baxter held the white cube of the AstroBug's Omni. Both women peeled off their half-masks and shook their hair free, but neither said a word.

Overwhelmed, Kyle struggled for words. "Darcy, I don't know what to say." He honestly didn't. He'd never had an experience like this before.

She looked away, taking a quiet moment to herself. Breathing audibly, in and out, she leaned against the food station, resting there as if the gravity was crushing her, or maybe it was her own grief.

Speaking softly, Baxter extended the white computer core to Kyle. "We brought the other Omni as a replacement. Corey said you needed it."

It? A replacement? Kyle felt stung. "Thanks, but he's gone. I have things running well enough." His sadness was followed by a flash of anger. He took the white cube and held it up accusingly. "*This* Omni's glitches are what made the AstroBug reel out of control! That's what caused this mess! I'd rather not rely on some ship-crashing knock-off of my friend."

Baxter backed away, surprised and confused. "What do you mean by 'your friend?' It's just an AI, another copy ..."

Standing at the pillar, Darcy turned to Kyle with misplaced anger. "We don't have time for this shit. Plug in the AI and do your fucking job! The *Odyssey* is coming, and the shield network is still down. Ten thousand lives are depending on us. Corey said ... Corey—" Her body was wracked with physical shudders.

After setting the X-Doc case on the deck, she collapsed into the pilot's chair. Working the controls, she raised the seat up to her station, as if to run away.

Baxter turned to him, concerned by Kyle's gray pallor. She got to work, opening the X-Doc case. "Heard you got banged up on the ride down."

Kyle closed his eyes. "It had to be done. After your ship went out of control, we needed to rescue—" He winced. What was the point? "It had to be done."

Baxter removed the cross-shaped automated medical device from its case. "Look, kid, the X-Doc can diagnose you and give us the best course of treatment, but we can't do that until the new Omni is installed." She opened the main console and extracted the charred, splintered old AI core with a show of reverence, dusted off the input portal.

Kyle picked up the AstroBug's core from where Baxter had left it. "Let me do it myself ... but it won't be the same."

His own Omni had always been there for him....

Growing up aboard the giant arkship, young Kyle Dyson still wanted to see and experience places from old Earth. His personal Omni echoed the same desires; they were of one mind.

He roamed the habitation ring by himself. Darcy and Corey were always together, while Kyle liked being alone. Except he was not actually alone, because his private Omni was always there with advice, an anecdote, an interesting bit of trivia, or just casual conversation.

Kyle could disappear into his own secret places, an out-of-the-way corridor or an empty storage bay where the airmoss had gone gray but the air itself was still breathable. His favorite place was a chamber with a small windowport, like a secret clubhouse where he and O could sit together and watch holoimages from the ship's library.

"This is the Grand Canyon in the southwestern United States," the AI's voice said. "One of Earth's most spectacular desert gorges cut by the Colorado River." Kyle had taken several self-directed geology courses, so he understood the erosion processes, but a conceptual understanding was far different from actually seeing such a spectacular place.

Now that Earth was gone, and the *Odyssey* was light-years away, he would never get a chance to experience it. These holos were all he would ever have.

Sensing his sadness, Omni had suggested, "Persephone will have landforms just as spectacular."

"And we'll explore them all, you and me," Kyle said. "Now show me more of Earth."

He and Omni viewed the spectacular fjords of Norway, the volcanoes of Iceland, the jungles of Indonesia, the sheer mountain peaks of Patagonia, the graceful deserts of the Sahara. They spent years getting to know Earth, so it wouldn't be forgotten. The AI had never actually experienced Earth either, so this was a shared experience.

One day, the comfortable routine in their private clubhouse was broken when a crewman, Mitch Siffredi, opened their secret clubhouse chamber for a routine inspection. Siffredi had dense, curly hair, thick eyebrows, and stern lines on his face. He had always viewed the three children as a personal affront to careful mission planning.

Now, when the brusque man saw Kyle sitting in the storeroom with his Omni, he scowled. "What are you doing here, kid?"

"It's not a restricted area." Kyle felt defensive. "Omni and I are undergoing training sessions."

"Then you should be in one of the educational chambers," Siffredi said. "This is a storeroom, not a playground."

"I'm not playing—I'm learning."

"Get out of here! I have work to do, and you're interfering."

Though he wasn't intimidated, Kyle scuttled away. He never

went back to that place, but he knew thousands of other secret hideouts on the *Odyssey*.

When he was fifteen, Kyle had turned his attention toward Proxima b. He did not imagine that the new planet would be the paradise that Earth had once been, but he was still intrigued.

Then the first high-resolution images arrived from the Forerunner mission showing the geoglyph. Kyle's attention was riveted by the clear enigma that stood out like a shout.

Now he hoped he lived long enough for a chance to understand it.

CHAPTER 25

As Baxter extended the X-Doc to Kyle, she was very worried about him—the kid looked broken and sick. But before she could wrap the medical unit's arms around him, he held up his hand. "Wait, that thing will knock me out. First, I need to show you what I found about the malfunctioning nodes in the shield network. I was working while Darcy went to rescue you."

Baxter needed to rest, too, but she summoned strength. "I analyzed it as much as I could in the AstroBug. What did you find?"

Kyle struggled to lean forward and pulled up a map of Persephone's dayside. "I came across the last thing my Omni was working on jointly with the Bug's AI. They were in contact just before the big surge ..." Wincing, he adjusted the display to highlight the non-functional sections of the shield network. "I compared the bad nodes and the metallic ore deposits from the *Forerunner* surveys. Look what happens when I show the geoglyph ..."

When he overlaid the malfunctioning points with the bizarre geometrical lines, Baxter pulled back in alarm. Every single corrupted node was located on top of a geoglyph line.

"*Forerunner* deployed all the shield towers from orbit, and they landed across the landscape," Kyle continued. "When the aeroshells folded back, the towers erected themselves where they landed. But according to this, any transmitter tower that happened to fall on the geoglyph has failed." He looked up at her. "And the geoglyph is a *big* pattern."

Baxter studied the screen. "Look, the rest of the nodes are at one hundred percent, but it's an integrated system. It all works together."

Darcy called up a dayside plot at her own piloting station. "We need the whole network at one hundred percent before the *Odyssey* arrives." She enlarged the projection. "The nearest malfunctioning shield node, Number 212, is just over the terminator line. Even if the AeroFox isn't flying anywhere, we can drive to the node in the TerraCat. We don't have any other choice. It's imperative we get it fixed."

The engineer's brow furrowed. "We need at least ninety-five percent of the nodes functioning or the network won't provide enough protection."

"Ten thousand people need to move down here, and soon," Darcy said. "We shoot for a hundred percent. You're the engineer —figure out a miracle solution."

Kyle looked frantic as he struggled to express himself. "Wait, you're missing the point! There's a connection between the geoglyph and whatever did this to our shield. There's a purpose behind it."

"A purpose?" Baxter cocked an eyebrow at him. "You're extrapolating an awful lot from a few straight lines and a mineral deposit."

Kyle frowned. "O and I discussed possibilities. Look, you're the radiation expert and you know how the shield works, but aren't you at all curious? Every node that touches the pattern has failed? And the strange surge that hit your Omni when it connected to the caretaker AI down there?"

Impatient with the conversation, Darcy finished mapping an overland route to reach Node 212. "We need to head out, Baxter. You two can write scholarly papers when it's all over."

Baxter had to admit she was intrigued. She pulled up an image of Proxima b's magnetic fields, which flared like a strange flower pattern enhanced by bright aurorae at the poles. "Considering the intensity of the directed pulse that hit the Bug, I wonder if this whole thing might be related to the magnetic field—which is huge, way bigger than Earth's."

Kyle seemed to sense a kindred spirit in her. "That would mean the geoglyph is interacting directly with the magnetosphere."

Darcy had obviously had enough. "Less talk, more action. The rover is ready to go. Command decision—I'm taking over the shield-repair mission." Her tone left no room for debate. "Baxter, grab your gear. You and I are going to Node 212 so we can figure out what's going on. I plotted a course through the mountain range and across the terminator. It's a five-hour drive. No time to lose."

Kyle slumped back, showing obvious pain. "And what am I going to do?"

"Get the new Omni installed and up to speed. We'll need him." Darcy continued in a rush. "Meanwhile, you let the X-Doc fix whatever the hell is wrong with you. All hands on deck! We've got no choice, and no time."

Kyle said in a small voice. "When you get over to the geoglyph, could you get me a sample of the material? Since you're going there anyway? I want to run some tests." He spasmed with a deep cough that felt like breaking glass inside of him. He wiped blood from the corner of his mouth. "I promise I'll use the X-Doc."

Darcy's nostrils flared. "Kyle, we need to focus on the engineering and repair the shield for the colony's sake. We can deal with the science shit later."

A flare of anger crossed the young man's face. "*Science shit?* Darcy, science shit got us here—this whole damned mission. And science shit is going to keep the colony alive. There's always time for science shit!"

Baxter interceded with a wry smile. "Actually, I'd argue that *engineering* shit is keeping us all alive. But, he's right, Darcy. Node 212 is on top of a major formation. If that might be what's causing the issue, we could use a sample. It won't take any extra time, once we get there."

As Darcy adjusted her envirosuit, Baxter could see the emotions roiling beneath the surface. "Fine. But while we're driving, I need you to create a firewall that'll block any further EMPs from messing with our shield. Protect all the transmitting towers. We won't have a second chance. Thousands of popsicles are coming down, and soon."

"Popsicles ..." Baxter muttered, offended. "I'll see what I can do."

Darcy grabbed her facemask and pulled on her pack. "Thanks to the two comm sats we deployed, we can stay in touch with you here on the AeroFox, Kyle."

Baxter scrambled after her, grabbing her own pack. She cast a quick glance at the injured young man as she headed for the airlock.

He gave her a weak reassuring wave as he held up the X-Doc, ready to wrap its mechanical arms around his chest. "I have everything handled here. I'm fine."

Baxter could see that he wasn't, but that was what both of them needed to hear.

CHAPTER 26

The TerraCat rolled over uncharted terrain in the dark, heading toward the perpetual terminator line between night and day. With wide, tough tires, the rover's auto-drive negotiated the rubble, and the bright headlights pierced the gloomy shadows. Endless bursts of lightning continued overhead.

Focused on the path ahead and wishing they could go faster, Darcy rode in self-absorbed silence. Following radar projections and detailed scans, the vehicle rolled into an ancient canyon with stark walls looming high above. As more than an hour passed, her tension turned into a dull ache, though her eyes and throat still burned. She tried to block out thoughts of Corey, but he was everywhere in her mind and soul.

She turned her grief into anger. The AstroBug had crashed because of a power surge in the shield network, and now Corey was dead. The geoglyph pattern that had always fascinated Kyle was somehow intertwined with the disaster. Maybe it had caused the deadly surge, like an aggressive attack. She couldn't wait to get there and see with her own eyes, then forcibly jump-start the whole thing.

Outside, as they reached the terminator zone, the whipping snow shifted to a murky rain. Rocks skittered down from the steep canyon walls, but the TerraCat's armor shrugged them off.

Riding beside her, Baxter remained quiet. Darcy figured it was out of respect or concern, or maybe just because the two didn't know each other well. The other woman was more than old enough to be her mother, although Baxter reminded her very little of Denise Clarke. Darcy didn't remember much about her mother anyway, except for a few bright and unforgettable moments from her childhood, and that final long, sad message.

With a compassionate expression, Baxter leaned over from the passenger seat. Her voice was still rough with cobwebs from hibernation. "I'm really sorry, kid. I only knew Jim Corey a brief time, but I enjoyed working with him. He was a real professional. I know you two had something special."

Darcy stared ahead, holding back tears. She wrestled with her thoughts and words for a long moment, then finally said, "Back at the AstroBug, the last time we were alone, all I did was yell at him. I found out he was holding something back from me ... something important."

Baxter answered in a warm and understanding voice over the background thrum of the rover's engines. "Honey, whatever was going on between you two, I'm sure it—"

Darcy cut her off. "Can you please just stop talking to me?"

The engineer folded into herself, withdrawing into the passenger seat. "I'll just rest ... still recovering." She looked away, closed her eyes, and tried to rest.

Darcy was angry at herself for her abrupt reaction, but she couldn't find the energy to make the effort at conversation. Tanya Baxter was a stranger, an unknown quantity injected into the stable world that Darcy had known all her life. But the disruption wasn't her fault. Darcy saw the weariness on the other woman's face as she dozed, the shadows around her eyes.

Darcy opened her mouth to say something, but thought better of it and sat back behind the controls as the canyon walls rolled past, slashed by intermittent rain. Finally, with no one watching now, she let her defensive walls melt. Pent-up emotions broke through as she gripped the control yoke hard enough to strangle it. Tears streamed down her face, mirroring the weather outside. She tried not to visualize the memories, but it did no good.

The TerraCat crunched over the uneven ground, dodging a canted slab of rock that had fallen to the canyon floor. Darcy drew a deep, shuddering breath, glad she could trust the auto-drive unit. "Safer this way," she muttered, patting the console. "You know what to do."

She closed her eyes and tried to sleep as well.

Inside the AeroFox, Kyle felt just as alone. Feverish from his injuries, he tried to focus on the geoglyph patterns and the gaps in the shield network, but his thoughts ricocheted in random directions, and he realized how often his AI had kept him on track, minimizing distractions.

He couldn't do this without O.

"Fine," he said, making it sound like a curse.

He winced in pain as he looked at the white cube Engineer Baxter had brought over from the AstroBug. Another Omni. He rolled it in his hand, resisting the temptation to hurl it across the pilot deck in frustration. But he needed the AI's help, even if it wasn't the same Omni.

Resigned but not really admitting defeat, he opened the access panel and slid the AstroBug's Omni—the other Omni—into the appropriate slot, locking it into place. He closed the housing cover and booted up the new AI.

"It won't be the same ..." he mumbled.

A soft, welcoming tone sounded, and a familiar infinity symbol appeared on the screen, blue instead of gold. The simulated voice sounded the same—almost—but with inappropriate cheer. "Ah—so this is AeroFox Two ... oh, and AstroTech Kyle Dyson! I'm here. I'm awake. It appears they made it away from the crash site. That's wonderful news."

A hot flush came to Kyle's cheeks. "Not all of them. The AstroBug exploded. We lost Jim Corey."

"I am so sorry to hear that. Please give me a brief status update, so I can better assist. I feel disoriented."

Kyle fought back his sadness. "Corey isn't the only one we lost. My personal Omni was also destroyed. You're going to have to forgive me if I seem ... weird when we work together. I was very close with my own AI, but I'm not used to you."

The synthesized voice paused as the avatar glowed, seemingly thinking. "I don't understand. We are both Omni."

Bitterness rose inside him. "No, not exactly the same. I got my first Omni Disc when I was four years old, and I did manual O-S updates until I was about nine. But I accidentally skipped one and never ended up doing it again. O developed his own personality, just like a real person, and now he's gone."

"Are you saying you never reintegrated your Omni with the ship's mainframe? This is fascinating."

Kyle shrugged. "I needed someone I could relate to. O was my best friend." He closed his eyes, and the pain of sadness seemed worse than the pain of his injuries.

"I am sorry for your grief, AstroTech Dyson. While I may not be the exact companion your Omni was, we both originated from the same initial program. I assure you that some of him is in me. Perhaps you and I can create a similar sort of friendship."

Kyle looked at the avatar with a glimmer of hope. "I should give you a chance. That's what O would have said." He tried to smile, but further words were cut off by a resounding coughing spasm. He tasted more blood in his mouth, felt something jagged twisting inside his body. What if it was more than just a few cracked ribs?

Omni was instantly concerned. "You are not well, AstroTech Dyson."

He grimaced. "If we're going to be friends, you should start calling me Kyle."

"Very well, Kyle. You are injured. Please make use of the X-Doc immediately."

"I got banged up by g-forces. Our X-Doc was ruined, and Baxter brought another one from the AstroBug. But that required the rebooted AI, and I was trying to figure out the geoglyph connection to the shield network, and I didn't want to let anyone down. The *Odyssey* and everyone aboard needed me. I couldn't just take a nap."

"That is a confusing chain of cause and effect," Omni said.

"Well, now that I've got you hooked up, I can take a break and get healed."

Moving stiffly, he dragged the spare X-Doc case over to his seat, which he set to the recline position. It felt like a personal battle just to lie down, and he was sweating with pain when he sprawled back. "Omni, could you run this medical thing for me? I'm not ... really at my best right now."

"Certainly, Kyle."

With painstaking slowness, he arranged the X-shaped device on his chest, and the armatures lit up as they moved into position and adjusted for a tight fit. The medical apparatus wrapped around his torso, and that made Kyle cough again. He could feel the tingle of the thorough scan pushing through his tissues. "How's it looking, Omni?"

The AI paused, as if loading up a bedside-manner protocol. "Not good, Kyle. These injuries are significant, and you are suffering from internal bleeding and organ damage. You should not have waited so long."

"We were pretty busy."

"Nevertheless, this internal damage is cause for concern. It would be best if you returned to surgery on the *Odyssey*. They have far more sophisticated facilities than the X-Doc."

"That's not going to happen." Kyle closed his eyes. "I thought I was tougher than this."

The AI put together a summary projection, just like O might have done. "You may be prone to organ failure due to your upbringing during the long space voyage, which could have had long-term cellular effects. Astronaut Clarke's extreme flying maneuvers added to those stressors on your body. We are fortunate that she was not equally affected."

"Yeah, great news. Will I be okay? I've got to get back to work on my shield calculations."

The artificial voice tried to sound reassuring. "I will complete my diagnosis and develop a treatment regimen. We can begin shortly."

His relief brought on a rush of sleepiness. "Sounds good to me. I just need a little rest, then back to saving the world."

Outside, muffled thunder raged.

CHAPTER 27

As the TerraCat toiled through the turbulent boundary zone, Darcy retreated into a deep sleep of exhaustion, but she could not escape her dreams.

She saw the *Odyssey* careening only a few hundred miles above the churning photosphere of Proxima Centauri on its final braking maneuver. Prominences flared around the ship, like serpents.

Darcy pictured herself inside the huge hibernation section, the entire front portion of the dumbbell-shaped ship. Countless pods held sleeping colonists, including her father. She rushed along a bright, sterile corridor among the sealed pods, all of which leaked tendrils of cold vapor. Inside those pods were optimistic settlers, and she could see each face through a clear viewport.

In her dream, Darcy hurried along the deck, frantic, looking into specific pods. Increasingly desperate, she moved from unit to unit, searching for someone. "I'm here! Where are you?" Her voice had an echoey quality.

Around her the ship creaked and groaned, like a death rattle. Structural damage—exactly what Corey had warned her about, what he and Captain Faraday had kept from her. The *Odyssey* was falling apart!

Darcy kept running, shouting, as the great arkship passed

through an enormous solar flare. The radiation surge sent the *Odyssey* spinning out of control, and large components broke off and drifted into space, glowing incandescent or melting under the flares.

She saw her mother drifting past in her bottle suit, doomed. Her mother tried to shout an alarm, but her comm batteries were dead.

Trapped in the hibernation deck, Darcy was overwhelmed with the sheer number of pods she had to search. She couldn't find the one she needed—until finally a name caught her eye. *Sebastian Clarke.*

As the arkship broke apart, she ran to her father's pod, pounding on the clear viewport, desperate to wake him up in time. "Dad!"

His eyes flew open. She shouted his name again, pounded on the pod's window, but he didn't recognize her. His face twisted, and she gasped to see his blank expression. Freezer burn!

Then the *Odyssey* exploded, vaporizing just above the red dwarf star.

It was just a dream, but the pain continued to be real.

Darcy had been only six years old when she lost her mother, and she hadn't understood what was happening at the time. Now, even after almost twenty years to process it, she still didn't understand, but the vivid events left an indelible stain in her memory, and they frequently haunted her dreams.

The gray blight had killed off most of the airmoss patches, and the dimly lit greenhouse domes failed to produce enough crops, or oxygen, to fully support the *Odyssey*'s habitation ring; but to Darcy and the other two children, everyday life seemed normal. Two years earlier, her father had gone into the hibernation pod, while her mother stayed awake to watch over them.

As a six-year-old girl, Darcy believed everything was the way it should be. Darcy remembered saying goodbye that day as her mother stepped into the bottle-suit hatch, for an important maintenance run. Laughing, Denise had pinched her little girl's cheek. "I'm going out to fix the solar collector for the greenhouse domes. That means we'll be able to grow more fresh food, and we need that."

Darcy had nodded, deeply interested. She liked the idea of more fresh food. Her mother whispered in her ear. "But I have a surprise, too. I might be able to fix something else...."

Denise had climbed into the bottle suit and sealed the hatch behind her. Captain Faraday took the little girl up to the bridge, where she could watch her mother through the biggest windows.

Denise emerged, standing in the oblong bottle suit fitted with articulated arms called waldoes, using the suit's thrusters to putter along. Her mother had showed off the waldoes, testing them, playing with them. Once she even let Darcy use the controls to open and close a pincer and flex a jointed arm. "The waldoes make me stronger than I can be by myself," she had explained. "It's how we get things done outside."

Drifting along, Denise worked to rig up a large reflector array, since the chemical lights in the greenhouse domes were no longer functioning well enough. As the thin, silvery solar film slowly unfurled, little Darcy watched her mother's bottle suit zipping back and forth. The bridge crew chattered as they tested the new circuits as soon as Denise installed them.

The little girl pressed her face against the bridge window. When her mother erected the concentrator array, it looked like a tapestry of stretched mirrors, curved sheets that would scoop glimmers of starlight and shine them into the greenhouses.

"Readings are optimal," said Stu McIntosh, an agricultural tech. "This might double our crop yield."

"Does that mean we can awaken more of the crew?" asked Ron Purvis, a quiet, short man at one of the bridge stations. "A full shift again? We really need the help."

Darcy remembered the hard expression on the captain's face.

"Not yet. But extra growing capacity means that the skeleton crew won't be on such thin ice."

The solar-mirror operation took well over an hour, but Darcy didn't get bored. She kept watching her mother's nimble movements among the *Odyssey*'s metal rigging.

When she finished erecting the collector array, her mother jetted farther along the ship's axis, heading toward the large disk in the front of the ship. "Since I'm out here, Captain, I'm going to run a new set of tests on our comm antenna. I might be able to fix it."

"Fix it?" Faraday replied. "We aren't sure there's anything wrong with the array. I don't think anyone on Earth is listening."

"We'll never know for sure, but I might get part of the answer," Denise said.

The bottle suit scooted along the axis to the spidery transmitting mast. Smiling, Darcy watched her mother extend one of the waldo arms to the comm array.

"I see a lot of pitting here, Captain. Some of the cables are exposed. I think we can fix this."

Faraday said, "If you're going to do more than run tests, we need to go back to the buddy system protocol. Wait there—I'll send Purvis out in a spare bottle suit to join you."

"It might be something quick and easy, like a loose wire or a damaged plate. Let me hook up this power coupling. There's a fair amount of energy coursing through—"

A loud burst of static roared through the bridge speakers. Through the window, Darcy watched sparks arc around the transmitter mast, engulfing her mother's bottle suit. The communications signal went dead.

"Mom!" Darcy cried.

Faraday raced to her own station. "Engineer Clarke, what happened? Can you hear me?"

Her mother's bottle suit had gone dark, and then it started tumbling, like a big crate rotating as it drifted along the ship's axis. As it came back toward the habitation ring, Darcy placed her hands against the window. A set of lights flickered inside the bottle suit, illuminating the interior enough that she could see her mother's tiny form, but it was just a dim emergency glow.

"Clarke!" the captain shouted into the comm.

After a few moments of terrifying silence and static, her mother's faint voice finally came back. "There, I rebooted the suit radio, but that's about all. My thrusters are dead. I have no control at all."

The bottle suit kept drifting like a wayward projectile. Darcy watched it pick up speed along the *Odyssey*'s axis, hurtling toward the habitation ring. Her mother was going to smash right into the wall!

But the bottle suit slipped under the rotating ring and flew past the *Odyssey*.

"My waldoes won't work. I'm deploying the magnetic cable." A silvery thread dangled from the bottom of the bottle suit, but it just flailed in the emptiness, never coming close enough to attach itself. "My jets don't function, so I can't maneuver. I'm just stuck here inside a big, automated coffin with none of the systems working."

"Mom!" Darcy yelled again. She looked behind her to see that Kyle and Corey had both come up to the bridge deck. Their eyes were wide as they absorbed the situation.

"I'm drifting, but the *Odyssey* is under thrust. You're going to lose me in just a minute," Denise said.

Captain Faraday was shouting orders, but all of her bridge crew just looked helpless.

"We can't possibly get out there in time, Captain," Purvis said. "At our velocity, she'll be long out of range. We're under heavy deceleration."

"What's happening?" Darcy asked.

Faraday barked sharp orders and she spun, saw Darcy, and her expression just collapsed. "I'll ... I'll explain later, Darcy. Please let us work now."

Stu McIntosh said in a hoarse voice, "Even if she gets her suit thrusters working now, she'll never catch up to us."

"Lock onto her with the telescope," Faraday said. "Don't lose her!"

One of the bridge screens showed the dim bottle suit, a tiny useless spacecraft tumbling end over end. It was far away from the *Odyssey* and getting farther every moment.

"What's going to happen to my mom?" Darcy asked.

"She's still able to transmit," the captain said. "She'll be able to ... to send messages as long as her air lasts."

"My god," groaned McIntosh. "It's just like the tragedy on Mars. It'll be—"

"Shut your mouth, Mister," the captain snapped.

Corey came up and took Darcy's hand. He was only five years old, but he knew something was wrong.

"Show me the bottle-suit manifest," Faraday said. "I want to see her energy levels, her oxygen tanks." When she looked at the numbers, the lines on her face deepened. "Six hours max."

As her mother drifted off into the gulf of space, she was able to transmit messages. After the bridge crew had tried their best, when everyone knew the futility of their situation, Denise Clarke had also grown resigned. She fell silent for a long while, then said, "I'm going to say my goodbyes. Record them so that my daughter and husband can listen to my voice."

"Understood, Engineer Clarke," the captain said.

Denise had sent a heartfelt message for her daughter to remember her by, and another one for Sebastian, although he wouldn't hear it until he was awakened from the hibernation pod.

Darcy had listened with tears streaming down her face. "Mom, why won't you come back?"

"I can't, baby girl. I'm out flying between the stars now, forever. I love you." Then she said to Captain Faraday, "Take care of my kids—not just little Darcy, but Corey and Kyle, too."

"Of course. You know I love all three of them."

"That's what I wanted to hear, Captain. And now I'm going to sign off. The air is getting a little thick and warm in here."

Faraday looked distraught. "You still have some time. Why don't we continue the conversation? Let us keep you company, just so someone's there with you."

"No, I want this to be my goodbye. Otherwise it could ... it could be something that I don't want Darcy to hear. Signing off now."

"Wait!" Faraday said, but there was nothing she could do. The bottle-suit transmitter switched off, and the *Odyssey* did not hear from Denise Clarke again. She would have drifted along for hours, her suit growing colder, the oxygen running out.

Maybe it was a blessing that they couldn't hear anything.

A jarring bump inside the TerraCat woke Darcy up. She looked around in disoriented panic. The landscape around them was rugged and garish, all shadows, angles, and rocks.

The calm female auto-drive voice said, "Sorry for the bumpy ride. I will adjust the suspension system to compensate."

Darcy rubbed her eyes, trying to remember where she was, and then she wished she could forget.

Baxter looked at her with concern. "You all right, kid?"

"I ... I'm fine. Bad dream." Darcy sat up, shaking off the painful memories. "Lots of bad dreams."

As she looked through the rover's windshield, she realized that the alien landscape was now lit with murky, ruddy light. They had made it through the churning terminator storm, and the uncharted vastness of the dayside spread out ahead of them.

CHAPTER 28

At least the TerraCat had coffee. Baxter removed the Autobrew device from behind her seat, popped a brewcap into the unit, and made a hot, fresh cup. Like magic.

She also retrieved protein bars and handed one to Darcy. "Keep your energy up. We've got a long day ahead of us." But her companion just stared at the alien terrain with a laser-like focus. Her hands twitched on the auto-drive controls, but relaxed, letting the TerraCat keep rolling ahead at its best speed.

"We cleared the worst of the terminator storm a while ago. Still another hour until we reach the first node," Baxter said. "You were sound asleep, so I let you have some time. I can't believe *I'm* the one who's awake for a change." She sipped from the Autobrew and let out a contented sigh. "I can dispense a coffee for you."

Darcy gruffly shook her head. "Can't stand the stuff."

Baxter sniffed. "Suit yourself. It's the only thing keeping me going."

Darcy accepted a protein bar, though, and started munching. "At least it's sunny. I've never actually seen a sky like this."

The big rover moved along on a steady course, and Baxter gazed at the exotic scenery. In the far distance, the gentle curved slope of a massive shield volcano swelled up from the plain, and a plume of smoke rose from its caldera. The TerraCat drove past dense patches of inky black vegetation with strange palmate leaves. The plants undulated under the dim red sunlight.

Darcy pointed out the windshield, drawing attention to a cluster of low artificial structures. "Hab modules, just waiting for our people." She lowered her voice. "We've got to get the shield working."

"Once we have the protection, our new home is ready and waiting for us." Baxter let out a low sigh. "From an engineering perspective, it's an audacious project, a whole colony infrastructure set up by itself."

The rover cruised past glistening salt flats and extensive shallow ponds of algae that were tended by automated farming units. More angular hab modules were scattered across the expanse, like breadcrumbs sprinkled over the dayside. Seeing the large, lumbering units at work and the hab module emplacements, Baxter marveled at the idea that the audacious colony scheme might happen after all.

She continued scanning the landscape. "The algae is growing well. Someday it'll convert the planet's atmosphere enough that we won't need to wear masks."

"Someday," Darcy said, sounding bitter.

Baxter pressed on. "Until then, at least we'll have something to eat ... if you can get used to it." She took another bite of her protein bar, which was improved by a swallow of strong coffee. "Green and brown slime ..."

"It's food," Darcy said, sounding defensive. "Fuel. What our people need."

"No argument from me," Baxter conceded. "But it's too bad you'll never have a lobster tail with drawn butter and a petite filet with sauteed mushrooms."

"We have mushrooms," Darcy said. "They grow just fine on the *Odyssey* even in the dim greenhouse light."

"Right, kid—barely any difference at all." She could never convey to this young woman all the things that had been irretrievably lost.

Baxter felt deeply sad that those kids had never known Earth's wonders, which humanity had taken for granted for far too long. Everything back home was gone now, and her husband gone along with it, because of his pig-headed decision to stay behind. Elwin had given up on the idea of going along, given up on Earth and on humanity long before it was absolutely necessary. Baxter had slept through the last fifty years. Saying goodbye to him seemed like just yesterday....

Darcy studied the projected route on the auto-drive console. "We better not need to drive to every single malfunctioning tower. I'm counting on you to do a big systemic fix."

Baxter nodded. "Already took care of it, kid. While you were dozing, I developed a software patch that'll reconfigure the shield nodes to block power surges like the one that hit the AstroBug. It's a cleanup and defensive program that will propagate through the network and reset all of the nodes. A solid firewall."

"We need a big sledgehammer of a fix," Darcy said.

Baxter finished her coffee and set the Autobrew to make another cup. "I even sent the patch back to Kyle Dyson for testing while he's resting with the X-Doc. He and his new Omni should have the whole firewall verified by the time we get to Node 212." On one of the TerraCat screens, she displayed a shield node and tower generator. The systems were all in the green. "We'll fix the shield in no time."

"Good." Darcy's voice still sounded hard, but then she looked over at Baxter, and her expression softened. "Thank you."

"It's why they woke me up in the first place."

In an awkward silence, they both stared ahead rather than at each other. Finally, Darcy spoke up. "What was it like on Earth—I mean really? All the reports looked horrible from those last days."

Baxter welcomed the conversation, though she responded with a heavy sigh. "The final days weren't good, sealed in our protected buildings against storms and severe climate upheavals. I spent the last couple of years working on the arkship project up in the orbital shipyards." She felt a pang as she remembered leaving stubborn Elwin behind. "We've got to do a better job with this planet, kid. Did the human race learn any lessons? We have to preserve this home so we can thrive here."

Darcy shook her head. "I can't imagine being stupid enough to destroy your own planet."

"People excelled in putting off hard decisions, and they let the next generation pay for it, and the next. When the facts were inconvenient, they denied the science, made up conspiracy theories, and distracted the leaders who could have forced action."

Baxter pressed her lips together in a scowl, remembering those difficult times. "The tipping point happened even before I was born. The permafrost melted and set off a runaway greenhouse effect." She shook her head. "There was no turning back. By the time the *Odyssey* launched, Earth was spiraling into becoming another Venus even before the stupid nuclear exchange...."

Darcy frowned. "Kyle showed us a lot of remarkable images and gorgeous landscapes. Niagara Falls, the Grand Canyon, the Eiffel Tower, the Great Pyramid, and a bunch more. I wish I could have seen those sights with my own eyes."

Baxter gave a wan smile. "If it's any consolation, I never saw any of them either. Earth was a really big place, you know."

"So I've heard." Darcy sounded wistful. "Until now, the biggest thing I've ever seen is the *Odyssey*."

Baxter mused. "I grew up in Illinois. My folks were farmers, raising corn for as long as they could manage it, but the major droughts ended that. Then they had big plans to go off to Mars, even signed up for the colony there, but they didn't make the cut." She sighed. "And then the colony failed anyway and everybody died. Mars is a much harsher place than Proxima b."

Baxter looked into the distance where she could see the glints of more hab modules. Someday, those would become homesteads....

"I was really excited to settle down and live here with Corey." Darcy slumped back in her seat and fought back tears. "But that power surge ruined everything."

The comm chimed with a message from the AeroFox. Kyle sounded more cheerful and energized than he had been when they departed. "TerraCat, there's good news, bad news, and weird news. Which one do you want to hear first?"

Glancing at Baxter, Darcy touched her comm implant. "Right now I could use some good news."

On the screen, Kyle was reclining flat in his crew chair with the mechanical X-Doc wrapped around his chest. Omni displayed a circuit diagram next to his face, but Kyle did all the talking. "We tested Dr. Baxter's new firewall software and simulated an EMP as powerful as the one that hit the AstroBug. It works—we can reset and protect the shield network!"

Baxter let out a sigh of relief. "Perfect."

But the young man wasn't finished. "I kept digging into what caused the problem in the first place. It didn't make any sense why those particular nodes went offline, what kind of virus could have infiltrated the caretaker AI network." He struggled to sit up, winced in pain, and the X-Doc held him down as it continued to perform its work. "That leads me to the, uh, weird news. Omni, show them the picture."

"Yes, Kyle."

The TerraCat's screen displayed Proxima b's magnetic field, juxtaposing it with the shield-node array, and the next layer showed the mysterious lines of the geoglyph. The primary points of all three lined up.

Kyle continued in a rush, "You were right. The planet's magnetic field and the geoglyph align perfectly." He coughed several times, but shook it off. "But we still don't know how or why they're connected."

Darcy was firm. "The science team can figure that out later, whenever we have the luxury. Right now, what matters is that the geoglyph is interfering with our shield, and our colony can't survive." She sat up. "The *Odyssey* should be in the middle of their braking maneuver right now. They're in communications blackout, but once they swing around the star and pull out of the gravity well, we need to tell them good news." Her voice hitched. "Or it's all for nothing."

"We'll get it fixed, kid," Baxter said with forced optimism.

Determined, Darcy spoke louder. "Omni, prepare to transmit an update to Captain Faraday. As soon as you are back in communication, send a priority burst, a full data dump. Tell her everything, the crashes and ... and Corey. That is a priority order. Ask for a report back, as soon as *Odyssey* is able."

"Understood," the AI said. "Priority order."

Baxter drew her brows together. "Wait a minute—you haven't told us the bad news yet, Kyle."

On the screen, the young man's expression fell. "Well, it's not as important as the fate of the human race, but it does hit a little closer to home—it's about me. The X-Doc report is not good. So, uh, my spleen is damaged, my liver is ruptured, and my lungs are filling with fluid. There's more, but that's probably enough detail to give you the picture."

Darcy straightened in alarm. "Dammit, you should have been strapped in! I didn't think you were hurt that bad. Oh, Kyle!"

Omni's voice broke in. "I believe these injuries were exacerbated due to a genetic defect caused by a lifetime of exposure to cosmic rays. The three children born during the interstellar passage have the potential to suffer this type of damage, including yourself, Astronaut Clarke. Kyle was apparently more susceptible than either of you."

"Crashing didn't help the situation," Kyle said while the X-Doc crawled like a crab down his torso. "It's not your fault, Darce."

Baxter leaned closer to the screen, concerned. "What do we do? Can the X-Doc fix you up?"

Omni said, "I am preparing to inject medical-grade nano-machines that will rebuild Kyle's organ tissue. The procedure will take several hours. It is somewhat intense and will require him to enter a rejuvenative coma."

Kyle brushed off the seriousness. "In the meantime, I'll keep working on—"

"No you won't, Kyle Dyson." Darcy took charge, using a stern command voice. "Lie back and let Omni do his thing. Nothing else. We've got this, do you understand?" Her face was flushed. "We already lost Corey."

"You sound like the captain." Kyle sulked. He took out his toy gyroscope and played with it as he leaned back and closed his eyes.

CHAPTER 29

In astronomical terms, Proxima Centauri was a dim, insignificant star, but right now it was the stuff of Gwen Faraday's nightmares.

The *Odyssey* shuddered as it plunged into the deep gravity well. Sparks popped and sprayed from half a dozen bridge systems —most of them noncritical, she hoped. The rattling and banging of overstressed support struts and groaning hull plates made her think of a slow-motion car crash that went on for hours.

Half of the skeleton crew were on the bridge deck, and the others were stationed at strategic positions throughout the giant ship, ready to implement emergency repairs. This was Faraday's ship, her crew, her colonists, and her responsibility. Dammit, she would hold this mission together by sheer force of will, if nothing else.

First Officer Kleve shouted out her report. "Deceleration thrusters on full. This is the point of maximum gravitational stress."

Faraday swept her gaze around the bridge, absorbing every detail. "Use attitude thrusters to keep us aligned—we have no wiggle room in this, people. It's like threading a needle with a giant redwood tree." She realized that the next generation wouldn't even understand the metaphor. But unless she got the arkship through this braking burn and the slingshot around Proxima Centauri, there wouldn't be another generation.

"Hang on, everybody. If something's going to break, it'll be now." She sucked in a quick breath. "Prayers, if you've got 'em."

The crew members remained intent at their stations, but she could hear a low murmur of soft and desperate entreaties.

The *Odyssey* rattled as it passed so close to the red dwarf that solar flares clawed up at them and magnetic field lines tried to ensnare the ship.

"Things have been breaking all along," muttered David Hamelin at the helm.

"We'll patch up what we need to, once we swing around the star," Faraday said. "We're almost there. Just need to hold it together around Dead Man's Curve, and then we can coast back to the planet. We've got extra rolls of duct tape on the supply decks."

More warning lights flared on the status panels, and the tenor of the groaning sounds changed.

"Not sure the duct tape is going to hold, Captain," Kleve said.

"Duct tape always holds." It was Faraday's form of a prayer.

On the main screen, the orbital track showed the extreme flattened ellipse of their orbit with one narrow end almost touching the red star.

"We're past perihelion," Hamelin shouted. "It's all smooth sailing from here."

Caught and slowed by the gravity, the *Odyssey* began to climb out of Proxima's gravity well leaving much of their velocity behind. The worst was over, but it wasn't all finished yet.

As if in a cruel trick, right after Hamelin's announcement, a new round of alarms sounded, a grating noise that made Faraday's teeth rattle. More sparks gushed from an unmanned station, and the console went dark.

"I thought I switched off all the damn alarms," Faraday said. Nobody needed the distraction, since they all knew the fragile house of cards the *Odyssey* had become. Even though she had hidden the true seriousness of the failing systems from most of the crew, she had told Jim Corey just before their mission to the planet. Someone needed to know there was a very real chance the arkship might not survive their braking maneuver. So much was riding on those three kids and Engineer Baxter.

Her skeleton crew was now fully aware of the crisis, with no sugar-coating, but these were the best personnel she could imagine. The bridge team rushed from station to station even as the deck shuddered and wall plates rattled.

As she gazed out the wide bridge window, Faraday shuddered to see the hellish bottomless pit of flares and bubbling photospheric cells. The alarm grated louder and louder. "Dampen that noise! None of us can concentrate. We already know the engines and the hull are in bad shape."

"That alarm's for the hibernation module, Captain," Kleve replied with heavy dismay. "A flare burst fried an entire sector, burned out the systems. A lot of hibernation pods were just destroyed ... all personnel inside are gone."

"An entire sector?" Faraday cried. "How many?"

Kleve stared down at her screen, squinted her eyes to focus on the number rather than the actual names. "One hundred fifty-three pods are ruined."

The stunned gasp on the bridge was louder even than the alarms. Faraday's eyes stung.

Kleve continued, "Should I send Brian Adducci and Killian Yar up the axis to see if they can reboot the life-support systems? Maybe do an emergency thaw?"

Outside of the habitation ring, the monstrous star filled the view, and Faraday knew they still had hours of extreme danger until they gained more distance. "Can't risk it. Those flares will cook them if our shielding flickers for just a minute." The weight in her stomach was heavier than the g-forces they were experiencing.

One hundred fifty-three out of ten thousand ... but they were still colonists, vital people who had been chosen for their particular skills, one hundred fifty-three people who were considered necessary cogs in the wheel of humanity's survival. Now they were gone, just numbers in her captain's log.

But they weren't just numbers. Not just personnel. They were names ... they were hopes and dreams.

"Let's keep the number to one hundred fifty-three and no more," she said. "The braking maneuver is over, and we're just coasting, but we still have a long ways to go. Lock down any systems that are failing. Reroute what you can. Plug any leaks, boost any backup systems, and monitor the hibernation module. Add electromagnetic shielding if you can to mitigate exposure to the rest of the pods."

Kleve stepped closer and issued a private report, though Faraday knew everyone could study the readings for themselves. "From what I can see, sir, we have about a fifty-fifty chance of even making it to Proxima b. And once we get into orbit, we'll need to start dropping hibernation pods in a mass exodus. This old hulk is on her last legs."

"The colony will be ready for us, Commander Kleve," Faraday said. "We can count on our team." She dredged up one last bit of optimism and forced a smile. "And this old hulk may have a few surprises in her still. Think of a marathon back on old Earth—runners would cover miles and miles, push themselves to the absolute limit, squeeze out every last drop ... but you can't collapse until you cross the finish line."

As she stared out at the ragged stellar flares, Faraday stroked the captain's console in front of her. "Almost to the finish line," she whispered. "Don't collapse just yet."

CHAPTER 30

The rover cast a long shadow as it drove to the shield node. Straight ahead, the metallic line of a geoglyph structure rose up like a wall many kilometers wide, its color ashen in sharp contrast to the surrounding brown terrain.

Darcy stared at the thing as if the geoglyph were a direct challenge to her.

Baxter, though, showed real wonder. "Those metallic lines are huge—no wonder they affect the magnetic field. If our transmitting towers are too close to them, I'm not surprised we experienced some failures."

Darcy pointed her laser ranger through the rover's windshield, concentrating on the priority of the colony's long-term survival. "They're a perfect source of metal for easy extraction. We could get real cities under construction right away."

Baxter gave her a look of surprise at the suggestion. "Kid, I saw enough strip-mining and clear-cutting on Earth. We can use a lighter touch here."

Before Darcy could respond, Kyle contacted them from the AeroFox. His voice sounded weak and wavery. "Omni just dispatched a full update to the *Odyssey*, as you requested. As soon as she receives it, Captain Faraday will know about Corey. I ... I added my own message, too."

"Are they in contact?" Darcy asked. "Do we even know if they survived the maneuver?" Her throat was dry.

"There's still a ton of static and interference from the star, but Omni got a brief snapshot. Let me send you what we know."

A schematic of the arkship appeared on the TerraCat's screen. The giant dumbbell vessel showed multiple red highlights that indicated severe damage. Omni's voice reported, "The ship successfully passed through perihelion, but the extreme gravitational forces caused a number of systems failures. The crew is working to stabilize the situation, but initial assessments suggest that some failures may be irreparable."

A red swath highlighted part of the hibernation module.

Seeing the schematic, Baxter paled. "*All* those pods?"

Omni continued, "The crew has begun emergency procedures. Captain Faraday expects to have a first wave of the settlers ready to disembark as soon as the ship enters Persephone orbit."

Darcy saw the look of disbelief on Baxter's face. "But we're not ready! Even if we do get the shield network up and running again—"

"We are ready," Darcy insisted.

"Even if my firewall works, the rest of the colony's not ready for occupancy yet! Nobody's checked the hab modules, the water filters, the energy grid. We were supposed to send down a vanguard, test out the systems, then send a few more people down. Baby steps. The *Odyssey* should stay in orbit for a couple of months as we do a staged disembarkation. We waited fifty years for this. We can't just unload all the hibernation pods at once! That's crazy."

"Plans change," Darcy said. It was obvious that Captain Faraday hadn't told Baxter about the severity of the situation either. She increased the rover's speed, rolling toward the shield node ahead.

Stressed and wrung out, Kyle broke in over the comm. "Wait, there's more major news. Omni, tell them."

The AI voice continued, "I've been using the new satellites to monitor the star. A major flare event appears imminent."

Baxter's eyes went wide. "Even if I can upload the firewall from Node 212, we'll never get the shield up in time. We'll be fried."

Darcy looked up at the always-turbulent ruddy sun. "Great. How long until the flare hits?"

"I can't give a precise estimate yet, but I am monitoring the star activity," Omni said. "I will update you when I have more accurate information."

Frowning at the angry red sun, Darcy thought not only of the flare storms, but also of the battered arkship out there and Captain Faraday trying to hold it all together.

Darcy remembered when her father finally went back into hibernation when she was sixteen, after being awake for an unprecedented ten years so he could raise his daughter. He'd given Darcy a long goodbye hug, knowing they wouldn't see each other again until they arrived at Proxima b. When Sebastian held her, she could feel his whole body shaking. "Take care of yourself, Peanut. I tried to be as good a father as I could."

She squeezed him, though at sixteen she had felt awkward. "You were a great father, and I learned so much from you."

He grasped her shoulders and looked into her eyes. His demeanor was intensely sad, and he gave her one more hug. "Captain Faraday will take care of you. Don't give her too much grief."

Darcy scoffed. "I won't. She needs me."

"We all need you, Darcy girl." Finally letting go, he climbed into the hibernation pod. "When we get to our new home, we'll set up our own place together. That's what your mother would have wanted." When he rested his head on the cushion, his face suddenly took on an odd expression. "Unless you're already married by then. Good lord, you'll be twenty-five or so!"

"I'll still be your daughter." She kissed him on the forehead and stepped back. "I'll try not to grow up too fast."

After he'd gone deep into sleep, she still visited him in the giant hibernation section with ten thousand other colonists in cold storage. She liked to look at his peaceful face, just to know he was there.

Her days were full with crew duties and advanced educational sessions, but Darcy began to think about growing up. Married by the time they set up their colony on the new planet? Was that what she wanted? The thought had never occurred to her. How could that even be a possibility?

She and Jim Corey would, of course, be together. They had been partners and close companions their entire lives. Among all the popsicles there were countless young men in their early twenties, all of them well-educated, healthy, chosen for their worth to a new colony and to rebuild the human race. Once they were awakened, Darcy would have more choices in a mate than she could imagine, but she had never doubted that her choice would be Corey.

Once, she had taken a shift on the bridge deck, alone with Captain Faraday. Darcy enjoyed the time for relaxed conversation with her long-standing mother figure. The *Odyssey* was still eight years out from their destination, but Proxima was a wine-red star easily seen ahead, not far from the bright double star of Alpha Centauri.

As she looked at the twin sister suns, she asked, "Do you think we'll ever go there, Captain? We know A and B have planets, maybe even someplace else we can settle." Darcy knew the *Odyssey* already carried a pie-in-the-sky Alpha probe to be launched for further exploration as soon as the colony was established.

The captain sighed. "We haven't even gotten to Proxima yet!

The last thing I want to think about is setting off on another voyage."

"When it's time, you can pass the candle to me, Captain. Corey and I can be co-captains, and Kyle will want to go along to do a bunch of science experiments."

The skeleton crew members went in and out of hibernation, but even the oldest people among them were only in their forties, a few early fifties because of special technical expertise. Faraday, though, had been awake for forty-two years.

Now she saw the weight of years on the captain's face. Faraday was by far the oldest person she had ever known. She noted the gray hairs mixed in with Faraday's tight locks, the weathered look on her dark skin, the crow's feet around her brown eyes.

"This one was quite enough for me," Faraday said.

"Don't worry, we'll get you to Proxima b, Captain," Darcy insisted. "Corey, Kyle, and I will take care of the hard work for you."

"I look forward to the hard work of retiring," Faraday quipped. "Only eight more years. I still have to get us the rest of the way there."

CHAPTER 31

The rover's auto-drive plotted a way to ascend the high geoglyph, which rose up like a dusty metal barricade pushed out from beneath the surface. Weathered dirt and debris covered its slopes, but a rounded, eroded hill would serve as a ramp for them to reach the upper surface, where the shield tower had erected itself.

Darcy felt tense as the TerraCat toiled up the incline. The rugged tires spun on the rocks and dirt, but the versatile vehicle made it. She felt a little dizzy to see the flat, smooth uplift stretching out ahead of them like a wide plain.

She let out a triumphant whistle. "Now we're going to make good time. Straight for Node 212."

Baxter was amazed at the improbable metal vein. "It's like a superhighway system."

"I've seen pictures of those back on Earth," Darcy said.

As they cruised along, their high vantage allowed them to see large shallow lakes and patches of Persephone's black weed. The endlessly distant horizon disoriented her. During her life aboard the *Odyssey*, Darcy had only ever seen the bulkhead walls just a few meters away.

Baxter pointed. "There it is!"

Darcy could discern the shield-transmission tower ten meters high, rising from the components of the protective black aeroshell that lay like enormous, dried flower petals.

"*Forerunner* dropped hundreds of shield nodes from orbit, so it's no surprise that some of the nodes landed on the geoglyph," Baxter said.

The TerraCat cruised right up to the base of the malfunctioning tower and drove onto the tough aeroshell components splayed on the ground. Darcy parked the rover, tires half on and half off of the geoglyph metal, and powered down the engine.

All business, she retrieved their halfmasks and AR goggles. "No time to lose. When that flare storm approaches, we'll have to find shelter as fast as we can." She donned her respirator. "Ready to go out there, Engineer?"

Baxter adjusted her own breathing mask. "Can't wait to start running tests." She retrieved the main toolkit while Darcy depressurized.

When the two emerged, goggles down and masks in place, Darcy saw her companion's obvious struggle with the heavy toolkit. "You want me to take that? I'm more conditioned than you are."

"No thanks, kid." With a grunt, Baxter settled the kit onto the mount on the back of her suit, where it snapped into place, distributing the weight. "I've got to get used to this gravity at some point. No better time than an emergency."

They trudged across the debris-covered aeroshell to the tower structure. Darcy looked up at the throbbing sky, remembering that not long ago she had walked across the dark, frozen night side. "It's a lot warmer over here."

Baxter adjusted her mask to make it fit more comfortably. "Once we get the shields up and running, this could be the Riviera of Proxima b."

"I don't know what that means," Darcy said.

Ignoring her, Baxter walked on top of the creaking polymer-composite aeroshell to the tower. Around them, without the wind, the environment was eerily silent, which Darcy found menacing.

Was there some presence lurking here that had sabotaged the shield nodes, corrupted the caretaker AI network? Something that struck the AstroBug and triggered the chain of events resulting in Jim Corey's death?

The high structure looked ungainly and graceful at the same time, all curves and reinforced struts that reached to the sky. At the base of the support truss, a power supply was connected to a computer interface screen, where the indicator lights all glowed red.

Huffing with the effort, Baxter lumbered up to the interface and dropped the toolkit to the ground like a boulder. "I'll pop the main board." She went to work, using a drill to remove screws. Even in the heavy gravity, her movements were swift and efficient from long practice. Setting the access plate aside, she reached in to disconnect a large computer node board.

Meanwhile, Darcy walked around the base of the tower to inspect it. The shield network consisted of hundreds of similar nodes and tower structures. Each one of them had been built in Earth orbit, packaged in a protective shell, then loaded aboard the *Forerunner* more than half a century ago. While the *Odyssey* and the other two arkships were in the last stages of construction, the unmanned mission had blasted away, carrying everything— *everything*—the colony would need.

Baxter held up the node board, turning it at an angle to watch the ruddy light reflect on the circuit patterns. A faint ripple of sparks discharged across the crystal pattern lines, then dissipated. "This node got hit by a pulse, too—probably similar to what fried the AstroBug." She activated a small screen above the node slots and checked the power flow. "This is odd. It's like there's energy coming from somewhere other than the fuel cells, flowing into the tower."

Darcy continued her slow circuit around the structure,

then came to an abrupt halt. "Engineer—better get over here!"

Distracted, Baxter plugged a diagnostic device into the node slot. "You can call me Tanya, you know." She tapped her wrist computer and initiated the check procedure.

"Dammit, *Tanya*—come here!"

Startled, the engineer set down the board and hurried to join Darcy on the sunward side of the tower.

The flat aeroshell material had been breached—violently—by a mutant outgrowth of metal, blobs of what looked like another geoglyph that had sprouted from the ground. The twisted, flowing metal had slathered up the sides of the antenna assembly like some insidious fungus.

Darcy studied the shattered aeroshell, keeping herself at a cautious distance. "Could the impact have melted some of the metal, and it flowed ... up?" In the ocher sunlight, the metal growth showed angles and planes, like a pyrite cluster.

"In this gravity? That makes no sense." Clearly fascinated, Baxter gazed up at the tower's spire. "The tower deployed just fine, so this metal growth or infestation happened *after* landing. The node was up and running—the *Odyssey* received nominal readings for almost two years once the shields powered up. But something happened to disrupt the node and mess up the network."

Darcy frowned at the aggressive metal growth. "I think we know what it was."

Baxter nodded. "I bet we'll find something similar at the other towers that went offline."

"And we're here now to fix it," Darcy said. "Your firewall better work like an exterminator." She removed a small rock hammer from her utility belt and poked at one of the metal-crystal shards. "This thing grew into the back of the node's computer system. Do we just chop it out?"

Baxter kept a cautious distance. "The metal looks almost organic, and that seems like years of growth. How could it change so fast?" She tapped on her wrist. "AeroFox, come in. We found something odd out here."

Omni's voice responded, "Please describe."

"Where's Kyle?" Darcy asked. "Is he in the X-Doc, like he's supposed to be?"

"Yes, Kyle is being treated right now. How may I help you?"

If Kyle had gone into his enforced healing coma, he would not be answering any questions now.

Baxter spoke as if delivering a scientific briefing. "We found the reason for the failure of Node 212. Geoglyph material ruptured the aeroshell and has grown inside the transmitter."

The engineer reached a gloved hand toward the exotic protrusion, but Darcy knocked her away. "Don't touch it!"

"It's just a weird rock."

Darcy couldn't put aside her suspicion. This anomaly had crashed the shield network; therefore, it was a threat. "We have no idea what this thing is. Don't underestimate how this planet can kill us—like Corey did." She fought down her bitterness and grief. "Let me grab a scan or two."

The AI voice responded with obvious curiosity. "Please send images. I will help process."

Darcy used the flash scanner on her wrist to collect a sequence of images as she paced around the metallic growth. "For a long time, this geoglyph has been keeping Kyle awake with crazy ideas. Maybe he's not so crazy after all."

Even as the X-Doc kept him pinned down for his healing, Kyle cracked open one eye so he could watch the video images Darcy transmitted. He was amazed by the unusual, angled growth extruded into the transmitter tower.

Kyle forced himself to sit up, no longer trying to sleep. His toy gyroscope rolled off his chest and onto the deck with a *clink*. He tried to speak, but his voice was an embarrassingly weak croak. "Get a sample ... an actual piece of the material."

Omni clarified for him, "Kyle is asking you to obtain a sample, but I must countermand the suggestion. Despite the importance of this discovery, you do not have time to perform scientific studies. Satellites confirm the increased turbulence from the star. The first major solar flare will arrive in less than an hour."

CHAPTER 32

Darcy whirled to look up at the dull red sun, as if she could see the swaths of radiation rolling toward them. She touched her wrist control to darken the AR goggles so she could view the churning orb through the filters. "Oh, my god."

In silence, they watched numerous flares writhing along the star's flank.

In the comm, Kyle's voice penetrated their awe and dread. "Guys, please—just one piece of the growing part! Chip off a little sample that we can analyze." His words had a wavering desperation. "It'll only take you a second."

Baxter looked down at the strange growth, then thrust her sharp rock hammer into Darcy's gloved hand. "You're stronger than me, kid. Use those muscles to break some of it off. I'll go get a sample container."

Darcy frowned at the unexpected tool in her hand as the engineer jogged toward the vehicle. "I'll try, but we need to find someplace to hole up." She was alarmed to see her wrist dosimeter already approaching the red zone. The readings had changed so much in only a few minutes! She grumbled under her breath, "Kyle, you better appreciate this."

She bent closer to the strange metallic encrustation and struck hard with the rock hammer, then she hit again and again. After everything that had happened in the past day, it felt good to release her pent-up anger, frustration, and grief. But the sharp tool bounced off, leaving barely a mark.

Darcy breathed heavily into her half-mask. "I've got no time for this!" Nervously, she glanced up at the red sun, then hacked away with redoubled energy. Finally, the hammer cut a deep gouge. Fragments of the pyrite-like mineral broke off and scattered like gravel onto the aeroshell's flat surface.

Baxter returned with a clear plastic tube, a soil-core container. "Darcy—stop! Jesus, we just need a piece! You want to smash the whole geoglyph?"

Darcy was shaking from more than the expenditure of energy. "If that thing is the reason the shield network failed, then, yes, I sure as hell do want to smash it." She clipped the tool to her utility belt, then glared at the boiling star low on the horizon.

Baxter said, "You can take care of the rest of it later. Right now, we've got to find some place to hunker down."

Darcy muttered, "If your shields were working, we wouldn't have to worry about a flare storm at all."

Baxter bent and started scooping the glittering shards into the soil-core container. "I'll get this. Go fire up the TerraCat. There was a deep crater a few kilometers back. We can wait out the storm in the shadow."

As she ran back to the TerraCat, Darcy saw the disconnected node-board lying next to the tower's access panel. She snatched it up, refusing to let the vital unit be exposed to the radiation flood.

Through her polarized goggles, the ruddy sky had an odd shimmer as the vast aurorae over the magnetic poles brightened. Her envirosuit issued a warning through the comm implant. "External radiation levels rising. Please find adequate shelter immediately." Her wrist dosimeter was now turning red. "Tanya, hurry up! The TerraCat doesn't offer much shelter, but it's a start. Let's move!"

Baxter finished gathering the samples and pushed herself to her feet with an audible groan. "I'm coming!" But then she stared at the metallic intrusion that Darcy had just hammered. The scar was already covered over.

"It's growing back! The gouge is gone!"

Darcy's skin crawled. "Get your ass into the rover, and we'll talk about it later!"

Baxter hesitated with the soil-core container, then sprinted toward the shelter. The cylinder swung wildly as she ran.

Darcy dropped into the driver's seat, telling the systems to fire up. The auto-drive responded with maddening calmness. She buckled in, ready for a rough ride.

Huffing into her facemask, Baxter entered the vehicle, carrying the soil-core container, and Darcy sealed the door. "Secure that thing in back and strap in." She added power to the rover's engine, polarized the windshield, and glanced at the warning screens, the countdown to the imminent flux from the flares.

Wheezing, Baxter collapsed into the passenger seat, cradling the transparent cylinder in her lap as if it might explode. "Didn't you hear me? Where you chipped off these fragments, the metal was already growing back, like it's alive. I don't think the geoglyph is just some upwelling metal ore. It's something else."

Darcy shot a suspicious glare at the soil-core. "Then get that out of here. Eject it."

Baxter sealed the lid tighter. "We've got the sample now. Nothing's going to happen—seems inert." She shook the cylinder and rattled the metallic fragments. "Like Kyle said, it needs to be studied."

An alarm tone thrummed through the rover, and the female voice of the auto-drive scolded, "Warning! Radiation alert. Find shelter immediately!"

Darcy snapped in exasperation, "That's what I'm doing!" She fired a frustrated look at Baxter. "Buckle in—and keep an eye on that shit!"

Darcy switched the auto-drive into emergency mode and

entered coordinates. "TerraCat, disengage safety overrides and prioritize *speed*."

"Proceeding to crater." The voice paused. "Maximum possible speed."

The rover's engines roared even louder, and the vehicle lurched—but it didn't move, as if something had locked it in place. As the whining vehicle shuddered, Darcy was jostled in her seat. The engine strained, but the Cat didn't budge.

Baxter looked confused. "What the hell? Why aren't we moving?"

"Engines are working fine. We should be racing away from here." Darcy scanned the control panel. "TerraCat, reverse. Full throttle!"

"Attempting to do so, Astronaut Clarke." The engine revved louder. "Encountering an obstruction. Our wheels are unable to turn."

Darcy called up the external camera, which showed that the rover's rear wheels had been grasped by a metal vise of geoglyph metal. The encrustation had flowed onto the tire, welding them into place. Now, more alien material oozed up from the ground, seizing the rover.

Darcy gasped. "Now that thing's coming after us!"

A synthetic voice rang through their comms. "Radiation reaching extreme levels."

Baxter lurched out of her seat and grabbed the rock hammer. "We better hustle. I'll go out there and hack away the obstruction if I can. Once I chop the wheel loose, you gun it and try to break us free. Manual drive." The engineer glanced at the red lines on her dosimeter. "And please don't leave me behind."

"Manual drive?" Darcy knew it was a foolish thing to be uncertain about. "I've never driven a vehicle."

Baxter turned to face her at the TerraCat's hatch. "You can fly a spaceship, but you can't drive a car?"

"We didn't have cars aboard the *Odyssey*!" Darcy snatched the rock hammer out of Baxter's hands. "Let me do the heavy lifting, while you handle the controls."

"Last time I drove a car was fifty years ago—but I'm up for it. Just get rid of that stuff around the wheels."

Darcy clambered out into the glaring red sunlight and ran around to the rear wheels. The fringes of the solar flare were already hitting the atmosphere.

The front wheels sat on the protected aeroshell section, but the rear tires had been parked on the surface of the geoglyph. The sinister metallic material had flowed up to encase the rear wheel. Now, Darcy was afraid the shiny material would shift beneath her boot and swallow her leg.

Angry and desperate, she started chopping at the alien metal, ripping off bright chunks. With one particularly hard blow, she cracked the solid encrustation—a chink in the armor! She wedged the rock hammer into the fracture, wrenched hard to pry apart the metal blob, and freed part of the entrapped tire.

She yelled into the comm, "I think I got enough of it. Move the wheels!" Then to her horror, she watched the broken substance begin to heal. "Hurry! It's growing back!"

Baxter worked the manual controls, and the TerraCat strained and surged. "I'm giving it everything!"

The trapped tire nudged forward, turned a quarter rotation, then locked into place again. Baxter put the vehicle into reverse, straining in the opposite direction, then forward again. The geoglyph metal groaned as it bent.

Up in the sky, Proxima glowed brighter. The flares were coming.

Darcy brought the rock hammer down with both hands, shattering the stressed metal. Geoglyph debris flew in all directions. "Try it now!"

The engine roared at full power, and the wheel groaned, then spun and squealed as it broke free. As the vehicle lurched ahead, Darcy ran after it and leaped into the open hatch, which automatically closed behind her.

Baxter sat at the helm, her jaw set, and the big vehicle spun pell-mell, racing back in the direction from which they had come, leaving the infested node tower behind.

Picking up speed, the TerraCat hit a rough patch that rocked them from side to side, but the stabilizers smoothed them out. Darcy struggled into the empty seat and strapped herself in. Her radiation detector was solid red.

Baxter rolled them down the debris ramp and off the metallic geoglyph uplift.

"Radiation levels rising," the auto-drive voice added helpfully.

Baxter slapped her palm on the steering controls, irrationally excited. "Even on Earth, I never drove like this!" She was panting heavily. "Am I even going in the right direction? Which way is the crater?"

In the mayhem, the soil-core cylinder had been knocked loose, and now it rolled around on the floor, filled with broken geoglyph samples. Darcy grabbed it, even though she was loath to touch the cylinder. She muttered under her breath, "That was a brilliant idea, Kyle. Just a little sample. It'll only take a second...."

Through the side window, she could make out a sandy ridge on the horizon, a distinct uplift. "Over there—that's the lip of the crater. It'll offer shelter once we get down into the shadow."

Baxter somehow managed even more speed. The TerraCat rolled directly across the flat terrain, then up over the ridge and plunged down the precipitous slope. Darcy held on as they careened into the blessedly deep shadow of the bowl-shaped crater.

CHAPTER 33

W hen Earth itself was falling apart in its last years, Baxter faced a more personal disaster as her marriage disintegrated.

Her husband Elwin was articulate and dedicated to his causes, but he was a very obstinate man. Although she didn't always agree with him, he never failed to make a compelling, thought-provoking argument. As a couple, they managed the careful dance of keeping their disputes an exchange of ideas without igniting into personal wars.

They were the perfect cliché—opposites attract. She and Elwin had even joked about it when they'd started dating. Tanya Baxter was a die-hard mathematics and engineering person who believed in clear answers, verified methods, and proven approaches; every problem, no matter how complex, had a concrete solution. Elwin was a nature writer who mourned for Earth's fading wilderness areas. She looked at him with starry eyes as he spoke to her about the "poetry of the universe."

But even with his grand descriptions of northern forests, Amazon jungles, and pristine tundra, she quickly realized that Elwin had never actually traveled anywhere, had not seen any natural wonders with his own eyes. He was merely an armchair adventurer. His journalism brought in some money and a dollop of fame, especially when he chose a controversial subject, but in the later years of their marriage he devoted more of his creativity to poetry, which earned nothing at all.

Baxter should have noticed the warning signs ahead of time, but by then she was smitten with Elwin. As an exceptional engineer, she earned enough for them to live comfortably in a safe enough shelter where they could hunker down during bad weather events.

Climate scientists determined that Earth had passed the environmental tipping point the year before Baxter was born. She, along with everyone else in her generation, never had a chance. Since her parents had been farmers in Illinois, she had grown up walking through struggling fields of corn, the plants turning brown, often suffering from a prevalent smut that destroyed the grain yields.

But Tanya was a brilliant engineering student, and at eighteen she received a full scholarship that paid for everything at Georgia Tech. Eventually, she and Elwin had moved in together. As she finished her engineering Masters, he would watch the weather reports, fascinated by the megastorms and massive hurricanes, the raging wildfires that ripped through the Western states. He said it inspired him to write, and he seemed moved by the apocalyptic nature of the spiraling crisis. The consensus of climate scientists said that even the most extreme mitigation measures could not rescue the planet from the brink.

Baxter was not a climate scientist, just an engineer, but she could see the data—any rational person could—and she believed it. Elwin was convinced, too, but he sat back with a fatalistic resignation to watch the end of the world from a front row seat.

But after hopeful images and data came back from the *Breakthrough Starshot* probe to Proxima Centauri, showing a planet that seemed viable for human life, Baxter threw herself into studies in high-energy physics. She believed that humans could survive on Proxima b much more easily than on Mars, if only the colonists could be protected from the solar flares.

For five years she immersed herself in her work to the point of drowning, and thus she didn't notice the malaise that was affecting her husband. Elwin became a cloud of gloom, endlessly fascinated with hurricane destruction and floods, and the panicked movements of entire populations that flooded out of low-lying areas. He would talk to her about revolutions and political instabilities, but Baxter didn't want to hear it.

She got herself assigned to the Forerunner mission, and she and her team designed the shield generators that would make Proxima b into a viable home. The arkship plan was the wildest of pipedreams, but it was better than giving up.

Elwin, though, had given up.

He endlessly argued with her that the Proxima Centauri mission was just a longer and more expensive way to die. But Baxter knew that Earth would become a hellhole like Venus in less than a century. There was no hope, no chance in staying here.

Because she and her team had developed the shield network, she and Elwin were offered a spot on the *Odyssey*, but he flatly refused. He had no interest in leaving Earth, shrugging off her arguments that he would absolutely die if he stayed on Earth. He insisted he would be there to watch, with or without her.

And so, it was without her.

Even though Elwin drove her insane sometimes, Baxter did love him. Yet her ultimate duty was to the survival of the human race, so she left him behind. Saving ten thousand people was just a grain of sand out of a population of nine billion, but they were the best of the best, the cream of the crop. She thought bitterly that maybe a fatalistic armchair nature poet was not the most vital need for humanity....

Baxter hated him for it, and she missed him now, but she put his memory away in a back corner of her mind along with any lingering regrets. No matter what had happened, Elwin was long dead.

And now Baxter was in another solar system, on another planet, in another crisis.

CHAPTER 34

S afe in the darkness of the crater, the TerraCat ground to a halt and sat shuddering. Sweaty in her envirosuit, Darcy just stared out the windshield. Baxter said nothing as she powered down the engine and locked the stabilizers. The rover groaned and ticked as it cooled down in the deep shadow.

Outside, overhead, the sky roiled with solar flares.

Clinging to routine duties, Darcy checked the panel. Her voice was hoarse, but she tried to keep her words even and professional. "Radiation levels are safe down here. We can ride out the storm." She swallowed hard as she looked at her distressingly red dosimeter.

Now that the cabin was pressurized, Baxter removed her goggles and facemask. "We'll need to be checked out by the X-Doc once we get back. That exposure was no joke. We should have—"

Snapping out of her funk, Darcy yanked off her glasses, heaved a deep breath of the cabin air, barely able to control herself. "Forget about the flares! What the hell happened on the geoglyph? I might not have grown up on Earth, but I know that rocks don't do that!"

Baxter shook her head. "Damn right they don't—and *you* want to mine the stuff and build cities with it?" She imagined tall, new buildings all suddenly writhing as the structural material came alive.

Darcy looked down, confused. "I didn't know what it was! Now how are we going to fix the shield nodes? The *Odyssey* is on the way!"

Baxter felt a flicker of relief when she spotted the node board that Darcy had rescued—now secured in a slot on the dash unit. "You were thinking fast."

"Never lose sight of the mission goal even when all hell is breaking loose." The young woman let out a shuddering sigh.

Baxter adjusted the node board in its slot and checked the readings, desperate to do something normal after their panicked drive. "You even uploaded my firewall."

Darcy lowered her head. "You saw how the alien metal had grown into the transmitting tower. The same contamination must be in all of the failed towers. How are we ever going to fix the network in time?" She drew a deep breath, hitched a sob. "There's no time!"

"We have to understand what the geoglyph is and why it's attacking us." Baxter looked around the cabin, saw the soil-core cylinder near Darcy's boots. "Hand me the samples."

Darcy grabbed the sample container and pushed it toward her as if it were poison, but Baxter was more fascinated than afraid. She slid the cylinder into a sample-analysis port in the rover's console. Lights winked on as the TerraCat began breakdown scans, but the vehicle had severe limitations. "This is too much work for the rover's computer. We need a full Omni to help—and Kyle should be in the loop, since this was his idea."

"We don't have time for a fun science experiment!" Darcy was barely able to contain her anger. With a rough gesture, she activated the comm. "AeroFox, do you read? Kyle? Omni? We're deep in the crater, and with all the flare activity scrambling the atmosphere, comms might be problematic. AeroFox, come in!"

Baxter used the controls to increase the gain, and Omni responded on a weak static-laden connection. "We can barely read you, TerraCat. Have you found shelter from the flares? Kyle and I were very concerned."

"We're riding it out deep in the shadows." Baxter looked down at the dosimeter badge, which glowed a deep red. "Made it just in time."

"Excellent." The computer voice actually sounded pleased.

"But we're not fine, and neither are the shield nodes," Darcy interjected. "The problem goes way beyond a software glitch. The geoglyph metal is alive—and malicious."

Baxter interrupted, speaking next to her. "Omni, we secured a sample of the material. It is much more exotic than we expected. Transmitting the data now."

Darcy said, "It attacked us, and it's intentionally disrupting our shield network."

The AI did not notice her concern. "Wonderful! I'm excited to see the sample. It sounds like a fascinating observation."

Darcy couldn't hold back. "*Fascinating?* The geoglyph didn't just damage the transmitter tower—it tried to eat the TerraCat! That alien metal is growing everywhere. It's an obvious threat to our future colony."

"She's exaggerating," Baxter said, "but there were some pretty tense moments."

Omni paused, as if surprised. "I obviously need more data."

Darcy gave Baxter an angry, disbelieving look. "How can you minimize it like that? We barely got away, and I was the one out there with a rock hammer roasting under the flares! You and I would have been cooked if I hadn't gotten the tire free. And now, if we can't get the protective shield working, our whole colony is toast!"

After Omni had received a summary of the logs, the calm AI voice said, "The geoglyph's response might have been connected to the rover's energy output. A similar thing could have attracted the material to the shield-generator tower as well, like a flower turning toward the light."

Darcy growled. "This wasn't a damned flower! We were attacked."

Hearing all this, Baxter felt oddly reticent. "We don't know what its motivations were. We can't be sure what the geoglyph was doing. For all we know, it was defending itself—from us. You were the one whacking it with a pickaxe, Darcy. Maybe that's what woke the thing up."

The young woman rolled her eyes. "And what did the tower do to piss it off?"

Baxter drew in a quick breath as an idea occurred to her. "Wait a minute ... Kyle said that the whole gigantic pattern has diminished dramatically ever since *Forerunner* arrived. After our shield network became active, the geoglyph shrank by about half. What if the shield is killing it?"

"Killing it? It's a bunch of fucking rocks!"

The AI voice responded immediately, laced with static, but still sounding offended. "Language, Astronaut Clarke."

Baxter shook her head. "Make up your mind, kid. Which is it —is it just rock and metal, or is the geoglyph some kind of alien monster?"

"Why can't it be both?"

Omni continued, "Your hypothesis is fascinating, Engineer Baxter. And we know that the damaged nodes are directly connected with the geoglyph lines. What do you suggest as a solution?"

Baxter concentrated on her sample analysis, as if Darcy weren't even there. "Kyle pointed it out himself. After our shield network began functioning, the whole geoglyph started shriveling up." She paused a beat. "Omni, can I talk to Kyle?"

The AI sounded sad. "Unfortunately, he lost consciousness while being tended by the X-Doc. I'd rather not wake him. However, I can find the images he was referring to. He and my previous Omni counterpart developed an extensive theory about the geoglyph. Just a moment ..."

The screen displayed an old, enhanced image from the

Forerunner. The geoglyph lines were grainy but still clear. For comparison, Omni played a sequence of images over time, then overlaid it with a new image taken by the AstroBug. The difference was obvious. The continent-wide pattern was much smaller and anemic.

Baxter whistled. "Like flowers drying up without access to water. It's obvious—we *are* killing it … something that's been here on this planet for untold millennia. Until we can figure this out, we have to keep the shield shut down."

Darcy looked at her in disbelief. "How can you suggest that? Right now we're hiding at the bottom of a dark crater, almost fried from solar flares—and that wouldn't have been an issue if we had the shield!" She held up her red radiation badge. "I almost died, and so did you. Ten thousand people need to move down here right away!" Her lips tightened into a hard smile as an answer occurred to her. "How about the opposite? What would happen if we uploaded your firewall and added a firmware update that *increased* power to the shield? Would that get rid of the destructive growths that damaged our transmitter towers? Can we pull the plug on that … thing?"

Baxter paled as she heard the outrageous idea, but Omni's voice responded, "I believe that would cause significant further damage to the geoglyph."

Darcy brightened. "To the point of destruction? If we can wipe the thing out, we wouldn't have to worry about it interfering with our colony."

"I believe so," the AI said.

Baxter was horrified. "You want to intentionally damage that extraterrestrial artifact, or lifeform, or whatever it is? We don't understand anything about it!"

Darcy looked grim and determined. "As soon as the flare storm passes, we're going back to Node 212 to complete our mission. We have to get the shield working again, at all costs. Captain Faraday is depending on us—and so it the rest of the human race."

"Wait a second, kid. This is a brand-new planet. You can't destroy an alien lifeform before we learn about it! How is the geoglyph even alive in the first place? What if it's sentient, for god's sake? If we do as you say, we could lose our only chance to study this marvelous anomaly."

Darcy was stiff as a statue. "I'm exterminating a deadly infestation that jeopardizes our entire mission."

Omni spoke up, "The damage to the shield towers may be unintentional on the part of the geoglyph. Or simply reactive. I agree with Engineer Baxter. This anomaly is an unprecedented discovery. Kyle and my counterpart were right to be intrigued by the mystery. It requires further study."

Darcy had clearly had enough. "You don't get a vote—you're just an AI." She straightened in her seat. "No, after the loss of Corey, I am in command of this mission. Omni, try and send another data-pac to the *Odyssey* describing our current situation. Include my images of the damaged node, the aggressive alien material, and the fact that this metallic organism has attacked us multiple times. Tell the captain that the geoglyph is preventing us from getting the shield online to make this place safe for habitation. Unless I can eradicate the infestation, we won't be ready by the time the ship arrives in orbit." Her mouth went dry. "Captain Faraday will know what that means."

"I can attempt the transmission, Astronaut Clarke, but the flares may make communication difficult, especially with possible damage the *Odyssey* suffered during the braking maneuver."

Darcy's voice was like steel. "That's why I'm initiating a response from here. Let the captain know that we are taking action to fight back and fix the shield once and for all. I won't let her down."

Baxter stared at her, trying to form words, but the AI responded first. "I must protest, Astronaut Clarke. This is not a wise course of action. Fact-based decision-making requires—"

Darcy pounded on the console. "Omni, shut up! I'm in

command here. Restoring the shield network is our absolute highest priority. End of discussion."

Cold and angry, Baxter turned to the comm. "Omni, how long will the flares last? What's our timeframe?"

"Four and a half hours, projected."

Baxter abruptly reached up to the comm controls. "Standby. TerraCat out." Before Darcy could argue, she switched off the transmitter and faced her companion. "All right, we have to cool our heels for at least that long before we can do anything outside—and in the meantime, you are going to hear me out, kid. You can't deny this is an absolutely unprecedented situation, and what we do here will have consequences *forever*! Is this some kind of vendetta you have against the geoglyph because of Corey? Destroying them won't bring him back."

"I know that!" The young woman flicked her eyes away, troubled. "I want this thing gone for bigger reasons than you can guess. And it has to be gone *now*!"

"Then tell me! What reasons?"

But Darcy ignored her. She snagged one of the portable Omni disks out of the charging cradle on the wall, then tugged her half-mask over the bottom half of her face, sealing it against her skin. "Put your oxygen mask on. I'm going outside."

Baxter touched the unit hanging around her neck. "Why? We need to stay—"

Darcy headed for the vehicle's hatch. "Because I'm going for a walk. I need some air! Isn't that what people used to say?"

CHAPTER 35

Kyle was awake again, despite the X-Doc's efforts to force him into a deep recovery sleep. The sample data was coming in, and no way was he going to miss this moment! He and his Omni companion had waited two years to study the geoglyph. And now Darcy was there in person, and it was stranger than he had ever imagined. Kyle squirmed in the reclined seat so he could watch the analysis of the sample from his monitor. He knew it! There *was* something mysterious and alien about the metal patterns.

But the data from the samples was maddeningly incomplete. He closed his eyes to think, wishing he could be in the TerraCat himself, not stuck over here on the cold night side. This was his holy grail! He couldn't be just some armchair researcher. But the rover's scientific capabilities were limited, which frustrated him further.

He still felt sick, but the arms of the X-Doc were like a straitjacket, clamping him down and preventing him from digging into the work. He and O had spent countless hours studying scraps of information about the geoglyph, and no one knew more about the patterns than he did. Darcy and Dr. Baxter would do their part on site, sure, but the real analysis and interpretation would have to fall to him. Darcy just didn't see the things he did, and he was afraid she would make a terrible mistake.

Enough! This was more important than getting himself patched up, and he couldn't afford to be unconscious during these critical hours. He disconnected the X-Doc's metal embrace, removing the sensors and implant tubes.

Omni's voice expressed alarm. "What are you doing, Kyle?"

"I've got work to do." With a sigh of determination, and a twinge of inner pain, he tossed the confining device to the deck. "You heard Darcy. She's going to kill the geoglyph before we even start to understand it." He crawled out of the couch where he'd been resting for hours, but his legs gave out and he collapsed hard onto the deck. He rubbed his thighs, which had gone entirely numb, but he managed to make his way toward the science station. "If she uploads the firewall to the transmitter, then the whole software package will propagate through the system. We'll never stop it, and the geoglyph will die."

The AI sounded stern and paternal. "I insist that you replace the X-Doc and return to bed. The nano-procedure is only eighteen percent complete. Your personal health is at stake."

"I'll take a sick day afterward." He pulled himself across the smooth deck, but his rubbery legs offered no help at all. "This is more important, buddy. My other Omni would have understood."

Conceding the point, the AI retracted the medical couch and deployed a stool and a keyboard. "The science station is ready for your use, Kyle."

He used the seat as leverage to haul himself halfway up, grimacing in pain. "You can help me do some of the work. The geoglyph isn't life as we know it, but it's alive—in some sense of the word. If we eradicate it, there's no going back. What do we know about the composition of that metal inclusion?"

Omni called up the TerraCat's data analysis of the sample. "It is composed of copper and iridium, the same materials that many quantum computers use, including myself. Yet, this metal sample appears to be self-organized, perhaps even self-aware."

Kyle shook his head in dismay. "And Darcy wanted to build roads and cities out of the stuff! What if it's a metallic life form? A planet-sized sentience? How much of the geoglyph have we already destroyed by having the shield active for the past two years?"

"Based on my calculations after studying the catalog of archived images, the geoglyph pattern has reduced in size by eighty percent since the time the shield network went operational."

Kyle was aghast. "Eighty percent in only two years? No wonder it's fighting back. What if it can't recover from this? This is the geoglyph's last gasp, trying to survive." He snapped his fingers as an idea occurred to him. "Wait ... we downloaded the system logs of the caretaker AI. Can we learn anything from that information?"

"I have those records, Kyle, but the caretaker AI's capabilities were extremely limited."

Kyle rolled his eyes. "Still, it must have kept records during the shield's initial months of operation. Pull those up and look for any anomalous readings."

The shield network data scrolled across the science station screens. Kyle saw multiple discrete energy spikes. Omni said, "On seven separate occasions, the geoglyph attempted to interact with the other AI."

"It was trying to make contact!" Kyle felt a chill down his spine. "When the shield built up enough low-frequency radio waves to block out the flares for *us*, it cut off the geoglyph's energy source. It began to starve. It must have extended tendrils into the tower nodes and attempted to communicate." He reached out to touch the screen. "Scroll forward to the first EMP that we encountered."

On the display, the levels rose to a massive peak, and then the data became so scrambled it was incoherent. Omni speculated, "Desperate to survive, the geoglyph must have sent the electromagnetic pulse as a means of protecting itself. Our shield generators were threatening it."

Kyle slumped on the stool, feeling increasingly emotional. He coughed hard, winced from all the ragged pain inside. He could tell the X-Doc was nowhere close to fixing his injuries, but he could hold on for a little longer.

"The *Forerunner* just dropped the shield nodes wherever they happened to fall. The geoglyph lines were in our way." His words were punctuated by a more severe, staccato bout of coughing. "Goddamn it, we're just like the white colonists bringing smallpox to the Native Americans, killing them and stealing their land." His eyes burned. "The geoglyph was just fighting back."

"Kyle, perhaps *I* could attempt to communicate with it? We share a certain fundamental commonality."

He felt excited by the possibility, then frowned. "The geoglyphs wouldn't be listening to radio transmissions. You'd probably have to be in direct physical contact. How do we make that happen?"

"Considering Astronaut Clarke's attitude, I seriously doubt she would assist us in that endeavor. She has a singular focus on the mission at hand."

"Darcy just doesn't understand. If she turns on the shield network again, she'll kill the geoglyphs. They are obviously a sentient lifeform!"

"Perhaps it is obvious to you, Kyle, but you have always had a different perspective from most people. You are open-minded to these possibilities and willing to accept a sense of wonder."

Damn, the AI voice sounded so familiar! A smile grew on his face. "You know, Omni, you're pretty perceptive yourself." Then a wave of dizziness drove him back, and he slumped forward and collapsed against the station.

"Kyle!" The AI sounded genuinely alarmed. "You must return to the couch and reinstall the X-Doc."

"I ... I'm okay. Can you raise the TerraCat? Please? Before Darcy does anything she can't take back...."

"Unfortunately, the flare is jamming communications, even with our new comm satellites in orbit."

Kyle mumbled a curse, but Omni continued in a grave voice, "You are rapidly approaching the point where the X-Doc will be unable to complete repairs. You cannot do both. I must insist."

The young man responded with a wan smile and drove back the pain. "I already made my decision, buddy. We need to figure out the geoglyph, before it's too late." He turned back to the science station, ignoring the X-Doc as he continued his work.

Kyle Dyson had never been good at making friends—not that he'd had many opportunities on a big, mostly empty arkship. The three *Odyssey* children had grown up as tightknit siblings, but that wasn't the same as actual "friends." He always felt like a pesky little brother around the other two.

As he grew up, Kyle talked with the adults on the skeleton crew, but with their heavy duties, they had little time for conversation or play. Every five years, a new shift would wake up or go down into hibernation.

Once, when Kyle had made a remark about wanting friends, O offered in his calm voice, "When the colony is established and all the hibernating settlers are awakened, there will be many people your age. You will have plenty of opportunities to make friends."

"I'm just a kid," young Kyle had said. "There aren't any colonists my age, and no children in hibernation."

"By the time we arrive in the Proxima system, you will be twenty-four years old, the same age as many of the hibernating men and women. You will fit right in."

Kyle brightened at the thought. That hadn't occurred to him. Then he grew intimidated. The thought of striking up a conversation and finding things in common with a complete stranger—thousands of complete strangers—terrified him. Every one of those popsicles in the huge hibernation section had been born on Earth ... and they had seen some of the places that he and O fantasized about in their virtual tours. Maybe that would be a way to start a conversation. He could ask them about the Great Barrier Reef or the Himalayan mountains, the Australian outback, the Siberian steppes.

Fascinated by the idea, Kyle had set off, taking his Omni disc. "Let's go to the hibernation section and have a look."

They rode the tram up the *Odyssey*'s long axis from the habitation ring to the much larger dumbbell section where ten thousand hibernation pods were packed together, connected by bright accessways.

O reviewed the arkship's database, the identities and ages, and offered possibilities for him. Because it had been such a rush to load thousands of colonists aboard the *Odyssey*, individual records were sparse, giving vital statistics and technical expertise, but nothing about hobbies, interests, or personality tags. Kyle wanted to find someone who might *like* him, and he could tell little from the information he had.

Carrying his Omni disc, he wandered from sector to sector among the hibernation pods, tracking down names that O had found for him. At one specific pod, he peered through the viewport to see a young woman with large lips and short reddish-brown hair. Her closed eyes were dusted with frost, but he imagined they would be green. Moira Stenzca, a specialist in soil composition. He pretended to know what her laugh would sound like.

"Will you be my friend when you wake up?" he whispered.

Of course, Moira didn't answer.

He moved to another one, Jared Quo, a tall young man who barely fit inside the hibernation pod. He had straight black hair, and even asleep he wore a thoughtful expression. Jared was a counselor, and Kyle thought he might like to talk to someone like that. Maybe they could even be real friends.

Somewhere in these ranks, his biological mother was also

hibernating. He had read up about Miranda Dyson, and although Captain Faraday or Sebastian Clarke had been careful not to speak disparaging words, Kyle wasn't impressed with what he knew about her, and he had little interest in meeting her. When she was revived at Persephone, his mother would be a few years younger than he was.

But Kyle didn't want a mother; he wanted to have people he could relate to.

O assisted him as he went from pod to pod, tracking down colonists that intrigued him for one reason or another. "Will you be my friend? Will you be my friend?"

When he finally stopped, Kyle had felt hopeful, optimistic. He was anxious for a new home on a new planet. He was anxious to be twenty-four, the same age as so many other colonists.

As he'd climbed back in the tram to return to the habitation ring, O had spoken up in a warm, serious voice. "I'll be your friend until then, Kyle."

CHAPTER 36

As the red star continued its flare tantrum, radiation rippled across the surface of Persephone, the empty hab modules and the colony infrastructure. Without the shield network functioning, the new settlement would be vulnerable to the frequent solar storms.

The crater offered enough protection for now, and all she could do was wait.

With her facemask in place, Darcy stalked away from the TerraCat, hunching down against the invisible radiation threat all around her. She was deep in the darkness of the wide crater, sheltered by the shadows. Always in the shadows ...

The last ten thousand humans needed to live here. They'd flown for fifty damn years to get to Persephone, and they didn't have another option. All those people couldn't simply shrug at some metallic freak show. "Sorry for the interruption. We'll just look somewhere else."

It was all or nothing. Us or them.

Fuming, she leaned against the rough wall of the crater. Kyle had always been clueless. He had a lot of knowledge from all the educational loops he absorbed, but not much experience or common sense. Darcy and Corey had grown up just as isolated, but at least they got along with the normal adult crew members.

Baxter's reaction to Kyle's crackpot concerns, though, was a surprise. Why would she protect the metal monster? The woman had lived on Earth, had designed the shield network herself. She had devoted her career to the survival of humanity, and she knew that no one could inhabit the new colony without her shield. What else were they supposed to do?

Now Baxter was willing to just throw it away, leave the *Odyssey* just hanging in orbit while somebody figured out a different solution. But the colony setup was *here*, on the dayside, deposited by the *Forerunner*. They didn't have any other options.

Darcy ground her teeth together. The old engineer knew better than anyone what was at stake! Why wasn't she furious that the geoglyph had wrecked those transmitting towers and disrupted the vital shield?

She pulled out the Omni disc and held it, pondering. No one could give her advice about this situation, but she still wanted support, a sounding board. She needed to hear her father's voice.

She called up an old recording: the last message Sebastian Clarke had made for her before going down into hibernation. As she stood against the rocky crater wall, she watched his familiar face on the small screen. "Hey, Peanut. I'm making this recording for you, just in case I don't wake up as expected. On this ship, you never know."

"Always the optimist," Darcy mumbled, but he had good reason for concern. Sebastian knew the *Odyssey*'s problems better than the other settlers who had slept obliviously the whole journey.

Darcy had played his message countless times, and her father's calm, rational voice always steadied her. How she missed him!

As the recording played, she glanced up beyond the rim of the crater to the sky. Out there, the massive geoglyph patterns must be basking in the flare storm, soaking up the energy. She resented the thing for it.

On the video image, Sebastian wore his crew uniform, relaxed and confident. He had left this recording without telling her, because he knew how important it was. She and her father had argued just before his scheduled hibernation. Now, so many years later, Darcy couldn't even remember the real cause for their quarrel. It had more to do with her volatile emotions than any specific event or comment. She was a sixteen-year-old girl and everything seemed extreme. She and Corey had also bickered at the time. She must have been difficult company.

Sebastian continued, "It'll be tough for us to be apart for the next few years, but it has to be done for the sake of the mission. I can't complain. I've already had more than my share of time awake with you. Ten years, and I got to watch you grow up. I want you to know what it's like to stand on a real planet, not just some metal spaceship with artificial light and recycled air. I want you to have a real home. I'll see you on Proxima b. We'll make it work." He mouthed the words "I love you," then signed off.

Darcy's eyes filled with tears. That was eight years ago, and it felt like he'd been gone forever. All she had was this recording and her memories, and she really needed him now.

Now in the crater beneath a storm of solar flares, she made a promise to the now-silent Omni disc. "I'm going to make sure this colony works, Dad. And I'm not going to let any weird metal thing ruin humanity's future."

CHAPTER 37

While Darcy stormed out of the TerraCat, Baxter turned her attention to the exotic, extraordinary life form. She felt chills as she considered how long those metal patterns had been here on Proxima b, growing into some kind of message or circuit. A brain pattern laid down under the perpetual glare of the red dwarf?

Part of the geoglyph had swelled around the shield towers, and she imagined it must have been curiosity at first, a vain attempt to communicate. But when the functioning shield began to kill the entire organism, the metallic thing had tried to defend itself. To survive.

Darcy Clarke just wanted to wipe the thing out because it was in the way—just like every short-sighted developer or industrialist from old Earth. Having seen how much ruthless destruction humans had done to their world until it fell off the environmental cliff, Baxter felt a particular horror to think of these refugees doing the same thing here.

Self-centered humans had caused the environmental collapse of Earth, killing not only their own race but all other species, too. *All of them.* Redwood trees, dolphins, elk, penguins, tulips, butterflies, bald eagles, humpback whales, and every single blade of grass.

Now, the last human survivors had reached another pristine and innocent place, which happened to be the home of a giant geoglyph organism. By erecting the shield network—*her* shield network—they were obliviously starting another genocide, willing to wipe out the only native life form without giving it a second thought or bothering to consider any alternatives. It was malignant narcissism on a planetary scale.

Elwin would have found it a matter for extreme pathos. He might even have written a poem about it.

Though the *Odyssey* was in bad shape, Baxter vowed not to let *her* work exterminate another species or wreck another world that was just minding its own business. No, she would figure out a different solution. Captain Faraday and the mission planners must have had a list of alternatives. The arkship would just have to stay in orbit until somebody figured it out.

First, she would try to understand the geoglyph.

Carrying the transparent sample container, Baxter also climbed out of the TerraCat. The strange pyrite-like lumps were quiescent, no more than shiny rocks.

Darcy had found a place to sulk against the wall in deep shadow. The young woman stared at her Omni disc and studiously ignored her.

Baxter trudged off in the opposite direction, toward the stark boundary of daylight on the opposite side of the crater where the rugged surface was harshly lit. Kneeling at the edge of the shadow, she edged the soil-core container into direct sunlight.

Darcy spoke into the comm, sounding annoyed. "Baxter, what the hell are you doing?"

"I'm conducting a little experiment. We've got to understand this thing."

As the ruddy glare shone down on the cylinder, the inert metal started to flex, move, and expand, like wax on a hot plate. Startled, she yanked the container back out of the radioactive glare, and the geoglyph bits hardened again into shiny rock. She rotated the cylinder to study the swift and obvious changes in the shards.

Darcy sprinted toward her. "Enough! You need to stop."

But Baxter pushed the soil core deeper into the glare again. "I want to see how the samples react."

This time, the growth was exponential, and the cylinder exploded as pyrite shards lurched out, growing to several times their original size. Baxter flung the shattered container away from her as she fell backward to the ground. The sample pieces tumbled onto the sunlit crater floor.

Under the glare, the geoglyph fragments stretched outward like tendrils expanding in a starlike pattern. They skittered in straight lines that suddenly turned at sharp angles, split, then drew more lines.

Retreating into the crater shadow, Baxter watched the pyrite fragments recreate a miniature version of the major geoglyph pattern. One of her boots also extended into the light, and two silvery lines of geoglyph material shot out to grasp it.

Darcy was suddenly there. Without a second thought, she kicked the alien metal, broke the tendrils, and dragged Baxter by the shoulders.

Her heart pounding, Baxter got to her feet and brushed herself off. "That was stupid—sorry. Not a, uh, well-thought-out experiment."

Furious with her, Darcy stalked back to the TerraCat, where she sat on the hood, brooding. "Yeah, whatever." She pulled out her Omni disc again and pretended to be absorbed in what was displayed on the screen.

Meanwhile, basking in the sunlight, the smaller geoglyph continued growing away from them. Still fascinated, Baxter watched the metal pattern growing in the sunlit patch of the crater floor. It became larger, more complex, but veered away from the cold shadows.

"We're safe, I think," she called to Darcy. "The organism is only active in sunlight. Must be why they only exist on the dayside."

"Organism ..." Darcy scoffed. "It's a dangerous and aggressive life form that sabotaged our only hope for survival. But now we know how to build the firewall and restore the shield nodes, so we can be protected from it. If it's them or us, then I choose *us*! Ten thousand colonists. What's left of the human race. We have our orders from Captain Faraday."

"Captain Faraday doesn't know the real situation." Her brow furrowed. "In all of human history, we've never encountered anything like the geoglyph. You're not even curious about it?"

"That thing killed Corey and it's ruining our colony." She turned away from the amazing metallic object on the crater floor. "No, not curious about it at all."

Baxter couldn't take her eyes from the angular planes and geometric patterns. "It's genuine alien life, can't you see? How long has it been here, covering the dayside? Does it think and feel?"

Darcy raised her head. "I just want the thing gone. We have to *live* here. It's not a theoretical exercise."

"How human of you—just wipe out anything that inconveniences us." Baxter went to the rear of the rover, away from Darcy. She felt melancholy, no longer giddy about the geoglyph. "Sometimes, it feels like the whole human enterprise is just one big tragedy, and I've seen a lot more of it than you have." She drew a deep breath. "I was hoping Proxima b would be a fresh start for us, and we seem hellbent on screwing it up again."

Though still tense, Darcy stared at the strange metallic structure. "I know you don't get what I'm trying to do, Tanya, but it's you who doesn't know the real situation. The *Odyssey* can't just wait in orbit until we figure a new solution. With or without the damage from the braking maneuver, the ship was dying. It can't support the hibernation pods anymore. Captain Faraday kept the magnitude of the crisis confidential from anyone but Corey—and he told me before he died."

Baxter slumped against the TerraCat's side. "Oh. It's starting to make sense now. I'm not surprised—all three arkships were built as fast as humanly possible, and a lot of it was totally unproven tech. The *Odyssey* was traveling hard for more than four light-years. But we need time to settle the planet."

"Time is what we don't have! The *Odyssey* has a week at most. The popsicles have to come down, all of them, because the hibernation disk is failing. The hab modules and the colony infrastructure are already here, ready and waiting for us. We need the shield functioning—period—or everybody dies. Where else are we going to go?"

Baxter did not have an answer for her.

CHAPTER 38

The TerraCat system interrupted their debate when their comm implants chimed. "We are receiving an X-Band transmission. Signal distorted, but I have amplified and clarified."

Darcy brightened when she saw the signal identifier on her wrist readout. "It's a message from the *Odyssey*. They're back in contact! I hope they received Omni's message burst so ... so they know." She felt a wave of emotions just to be in contact with the captain again. Faraday would give them direct guidance, issue orders to Baxter, and put an end to this nonsense once and for all.

She turned her back on the growing metallic monstrosity on the crater floor and ducked back into the rover. Baxter followed her, and they sealed the hatch to repressurize the compartment. A staticky screen image appeared on a side monitor.

"It is just a message," the system said. "Two-way communication is not possible at this time."

Captain Faraday was at her bridge console—tired, haggard, angry, as if she had been through hell and back, which was probably an adequate description. The *Odyssey*'s bridge deck flared with emergency lights. Crew members scrambled around, attending to multiple system failures.

"Darcy, I hope you're receiving this. We've boosted the signal as much as possible to cut through the solar flares. That storm is wreaking"—a burst of static garbled her words, and her image distorted before sharpening again—"can't believe Jim Corey's dead. I'm so sorry. I think of all three of you as my kids, always have." Her voice hitched. "Kyle's injuries sound serious. The idea of any of you being hurt is devastating to me. We've ... lost quite a few on *Odyssey*, too."

Her image blurred, snapped back into focus. "When I signed up for the mission, I knew all the risks, but you three were born into it. You never had any choice." She lifted her head and seemed to look directly into Darcy's eyes. "Regardless, I know you're doing your best. I hope you've made progress on the shield. We are all counting on you ... every single person aboard the *Odyssey*."

Listening to her now, Darcy was reminded of the many serious, private conversations they'd had together. "We're past the braking maneuver and on our way to you. The *Odyssey* is limping, but I think we'll get there. The fact is, things are getting worse. Much worse. This ship won't last long once we enter orbit. We have to get all the hibernation pods offloaded. Not a moment to spare."

In the adjacent seat Baxter looked away, but Darcy ignored her.

Faraday continued, "Because of cascading system failures, I'll be forced to awaken many of the settlers earlier than we planned. Once in orbit, we'll only have hours to start a full-scale emergency offloading effort. We'll fill up our fleet of AstroBugs, all forty-eight of them, with hibernation pods."

The captain looked down at the instruments in front of her. "If Engineer Baxter can't get the shield network running, we'll have to dump the AstroBugs on the dark side until we sort it out. That was the mission backup plan. Staying aboard the *Odyssey* is not an option."

With a hardened expression, Darcy turned to Baxter, who had gone pale. "That's why we need to fix the shield nodes. Now. Geoglyph or no geoglyph."

Faraday's transmission continued, "*Odyssey* will be in orbit by eighteen-thirty hours tomorrow. You've got a ticking clock."

"No pressure," Darcy whispered.

More static surrounded the image. Behind Faraday, two crewmembers rushed to a console that had just gushed a stream of sparks. "Faraday out." The transmission ended.

Darcy stared at the blank gray screen. "There you have it. Are you going to help me upload the firewall as soon as the flares pass, or are you going to kill everybody aboard the *Odyssey?*"

The engineer flinched. "The captain already said there's an alternative. We can land the fleet of AstroBugs on the dark side, use them as temporary habitats. We've both been over there. It's survivable!"

"Don't be ridiculous! All the hab modules are over *here*. All the algae ponds, all the pumping stations, the entire power grid. Why would we go live in the cold and dark? That was never anything more than a worst-case scenario."

Baxter raised her eyebrows. "Really? Worst-case? You need to think outside the box, kid—none of our planning considered a sentient life form already here."

Darcy was adamant. "The captain is counting on me."

Ever since Sebastian Clarke had gone into hibernation when Darcy was sixteen, she, Corey, and Kyle made a habit of eating meals with the captain. One time they were sitting in a small mess chamber enjoying a mushroom-and-yeast stew when Faraday had an epiphany.

The captain was chatting about some old Earth entertainment program, a children's show that made no sense whatsoever to the three kids, then she stopped in mid-sentence, just staring at the three. Her face had split in a grin. "I see you every day, but I don't ... *see* you. You aren't children anymore."

Darcy let out a quick, loud laugh. "Yeah, we haven't been for quite a while."

Faraday's brown eyes looked very tired. "You've been doing regular adult crew duties since you were eleven years old. You're genuine, vital crew members, and when we set up our colony and thaw the popsicles, there'll be thousands of colonists your age."

"You mean we won't be special anymore," Corey said.

"We're still special," Kyle interjected.

Faraday rose from her seat. "I need to make sure you're prepared for any and all duties and qualified on numerous systems. I'm going to start you on an expanded duty roster. You never had any real-world experience on Earth, but you've been awake longer than anybody but me, and I'm going to turn that into an advantage."

"More work and more duties?" Corey asked.

"Don't forget our school hours," Kyle said.

Darcy pushed aside her now-empty bowl of stew. "We'll need to hibernate just to rest from all that."

But Faraday seemed more energized than she'd been in quite a while. "Bottle suits, so you can learn how to do outside inspection and repairs. If you know what you're doing, you can just fly free. It's quite a rush."

"Bottle suits!" Corey exclaimed. "Now you're talking."

Darcy could never forget the horrible day of her mother's accident, even though she'd been only six, but she had always longed to explore outside, to flit around the superstructure to gain perspective on the enormous ship that had been her entire world. "I'm all for that."

"I ... I'll stick with the simulators," Kyle said.

"Not the same," Faraday insisted, and her expression grew warmer. "Your Omni will be right there with you."

"You should know the ropes too, Kyle," Darcy said.

Corey clapped the young man on the shoulder. "We'll watch out for you, buddy. Nothing's going to happen."

So, they had spent two weeks in the simulators, then Captain

Faraday declared that they were ready. When they had climbed into their booth-sized bottle suits, Darcy's pulse was racing. She glanced through the suit's side window to see Jim Corey smiling at her in the adjacent unit. She blew him a kiss, and he flushed before doing the same.

Once the bottle suits had sealed, pressurized, and detached from the hull, Darcy and her companions had used their maneuvering thrusters to drift along. As they glided along the axis of the dumbbell-shaped ship, Darcy used her jets to rotate so she could look at the gigantic engines that glowed with constant deceleration thrust. As a cluster, they moved away from the central habitation ring and then up front to the gigantic, shielded disk that held the thousands of popsicles. More exciting, though, Darcy looked beyond the ship out to the stars, an infinity of diamonds, the great white river of the Milky Way.

Together, they cruised along the *Odyssey*, supposedly inspecting the vessel for unknown damage, but really just reveling in the size of it all.

"This is quite an experience," Kyle admitted.

Darcy couldn't contain her excitement. "We should do this more often, Captain!"

Faraday replied, "With such a small skeleton crew, we usually only have one person certified for extravehicular activity, with me as a fallback. Now I've got you three, in case we need an emergency repair crew."

"We'll be ready, Captain," Corey said.

"You have to admit it's marvelous out here," Faraday said.

"It is," Darcy chimed in.

They spent two hours outside before they finally returned. Darcy had been giddy the whole time, but now she felt drained and exhausted. She went to her quarters, stripped down and wiped off with bathing cloths. Uneasy but determined, she called up her mother's last message again. This time she was able to watch it.

As she played Denise Clarke's final words to her daughter, Darcy thought she understood what she was saying.

Only moments after the *Odyssey*'s transmission ended, Omni's voice came over the comms. "AeroFox to TerraCat—I'm calling about Kyle! It's an emergency. He refused treatment from the X-Doc and is now non-responsive. I need your help. You must return."

CHAPTER 39

The TerraCat thrummed as the big wheels carried it across the shadowed crater floor. Above, the flares had abated enough to make travel possible again, but it would be a long and frantic drive back to the AeroFox.

Behind them in the slice of coppery sunlight at the bottom of the crater, the new geoglyph continued to grow slowly, all angles and planes.

The vehicle ascended the steep inner wall and crossed over the rim to emerge into the blazing red sun. Turning about, they accelerated toward the line of twilight and the distant terminator storm. Darcy vowed that she would not lose Kyle and Corey on the same day, and Baxter couldn't argue with her.

Baxter tried to coax as much speed as possible across the uneven terrain. Kyle had not looked well when she and Darcy had headed out to Node 212, but the X-Doc should have taken care of his injuries. She knew that wouldn't help, though, if Kyle refused to wear the medical device and accept the healing procedure.

"The auto-drive probably has some sort of governing routine against speeding," Baxter said. "I'm going to keep it on manual for now."

Visibly worried, Darcy agreed. "We're not sightseeing. We're hauling ass."

The TerraCat rushed past the clumps of inkweed and sprawling pools of algae, but Baxter focused only on the smudge of shadow on the horizon. She figured she could cut their travel time by half an hour at least, since they didn't have to plot a course and pick out a feasible route this time. The TerraCat could just retrace its previous path.

Though the hours seemed interminable, they quickly reached the terminator line and pushed into the whipping wind at the interface layer. Webs of lightning skittered overhead. The rover's bright headlights stabbed ahead into the gloom, illuminating the hellish terrain. They wound their way through the rocky canyon, out of the warm sheeting rains, and into flurries of snow.

"See, it's practically a paradise," Baxter said. "We can live here, if we need to." Darcy didn't even smile.

She swerved to avoid a boulder, then lurched the other direction to avoid a steep drop-off. Darcy clutched her abdomen and groaned. "I'm not sure if I'm sick from radiation or your driving."

Baxter glanced at her dosimeter, which still glowed red. She closed her eyes to push back a brief bout of nausea. "Kyle isn't the only one who'll need the X-Doc when we get to the AeroFox."

When the headlights finally shone ahead to where the Fox's pulsing beacon flashed on the horizon, Darcy touched her comm implant. "Omni, we're almost there. Any word from Kyle?"

Oddly, the AI sounded almost evasive. "He is ... still unresponsive, Astronaut Clarke."

When the TerraCat ground to a halt outside the spacecraft, Omni already had the outer airlock open and waiting for them. Baxter bounded out of the rover, with Darcy right behind her.

After they cycled through the airlock to the Fox's interior, Baxter rushed into the pilot deck, where she found the young man slumped motionless against the science station. His skin was gray, his expression slack. "Kyle!" She pulled off her glove and pressed her palm against his forehead. He felt cold, much too cold. When she touched him, he slid like a rag against her arm.

Darcy sealed the airlock hatch and ran to join her. "Oh my god! This is worse than I—"

Baxter caught Kyle's limp body in her arms and gently lowered him to the deck. She knew the terrible truth, but she checked anyway for a pulse. Found none. "He's dead, Darcy."

In disbelief, Darcy dropped to her knees. Tears sprang to her eyes, and she kept shaking her head from side to side. "No! That's not possible!"

Baxter looked up at the screen that showed the AI's blue avatar. "Omni, what happened to the nano-treatment? Why didn't it work?"

"The treatment required him to be comatose for an extended period so the nanomachines could complete their work. Kyle halted the procedure and removed the X-Doc so he could continue working, which he considered more important. I strongly advised him against this, but he refused to follow my instructions. He knew the consequences, but he insisted on compiling data on the geoglyph and sending another message to the *Odyssey*." The AI voice hung for a moment, then added in a deeply remorseful tone. "Not long afterward, he succumbed to his injuries. I watched him die, but could do nothing to help."

Bitter and grief-stricken, Darcy wrapped her arms around her abdomen, obviously sick herself. "If only we'd gotten here sooner!"

The infinity symbol dimmed. "It would not have mattered. His life functions had terminated even before I contacted you in the crater."

"What? He was already dead before we even drove over here?" Darcy was astounded. "You lied to us!"

Baxter understood, though. "Omni didn't lie—just misled us. He said Kyle was 'non-responsive,' and that was true. We both heard what we wanted to hear." She narrowed her eyes and looked at the infinity symbol. "But why would you do that?"

The AI responded, "It was Kyle's final request to force you to return here. He was willing to die for this. Please don't be angry with me."

Darcy's nostrils flared. "I'm angry at Kyle, not you. He should have put on the damned X-Doc. Why would he sacrifice his life over a bunch of metal lines?"

Omni continued in a soft voice. "I will let him explain it in his own words. He recorded a message for you. Do you want to see?"

Darcy hung her head, as if afraid of the prospect, but Baxter steeled herself as she cradled the young man's body. "I do."

The screen at the science station displayed Kyle's wrung-out face. He wore an unconvincing smile, but his words wheezed out as he made a visible effort.

"Hey, guys ... Glad you came back, and I hope I got you here before Darcy uploaded that damned firewall." He was covered in a fevered sweat. Another window on the screen displayed a stream of data. "So, uh, I've been busy—too busy to take a time out with the X-Doc. As Darcy said, it's all or nothing. This is our one chance, and we have to get it right."

Darcy's eyes glittered with tears, but her gaze was hard. "Stupid ..."

"In addition to analyzing your sample of the geoglyph material, I reviewed the logs of the shield system's caretaker AI. It's very clear—the geoglyph did attempt to communicate several times, but no one answered."

The technical display showed multiple energy spikes in a repeated pattern. Kyle matched the signals with similar data from all of the other malfunctioning shield nodes. "Only when those attempts failed did it strike out to protect itself. Dr. Baxter's shield was killing it. It shrank by eighty percent in just the two years we had the shield on."

His breath rattled as he tried to suck in enough air to keep going.

"The geoglyph is alive and sentient—a single giant organism, like the mind of Persephone." He coughed repeatedly, wiped blood from the side of his mouth, but he reached out to the controls to display an orbital image of the complex circuit-like formation across the dayside.

"It's a living solar cell that occupies that entire hemisphere. A vast array evolved to absorb solar flares, living off the energy. It might even power the volcanoes, like a giant generator—that's part of why this planet has such a thick CO_2 atmosphere." He rubbed his eyes, quelled another bout of coughing. "I couldn't let you kill it."

Still cradling his lifeless body, Baxter spotted Kyle's toy gyroscope on the deck beside the science station.

He wheezed. "We've been wearing blinders for so long, just assuming that *Forerunner* would deliver the colony as expected, that the shield network would work perfectly, that we'd move right in without any impediments.

"But the mission planners always had a Plan B, and C, and probably all the way through the alphabet." He leaned closer to the imager. His eyes were bloodshot. "Right here, the night side, is *livable*. At least for a while, and it's way better than what Earth turned into. Captain Faraday has a backup plan, a fully planned exodus to set up temporary bases over here, for years if necessary. O and I found them."

Baxter looked at Darcy, who was stubbornly shaking her head. "No, our colony is already set up on the other side."

As Kyle continued, his words had obviously become more of a struggle. "Guys, don't be mad at me. I couldn't let you murder the ... soul of the planet. When we colonize Persephone, we'll have to learn to live with it. We have to—"

Darcy stalked toward the science station and cut off the recording. "Great, now Kyle has a new imaginary friend!" She looked at Baxter, her eyes glistening with desperation. "If we don't get those nodes working—and soon—all the colonists on the *Odyssey* will also be toast." She paced the deck, a mass of conflicting emotions. "I don't give a damn about hurting the geoglyph's feelings!"

Baxter rested Kyle's body against the bulkhead so she could stand. "But we attacked it first. If we're justified in our actions for our survival, isn't the geoglyph justified, too? By cutting off the solar flares, we were starving it to death." Sickened, she shook her head. "I created the shield to protect lives, not destroy them. But now, with one fell swoop, I am exterminating a sentient life form—maybe the only one of its kind in the universe—and destroying the delicate ecosystem of another world. I don't want the extinction of a species on my conscience."

Suddenly suspicious, Darcy glared at the glowing blue infinity symbol. "Omni—you said Kyle sent another message to the *Odyssey*. Did you first provide the complete data summary and the urgent request that I put together for Captain Faraday?" She hardened her voice. "Does she even know the threat the geoglyph poses?"

The AI didn't sound guilty at all. "From an objective point of view, your statement was full of half-truths and assumptions. That's no way to do science, Astronaut Clarke. Facts matter. I included all of the data about the situation, and Kyle also made a very compelling case to consider an alternative plan, at least as a temporary solution."

Darcy bristled. "Omni, you disobeyed a direct order! We have an enemy on this planet, and it doesn't want us here."

"I doubt the geoglyph entity is so discerning about what happened. While it may perceive computer intelligences like me as a form of life, humans would be incomprehensible to it. It has no experience whatsoever with organic biology."

Darcy continued pacing the pilot deck, but she looked broken by her inconceivable losses, cast adrift in a deadly storm. She looked at Kyle's motionless body in disbelief, then hung her head and turned to Baxter. She sounded defeated. "Right now, I need your help outside, Tanya. This is something only we can do."

Baxter felt impossibly weary, beyond just the lingering malaise from hibernation. "Help with what?"

Even on her young face, Darcy's expression made her look infinitely old. "Something Corey never received. We can give Kyle a decent burial."

Outside the AeroFox, standing in the alien night, Baxter and Darcy worked together in silence as they chipped rubble with their rock hammers. They carried boulders over to pile the final stones on Kyle Dyson's burial mound.

As a finishing touch, Darcy placed Kyle's toy gyroscope on top of the cairn. "He insisted on calling this planet Persephone," she said. "We should honor that."

Baxter's eyes burned behind the AR goggles. "Persephone it is." Her body was worn out, filled with a thousand aches. "But if you and I don't want to end up here in our own graves after that massive radiation exposure, we'd better get back into the AeroFox and take turns with the X-Doc."

Darcy looked down at the mound for a long moment. Snow was already collecting in the crannies. "Agreed. We have to stay alive to do what we need to do."

CHAPTER 40

As the *Odyssey* cruised farther from the red dwarf, Captain Faraday was heartbroken by what had happened to her beloved ship. Behind them, the cauldron of Proxima Centauri was like a sore loser, throwing up a tantrum of flares.

The braking maneuver had slowed the giant vessel enough for David Hamelin, her helmsman, to guide them toward a safe orbit around Proxima b. Like a marathon runner collapsing just over the finish line, they would take up their position over the planet, but it would be the arkship's last gasp.

As bad as things were here, Faraday now knew that her team on the surface was also in big trouble. As soon as they had a communication link out of the flare storms, she had received the summary burst transmission from their Omni, the awful details of Jim Corey dead, Kyle Dyson severely injured, the AstroBug destroyed, the AeroFox damaged. And the shield network still wasn't functioning.

She hadn't even considered this worst-case scenario.

And then the second astonishing message with Kyle's revelations about the geoglyph, the incontrovertible evidence that it was indeed some kind of alien life form, a presence that had tried—and failed—to communicate with the human outsiders who had already nearly killed it.... Kyle had begged her to look at the alternative plans that had already been built into the mission, sending her detailed readings about the dark portion of the planet, a temperate zone near the terminator line.

The *Odyssey* did not have any truly good options. But this was better than no options at all.

Now, as the arkship lumbered toward the planet, Faraday couldn't help but think of a bedraggled shipwreck victim crawling up onto the shore of a desert island. Immediate safety, yes, but then the real struggle for survival would begin.

Commander Kleve stepped up to her bridge station. "I've got a first-cut summary of our damage report, Captain."

Faraday's stomach twisted as she saw column after column of red zone indicators. "Do I have time to absorb all this in the next day before we get to orbit?"

"Probably not, Captain. That's why I highlighted the most significant failures."

The first officer touched the screen, reordered the lists, and Faraday let out a gasp. Three of the major power-regeneration cells had exploded. The external comm array with the transmitting masts and receiver grid had shorted out and melted. One of the water-recirculation systems had burst, spraying thousands of liters into space. The *Odyssey*'s primary life-support systems were offline.

"We have maybe three days of air," Faraday said. "Good thing this ship is huge."

"My engineers can goose it a little bit," said Kleve. "Our skeleton crew will have heat and power and breathable air for another week maybe, but that's all."

"Maybe we should all just hold our breath," Faraday muttered, then she straightened and raised her voice for the whole bridge crew to hear. "We have absolutely no room for error. Forget the rest of the system failures and put everyone to work on life support to buy us some extra time." Her mind spun as she considered how much effort would be involved in reawakening ten thousand colonists from hibernation pods—under normal circumstances! When Tanya Baxter had been revived, she'd been slow and sluggish for a couple of days. What would happen when thousands were revived at the same time?

Her stomach knotted further. How many of those ten thousand would be gibbering casualties of freezer burn, just like Captain Premanik? "This operation would have been a nail-biter under the best of circumstances, and these certainly are not the best of circumstances."

"They're the best we can make them, Captain."

Faraday found her resolve. "As we always do." She activated the comm to the front section of the dumbbell-shaped vessel, hailing Brian Adducci, the hibernation chief. "Do we have a systems report, Brian? How are the popsicles?"

"They're not having their best day, ma'am," Adducci said.

"I saw the pod failures on the monitor, but I couldn't pay attention to them during the braking maneuver—one hundred fifty-three lost," Faraday said in a somber voice. "It's safe enough now for you to run a check on the rest."

"That was just the first wave. There's an entire sector offline, at least six hundred hibernation pods."

A wave of nausea swept over her. "Six hundred more! They're all dead?"

"Not necessarily, Captain. I've just lost readings, so we have to manually check the pods. At first glance from random spot checks, the units still seem to be functioning, but they just don't show up on my screen."

Tears of relief sprang to her eyes. "That's something at least."

"Well ... it's not all good news, Captain. We did lose some of them."

Faraday rose from her console. "I'm on my way up there. I need to see this for myself." She glanced at the seven people still with her on the command bridge. "Keep plugging leaks and taping struts. Do anything necessary to hold us together until orbit." She drew a breath and headed out of the bridge. "I also need a full plan for deploying the AstroBug fleet to take colonists down, whether they're awake or frozen."

Because their external comms had melted, she had no way of knowing what Darcy Clarke and Engineer Baxter were going to accomplish. But she was already putting Plan B into motion for a base on the dark side, where they could install generators to keep the hibernation pods running in the interim....

First rule of leadership: nothing ever goes as planned.

Faraday rode the swift tram car up the axis from the central habitation ring. When she reached the hibernation section, she emerged to walk among the corridors of countless pods, like an enormous warehouse for frozen people. Popsicles.

Adducci came to meet her, looking grim. "Three of my people are identifying pods that are burned out and offline. We have no hope of reviving those inhabitants. We ..." He swallowed. "We already tried."

"How bad is it?"

Adducci spread his hands. "You want the optimistic answer or the pessimistic one?"

"Isn't it the same number?"

"Everything is relative, Captain. I could say that a total of three hundred ninety-six people just died during our braking maneuver."

Faraday's heart already felt like stone. "And the other way of saying it?"

"I could say that out of ten thousand colonists, we lost less than four hundred—four percent—which is kind of a miracle considering what we just went through."

She nodded. Still, 396 men and women had left a dying Earth on this last hope. They had surrendered themselves to the hibernation pods, lying back into that long sleep and trusting that their captain would get them safely to their destination.

Michio Sakamoto, her lost love, had made the same promises to his passengers, but the *Valkyrie* never even managed to leave

Earth. She and Michio had made similar promises to each other. She hated breaking promises.

"Three hundred ninety-six souls, Mr. Adducci," she said. "I don't want that number to go higher."

"I guarantee you that's not the final tally, Captain. Once we finish auditing the dark sector, we're bound to find more pods that failed."

"Just ... do your best." She looked at the endless array of cubicles. So many people. So many plans for the future. "And give me an honest answer, no matter how bad it is."

Adducci nodded and got back to work.

Faraday headed to the tram that would whisk her back to the habitation ring. She was already calculating how many of her people she could reassign from the emergency life-support and power-grid repairs. She needed to determine the best way to move thousands of colonists all at once, reviving as many as their outpost could support. It all depended on whether the shield network functioned or not ... or else 396 casualties would definitely not be the end of the story.

CHAPTER 41

Leaving Kyle's burial mound, Darcy felt a renewed determination, even after the somber moment. She would not fail, would not let the captain down ... and she would not let the damned geoglyph destroy the future of the human race.

Less than two days on the planet, and Corey and Kyle were both dead. She would not let ten thousand more die because she didn't fix the shield network, especially with the node board and the firewall already at hand.

As they returned to the AeroFox airlock in the skirling snow, she gave Baxter a hard look. "We need to upload your patch and get those nodes working again. The geoglyph has already cost us too damned much."

The engineer blocked Darcy from entering the airlock. "Kid, if we knew there was a living organism covering half of this planet, we would never have suggested the mission at all. This whole Proxima b colony wouldn't have been an option."

Darcy stood before her in a face-off. "I don't agree—nor would Captain Faraday. Some decisions are hard, but we have to do what's necessary. It's the geoglyph or humanity. Our hab modules are all sitting over there. If we don't turn the shield back on—now —then our species goes extinct."

"There are other possibilities," Baxter insisted. "Kyle pointed us to the mission's plan B already, and I think Captain Faraday knows. Since the *Odyssey* is out of touch, we can't confirm what their situation is right now."

"Well, I know what *will* work, and I'm not in the mood for academic arguments."

Baxter braced her hands on her hips. "So, humans are just automatically more important? Tell an ancient sentient lifeform, 'Sorry, but we're taking this planet now?' Because it's too inconvenient to look for another solution?" Her eyes flashed behind her goggles as she huffed. "So much for the *Odyssey* carrying the best part of humanity! What you're planning to do is the same thing that happened over and over again on Earth. Entire indigenous tribes were wiped out by conquerors who believed they were 'doing what they had to do.' Genocides were carried out without a second thought because those poor people happened to live near some valuable resource."

Darcy reeled as she heard the older woman's pig-headedness. "You're talking about human beings, and the geoglyph is just a strange rock—and a hostile one. This is completely different."

"Is it? How many conquerors considered the indigenous people to be less than human? Or at least less important than whatever goals they got in their heads. You saw the energy surges —the geoglyph was trying to communicate. It's not just a rock."

Darcy considered shouldering the other woman aside to force her way into the AeroFox's airlock, but she tried a different tack. "You yourself designed the shield network because you knew it was the only way for us to survive here. The only way!"

"Yes, I did. But things have changed."

Darcy wanted to scream. "No they haven't! Not for humanity —the last survivors of our race! We can't give up everything just so we don't bother some stupid rock-thing! It might be no more intelligent than ... than mold!"

"You didn't watch humanity ruin their first world," Baxter muttered. "I'm not saying we give up. You heard Kyle. Maybe he had the right idea. We could land everyone here on the night side, set up a temporary outpost and leave the other hemisphere to the geoglyph—until we figure this out."

Darcy scoffed. "That's not a serious suggestion! The algae farms and hab modules are all on the dayside. It's not like we can just move them over here! Where would we live? How would we eat? And what sort of life would that be? We didn't spend fifty years getting here—and Corey, and Kyle, and my mom all dead along the way!—just to huddle in the dark."

Baxter sounded just as exasperated. "It doesn't have to be permanent. The dayside isn't exactly the Garden of Eden, either. We were nearly broiled alive by flares only a few hours ago. From an engineering standpoint, it wouldn't be any harder for us to survive over here."

Darcy spread her arms to indicate the nearby rumbling volcano, the snow and ash drifting in the air, the jagged line of mountains near the roiling terminator storm. "I've spent my whole life training to live on the dayside. The Forerunner mission came here to set it all up. We need to settle there, use those resources, those hab modules. It's supposed to be our home!"

Baxter gave up, backed into the airlock. "I'm not going to argue about this. We will sit tight and wait until Captain Faraday arrives. We'll let her decide."

But Darcy kept hearing the tick of the countdown clock in the back of her mind. "The captain trained me and drilled her priorities into me. She's responsible for her ship and everyone aboard—not the geoglyph!"

And Corey and Kyle were already both dead.

"Nobody even knew what the geoglyph was until now, Darcy ... and we still don't know, but that doesn't mean we should just kill it. The captain will understand that."

Darcy thought of all her deep conversations with Faraday, listening to her reminisce about Earth, the people she would never see again, the beautiful landscapes. The captain carried the weight of a race's survival, and decades more command time than she had expected.

Baxter had been oblivious to it all, frozen in her hibernation chamber and still not caught up with a half century of current events.

"You're not thinking straight." Darcy's voice held a clear undertone of threat. "Maybe you suffered from a little freezer burn. Or maybe it's the effects of the radiation exposure."

In the distance, a jet of scarlet lava erupted from the uneasy volcano. Molten rock crawled down the rocky slope and struck an inclusion of old ice, creating a steam explosion.

Baxter tried to place a conciliatory hand on Darcy's shoulder. "Look, kid, you're emotionally compromised, and it's obvious why. You were exposed to even more flare radiation than I was. Even Omni thinks your grasp of the situation is fragmented and extremely biased."

Darcy flinched from her grip, but the older woman wasn't done. "I'm sorry. I'm going to have to take provisional command of this mission to prevent you from doing anything rash and dangerous. I'm sure Omni would agree."

"Omni is an AI. He doesn't get a vote." The wheels of a plan suddenly clicked together in Darcy's head—a snap decision, as a commander needed to make. She couldn't count on Baxter to do her job or to follow the right priorities. The engineer who had designed the shield network was now willing to let thousands of colonists die while she contemplated her navel and pondered esoteric subjects.

Just like Kyle and his pet Omni used to do.

Darcy didn't hesitate. While Baxter tried to sound oh-so-reasonable, she swung her fist and punched the other woman hard in the stomach, a blow that knocked the wind out of her. Caught off guard, Baxter gasped and collapsed to the ground just below the AeroFox's airlock, unable to breathe.

Defiant, Darcy marched back toward the TerraCat. "We wasted hours driving over here because Kyle was being foolish, and now it'll take me that long to get back to the shield node. But I have to take care of this once and for all." As the engineer struggled to get back to her feet, Darcy climbed into the rover. Through her comm implant she could hear Baxter wheezing.

She sealed the hatch, activated the auto-drive, and rolled out. She barked orders to the auto-drive unit. "Get me to Shield Node 212, best possible speed. We've got work to do before the *Odyssey* arrives."

Suddenly, Baxter lurched in front of the vehicle, blocking the path. Bright headlights splashed across her envirosuit. She planted her feet, waving her arms. "Stop! Darcy, stop!"

Detecting the obstacle, the auto-drive automatically ground to a halt. Darcy worked to override the controls, glaring at the other woman through the slanted windshield.

The light beams swerved as the rover shifted course and dodged her. Baxter ran forward, banging on the hood, but the TerraCat kept accelerating, and she couldn't keep up with it.

The calm auto-drive voice said, "Destination acquired, Astronaut Clarke. Arrival in three hours and twelve minutes."

CHAPTER 42

As the rover spun about and roared away, Baxter dropped to her knees on the icy rock. Wheezing to catch her breath after the sucker punch in the gut, she kept yelling into the comm for Darcy to stop, even resorted to begging—something she hadn't done since she'd tried to convince Elwin to come with her on the *Odyssey.*

But the young woman silenced her comm implant, and the TerraCat vanished into the distance.

She stumbled back toward the landed scout ship. "Dammit!" There had to be something she could do!

Baxter felt like crap with the heavy gravity, the lingering hibernation sluggishness, the radiation exposure from the solar flares, not to mention the frustration. Each movement was a painstaking process, but she couldn't afford to give up. *The planet* couldn't afford it.

She cycled through the AeroFox airlock and yanked off the facemask.

Omni's voice sounded concerned. "Engineer Baxter, what happened out there?"

She pulled down her envirosuit hood, shook her dark hair loose. "Darcy took off in the TerraCat, heading back to the shield node. I ..." She wheezed in and out, glanced down at the angry red of her wrist dosimeter. "I couldn't stop her, and she is going to do something stupid."

"This is very concerning. Astronaut Clarke has the firewall program that can overwrite and activate the shields." The AI paused, as if Baxter didn't already know the stakes of the situation. "She must not reprogram the nodes, or the geoglyph will be destroyed."

Baxter leaned against the inner airlock door, dredging up every scrap of energy she had left. "I tried, but I'm not big enough to stop a speeding rover."

Omni projected a schematic of the TerraCat on the science station. Kyle's station. "Perhaps we should try a different approach. I might be able to remotely access the TerraCat's self-drive system."

Baxter flashed a hard grin. "Good idea, Omni. Darcy can't drive the thing herself. Do it!"

Grinding its way through the darkness and snow, the rover rolled along, retracing the known route. After three trips, the TerraCat was practically forging its own road to Node 212.

As the auto-drive avoided any hazards ahead, Darcy slumped in the seat, feeling the afterwash of adrenaline and sick from the radiation. Her body was shaking as she grappled with what she had done, and what she was doing now. This decision was more consequential than anything she had done in her life, with the fate of the last human survivors in the balance. She pushed her thoughts into laser focus. Corey and Kyle were both gone, so she had nothing to lose ... and yet she had everything to lose.

Miserable, she put her head in her hands and closed her eyes, lost in thought and a fog of radiation sickness. She paid no heed to what Baxter had said, or even Kyle's delusional ideas. The young man had always been enamored with the rock thing, just as he had been best friends with his pet AI.

But Darcy had seen nothing in the geoglyph's actions to make her consider it some innocent victim rather than an alien threat. She had seen the willful damage it wrought on the shield nodes, that aggressive outgrowth of living metal that ruined the transmitter tower. The geoglyph's actions would be a death sentence for the *Odyssey* colonists, including her own father....

She had watched the dangerous metal attack Baxter's boot, seize the rover tires. It was a monster, an adversary. And it was responsible for Jim Corey's death.

Despite her urgency, the TerraCat could only move so fast over the rugged terrain. It would be hours before she reached Node 212—and that didn't leave much time before the *Odyssey* arrived.

"Come on, come on!" she said.

Suddenly, the sound of the engines changed, and the vehicle dramatically slowed, then ground to a stop. The headlights spilled into the cold, shadowy terrain, but the auto-drive system had gone offline. "TerraCat! Why aren't we moving?"

The engines hummed again, and the rover swerved to the left, turning around so that it could drive back the way they had come.

"Where are you going? Reverse course! We need to get to the shield node!"

Instead of the calm feminine voice of the auto-drive, Omni's male tones emerged from the speaker. "Engineer Baxter and I are bringing you back to the AeroFox, Astronaut Clarke. Once you return, we want you to take a stress pill and think things over. It will be for the best. You must undergo X-Doc treatment for your radiation exposure."

With a flare of rage and desperation, Darcy saw the AI's blue infinity symbol on the auto-drive screen. "You son of a bitch!"

She pushed herself to her feet, fighting a wave of dizziness and nausea. When she yanked the comm uplink unit out of its socket and deactivated the virtual pilot, the rover screeched to a stop, throwing Darcy to the floor. In disgust, she tossed the disconnected unit into the back of the compartment. She would just have to drive herself.

Sweating and shaking, she climbed back into her seat. She scanned the TerraCat controls, remembering how Baxter had driven the heavy vehicle away from the flare storm. She steeled herself and punched the MANUAL MODE button, then pulled the safety restraint back across her chest and locked it in place. She called the navigation chart onto the main screen.

"I can do this." She had maneuvered in a bottle-suit, had piloted the AeroFox, and she was qualified on the much larger AstroBugs. How hard could it be to drive a ground vehicle?

The rover's wheels spat gravel and ice chips as she pulled it back on course, racing to Node 212.

Baxter groaned as she watched the TerraCat's blip start moving again on the map grid.

Omni said, "It would appear that Astronaut Clarke has disabled the self-drive. I'm sorry, Engineer Baxter. I can think of no other way of stopping her. Kyle would be very disappointed."

Not ready to give up, Baxter tried to use a direct beam to the rover. The Omni link might be disconnected, but she might be able to get through to Darcy's comm implant. "Darcy, I know you can hear me." She made herself sound calm and conciliatory. "You need to do the radiation therapy, or you'll die—just like Kyle! I can see my own dosimeter readings, and I know you got even more than I did."

Silence. Baxter worked her jaw in frustration. "Talk to me, goddamn it!"

Now the entire screen went blank. Omni reported, "I'm afraid she has disabled her comm implant, too. We are cut off."

CHAPTER 43

Knowing she could not stop Darcy's brash act, Baxter felt as if someone had punched her again. With a single software upload, the young woman could annihilate a vast alien life form.

Baxter swayed as a wave of nausea welled up inside her. Her skin flushed hot, and her insides twisted. The ominous red dosimeter seemed to be mocking her, and she knew damned well the radiation damage had already been done. Her condition would only worsen.

She staggered to the ship's small lavatory, and her legs buckled as soon as the privacy door whisked shut. She vomited into the toilet receptacle, gripping the wall rail. She winced her eyes shut. "No, I will not cry!"

Baxter pulled herself to her feet again and ran water in the sink, splashing her face, rinsing her mouth. When the foul taste was clear, she smeared more water over her eyes, then stared at herself in the mirror. She had to figure out what else she could do.

Emerging from the lavatory, she said, "Omni, play Kyle's message from where we left off. I want to hear what else he had to say."

The young man's sickly image appeared on the monitor. "I did this to protect the geoglyph, Darcy," he continued. "Persephone is its home. We have to learn to live with it, think outside the box. It won't be so bad."

Baxter shook her head, whispering, "Yeah, that's exactly what I told her." She wondered how clearly Kyle had been thinking at the time.

His voice was low, barely a whisper. "My decision probably doesn't make sense to you. You and Corey never really got it when O and I shared exciting ideas about the geoglyph. But ... I'm *nothing* in the face of this discovery." His lower lip trembled as he fought back tears, and the passion rose in his words.

Baxter suddenly realized that Kyle knew he was going to die.

"Honestly, I've lived an amazing life," he said. "I'm a human born between the stars, and yet I made it to Persephone."

His voice grew thinner, as if he had lost the energy to speak. The young man was fading, clearly in his final moments. "I want to name this planet after the goddess of the underworld, because it's our entrance to the galaxy ... a gateway to the unknown." He lifted his chin, showing pride. "The discovery of the geoglyph is just the beginning of what we can accomplish here. But we have to do it right this time."

Kyle flashed a final weak and reassuring smile and ended with crucial words, which Darcy unfortunately never heard. "*Try* and work with Dr. Baxter. Together, you can find a way to protect the mission and the geoglyph at the same time. Captain Faraday always warned us against taking the first and easiest solution. You can come up with something that works—I know it. I wish ... wish I could be there to see it. Good luck." He signed off.

When his recorded message ended, Baxter wiped away tears. She felt ill in so many different ways, and she fought down another urge to vomit. "I don't have time to be sick." She steeled herself, turned back to the science station. "Omni, show me your projection of what will happen to the geoglyph if Darcy installs the firewall."

"It's quite discouraging, Engineer Baxter." The AI displayed the geometric patterns across the dayside, which were already drastically smaller than what the first *Forerunner* images showed. "With the damage previously done by the shield, a new onslaught like this will kill it."

Baxter gripped the console to fight off dizziness. "By the time the colonists settle into the hab modules, the geoglyph will be past the point of no return." She looked up to the piloting controls in the deck above, but the task of climbing that far seemed insurmountable. "Omni, take me up to the pilot's station."

The reclining seat descended on its support, and Baxter let herself collapse in place, drawing deep breaths as the AI raised her back up to the helm. On the console, she noticed the old photo of the little girl standing between her two parents in the hibernation deck. Baxter stared for a long moment, saw Darcy's bright eyes, the happy smile ... the warm and proud father, the mother full of hope.

Sadly, she called up a 3-D model of the planet, showing the present location of the AeroFox, then rotated it to display the hundreds of shield nodes across the dayside. All those points would intertwine with the planet's magnetic field to protect fragile human life. The shield—*her* shield—was powerful enough to block out terrific radiation storms ... and powerful enough to suffocate an alien sentience that spanned a continent.

Baxter focused on Node 212 closest to the terminator line. That was where Darcy was headed.

It was time for desperate measures. Reckless measures.

Engineering measures.

She plotted a parabolic trajectory from the AeroFox to the shield node. "Omni, have a look at this. We're basically trying to hit a bullseye three hundred kilometers away. How much thrust do we need to get us there?"

"Are you aware that our engines are inoperative?" The AI called up a schematic of the crashed scout ship, highlighting the faults.

"I'm an engineer—I'm going to fix it."

The damaged sections flashed a brighter red on the schematic, as if to mock her. "Yeah, right," Omni said.

Baxter was surprised by the AI's sarcastic tone. "It's a typical dual-mode propulsion unit. How hard can it be? I've worked on systems like that for years."

Though it seemed impossible to get herself moving again, Baxter fitted her envirosuit hood, adjusted her AR goggles and her facemask, then grabbed a basic toolkit and diagnostic scanner. She couldn't let herself slow down. Every minute, the TerraCat was getting closer to the shield node.

Outside in the cold again, she worked her way around the ship, noting the battered hull. Luckily, the AeroFox had a sturdy, durable design, and most of the ugliest marks were just superficial. At the engine access panel, she called up the details in her augmented goggles. Darcy had already pulled the ruined line-replaceable unit, and now Baxter scanned deep into the damage, trying to calculate how to fix it.

"I can print a new LRU," Omni said, "but that is just the beginning of the necessary repairs. Where will you find the remaining parts?"

The third comm satellite was mounted to the side of the craft, the one Darcy had been about to deploy when the AstroBug crashed. The sat was still locked in its launching cradle. "I've got my spare parts right here. The electronics should all be intact, shielded inside the satellite. I'll reroute and use what I need."

Omni sounded skeptical. "A repair of this type typically requires up to thirty—"

"We don't have 'thirty' of anything. If we don't stop Darcy, she'll kill the geoglyph ... and she'll kill herself from radiation exposure. I'm an engineer, dammit. Machines. Electronics. This is what I do." She was already at work on the satellite's external panel, exposing the dense circuit boards.

"Yes, Engineer Baxter. You do not, however, pilot spacecraft."

She inspected the large satellite, envisioned how to repurpose the components inside. "You've got our roles wrong, Omni. *I* fix it. *You* fly it."

"Perhaps that will work—but only *after* you connect yourself to the X-Doc and undergo the rad procedure. You have sufficient time, given Astronaut Clarke's rate of travel. I ... I can't lose you, too."

Baxter was just about to insist on doing all the repair work first —but that was exactly what Kyle Dyson had done, and he had let himself die. She stalked back around to the airlock hatch. "Okay, but you better program the doc for an express cycle. I've got things to do."

CHAPTER 44

After passing through the turbulent line of storms, the TerraCat pushed into the orange daylight. Darcy drove along at a speed greater than she could handle, moving erratically, and the rover kicked up dust, bounced over rocks, and threaded shallow ravines.

Radiation sickness was making her delirious—or maybe it made her see more clearly. She was sore, weary, nauseated, sleep-deprived, and wrung out with grief. She wiped her forehead, smearing the fever sweat. The terrain blurred in front of her vision, but she shook her head and made herself focus.

Not much time!

Ahead, the coppery sunlight glinted on a large spacecraft that landed not far in front of her. She squinted to make out what it was, and her heart lurched—had the *Odyssey* arrived? Was this another AstroBug, the start of the main exodus operation? She would have help at last! The node board inside the rover carried the firewall, the miracle cure that would restore the shield and save the colony. There was still time, but she couldn't do it all herself.

Her vision doubled, and she rubbed her eyes, staring harder at the landed spacecraft. She slowed the rover, discerning fuzzy mirage lines around the big disk-like craft. Yes, it was an

AstroBug, just like Corey's! The *Odyssey* had forty-eight of the vessels, which would be used for the colony setup.

No, she realized that it *was* Corey's ship!

She must have lost consciousness, because when she blinked again, the new spacecraft loomed directly in front of her. She hauled back on the manual drive controls, pulling the rover to a halt as she stared in disbelief through the dusty windshield. Yes, this was AstroBug Five.

But it had exploded while trying to rise from the frozen lake. She had seen the fireball herself, and Jim Corey was inside.

And yet AstroBug Five was right in front of her now, intact, shiny and new, silhouetted against the ruddy glow of Proxima Centauri, low on the horizon.

Adjusting her facemask and goggles, she opened the hatch to stumble out into the desert. Sweat prickled all over her body, and she wavered on unsteady legs. Amazed, she strode over to the spacecraft. Was this real? What was the Bug doing here? How was it intact? And why was it blocking her way to the shield node?

She took two wavering steps toward the apparition, paused— and the AstroBug's ramp extended in clear invitation, its airlock door open and waiting for her to come inside. Unable to stop herself, she stepped to the lower hatch.

Jim Corey was there, standing in the airlock chamber. He was smiling, healthy, alive, dressed in his gold and black flightsuit. Grinning, he raised a hand to wave. She realized he wasn't wearing an oxygen mask or an envirosuit. How was that possible?

Darcy longed to throw herself into his arms, but something held her back. This wasn't right. "Corey ...?"

Without a word to her, he turned and disappeared into the ship. Darcy hurried after him, calling his name again. Inside the AstroBug, he stood at the end of the accessway, leading her on. He gave her a smile as she tried to catch up, then he climbed the ladder to the cockpit. She tried to keep up.

Corey took his seat at the pilot station, running a palm over the smooth panel, caressing the controls. He let out a wistful sigh and finally spoke aloud. "God, I loved this cockpit, Darce—I belonged here. In fact, I was looking forward to this ship being our home together for a while. We could just live aboard the Bug, me and you, until our hab module was ready."

Darcy stood at the top of the ladder, looking across the cockpit. Something was holding her back. She didn't know whether to be happy, or sad, or afraid.

Corey swiveled his seat to face her. "Sorry I put you through all that. Persephone is a strange alien place. Different rules. How are you, babe? Did you miss me?"

She began to weep, and her voice was raw. "How do you think I am? I hate this fucking planet, and I hate that alien thing that's trying to kill us all! This is no home. There's no point going on without you."

He made a gentle, scoffing gesture. "Sure there is."

"Then tell me what to do!" Her skin felt hot, and she could barely see through the warm tears in her eyes.

"Ah, there's my feisty Darcy!" He chuckled, then grew serious. "You already know what to do."

"I know I have to fix the shield, no matter what it takes. The captain is depending on me ... the whole human race is depending on me. It doesn't matter what happens to that metal thing."

"The geoglyph," Corey said.

"Kyle wanted to protect it, coddle it like a pet or something. And he's dead now, too! He just let himself die because he was obsessed with that geoglyph. Do you know that?" She sounded like she was accusing him.

"Kyle never could see the big picture the way we can." He pointed at her. "The way *you* can, Darce. You know this is up to you. Your most important decision ever."

Darcy could admit her doubts to this man, even if she could never express them to Tanya Baxter. "But what if Kyle's right? What if I'm wiping out something that's existed for billions of years, just so we can have a new place to live?"

"New place to live?" He raised his eyebrows. "We're not

talking about a vacation home. This is humanity's last chance, babe. Survival of the fittest. There might be other planets around Alpha Centauri A and B, but we'll never get there. Persephone is *it*. The geoglyph is aggressively denying us our only protection, and we've got to be stronger than it is. The superior species has the upper hand. It's time for you to finish this thing once and for all."

Without moving, as if she had forgotten to blink, Corey was suddenly standing right behind her. He put his arms around her, pulled her close in an embrace. It felt so good, so reassuring. She closed her eyes, let herself be wrapped in his presence, felt the warmth of his touch. He kissed her ear, and she spun to face him, kissing him passionately.

And then she found herself standing alone in the empty desert outside of the TerraCat. The terrain was empty. The AstroBug and Corey were both gone, leaving untouched sand and rocks, not even a hint that they'd been there.

Reeling, she dropped to the rough ground, sobbing into her facemask. She pounded her fists in the dirt, grabbed handfuls of sand. It was just a hallucination, a feverish wishful dream. She hated Persephone!

But Corey had been right about one thing. Darcy knew what she had to do. Maybe it was just radiation-caused delirium, an internal debate manifested in a visible way. But she *knew*, with or without the specter of Corey giving her advice.

Darcy returned to the rover, more resolute than ever. As she buckled into the driver's seat, she looked at the modified node board plugged into the dash unit. Her secret weapon against the geoglyph. "TerraCat, access the node board."

"Accessing." The calm female voice was unaffected by the magnitude of events around them.

A wave of nausea hit Darcy hard, and she pressed her lips together, breathing through her nose to force the sickness back. She could not vomit inside her facemask. Her heart pounded as she gasped out, "TerraCat, I want you to ... I want—"

Then she couldn't hold it back. She tore off the oxygen mask and vomited into the adjacent seat well. She retched twice more before wiping the side of her mouth, forced herself to pull it together. "I want you to recalibrate the board programming."

"Specify parameters."

"When it's reinstalled in Node 212, the board will access the entire shield grid and permanently upload the firewall program in all active towers." The console screen displayed a map of the entire network covering the dayside. "Increase low-frequency output to two hundred percent. That'll turn the shield into a fortress—just in time for the *Odyssey* and our people."

She pounded the steering column in frustration. "I'm gonna kill that thing."

Darcy stared through the windshield at the empty spot where she had seen the AstroBug and Corey. He was right—Darcy knew what she had to do. And she finally felt she was able to let go. "Goodbye, Corey."

She activated the manual controls again and drove forward.

CHAPTER 45

Inside the AeroFox, Baxter was a mass of fidgeting frustration as she tried to lie still for the emergency radiation treatment. The X-Doc's armatures were wrapped around her, and she counted down the seconds, counted down the minutes, then lost count and cursed under her breath. She couldn't hurry the machine, but it was taking its sweet time.

With each minute, Darcy kept driving to the shield node.

The medical device was locked over her torso, and its arms continued working around her abdomen. The designers likely intended it to feel like a warm and comforting embrace, but there was something threatening about it. Baxter couldn't move, couldn't *do* anything. No wonder Kyle had given up in desperation.

She counted to sixty again and stretched out her arm for the Autobrew device, which she had wisely left within reach. She made another cup of coffee and sipped a mouthful of warm, strong coffee.

From where she lay in the pilot seat, Baxter could see the photo of the little girl and her parents. Darcy and the other two miracle children were babies born in transit, twenty-five years away from destination ... just kids with no memories of Earth, who had been trained all their lives and yet unprepared for real life, real society.

"They're still just newborns ..." she said under her breath, then smiled as an idea occurred to her.

"Excuse me?" Omni asked.

Baxter forced herself to remain still as the X-Doc continued its ministrations. "Darcy, Corey, and Kyle called the hibernating colonists 'popsicles.' It was a little insulting, so I promised I'd come up with a suitable nickname for the three of them."

"A metaphor," the AI said, as if reaching an epiphany. "'Newborn'—a child just entering the world."

A shadow of melancholy settled over her. "All three of them thought they knew what they were doing, but they were still pretty wet behind the ears. Newborns."

Omni sounded protective. "For many years Corey, Darcy, and Kyle did an excellent job integrating with the captain and the skeleton crew."

"We never should have tasked them with a mission like this. Way too much to ask, way too much at stake." Baxter pushed aside the sadness, felt impatient again. She really wanted to tear off the X-Doc and try to launch the AeroFox. Now. "How much longer is this damned thing going to work on me?"

"The initial X-Doc cycle will be completed in three minutes."

"That's a relief." She waited out the longest three minutes she had ever experienced.

Outside in the dark, wearing her facemask again, Baxter felt revitalized, but nowhere near as good as new. The coffee seemed to help as much as the X-Doc did. She was ready to get to work.

On Earth and in the orbital assembly yards, when she'd loaded the shield towers in their aeroshells onto *Forerunner*, Baxter had her team, the best engineers anyone could ask for. But now she was the whole team, a solo repair operation that would prepare the AeroFox for one brief, final flight—she hoped.

As Baxter trudged around to the side of the scout craft, Omni released the comm satellite from its cradle, and the large trapezoidal device dropped to the ground in a cloud of dust and snow.

Baxter inspected the satellite's nose and the packed solar array, then removed a rear panel to expose a treasure trove of panels and spare parts. "This'll do nicely." She yanked out a board, turned it back and forth. "This will take the place of the LRU, and this ..." She traced connection paths with her gloved fingers. "This flow regulator should be the last part I need to get the craft back on track, just like nothing ever happened."

As she carried the parts to the engine access panel she had left open, Omni let out a very convincing sad sigh. "Yes, like nothing ever happened ..."

"Are you okay, Omni?"

"According to my diagnostics, I am back to normal parameters, but I was pondering Kyle's death. I was just getting to know him, and I liked him a lot. Did you know he had a unique friendship with his personal Omni, which had developed an independent personality? Kyle called him 'O.'"

"I never really thought about it." She set the components on the frozen ground and inspected the damaged section of the engine. "You're all just Omni, as far as I'm concerned."

"The surge that hit the AstroBug destroyed Kyle's personal Omni. He was very sad about it." The AI sounded on the verge of tears. "Kyle's dedication to science and uncovering the truth was admirable. I have reviewed all of his theories about the geoglyphs. It meant so much to him."

As she installed the new components, Baxter paused. The young man had realized the significance of the geoglyph long before anyone else. Kyle's imagination, determination, and maybe even a little naivete had let him understand the wonder of the ancient alien life form. And he had not been so quick to kill it, as Darcy Clarke was.

"If the human race had more people like Kyle, we probably wouldn't have destroyed Earth." She sighed.

Omni sounded very wise. "Humans do seem to let fear and ignorance drive their actions far more than reason."

Baxter reconfigured two connectors for the substitute LRU and pushed the board into place in the side of the AeroFox. "You got that right."

"Engineer Baxter, we must not let Kyle die in vain."

"We won't." She installed the second replacement unit, checked the power couplings. The indicator lights all flashed green. The AeroFox was ready to go. "We won't."

Baxter strapped herself into the pilot's chair, thinking of how Darcy must have felt when she tried to drive the TerraCat for the first time. "Here's the big test, Omni. Cross your fingers."

"I will do so, figuratively."

She powered the engines at low thrust, igniting the reaction chambers. On her screens, she watched the output levels blip up. The side-mounted engines fired, sputtered, then faded.

Baxter throttled back, sweating. When she displayed the engine sensors, one section flared red. "That was only at five percent. I'm scared to push it any further."

She thought of the AstroBug heaving itself up out of the frozen lake, then the explosion....

"If you intend to move this craft, Engineer Baxter, we will need significantly more thrust." An orbital diagram appeared on the screen, showing the planet, the AeroFox's position on the night side, the destination point of Node 212 on the other side. A tight parabolic path connected the two points, arcing up above the atmosphere and then down again.

Baxter set her jaw. "Supplement with the plasma engine."

The rumble grew louder, and on screen, the warning indicators switched from red to green. "Done," Omni replied.

"That's the ticket." Baxter's fingers hovered above the main engine activation panel. "Do or die ... fish or cut bait. Choose your own cliché." She sighed. "Prepare for a ninety-second burn—firing!"

A bright exhaust plume erupted from the side-mounted engines, dispersing snow and frost from the alien landscape. Beneath the AeroFox, an intermittent blue glow shone from the plasma engine at the base, building power, blasting dust, ice, and gravel in all directions.

The spacecraft trembled, then lifted just barely off the ground, shaking with the effort. Then the glow died and the thrusters failed. The AeroFox settled back down, stuck.

On the screens, a section of the engines flashed red again.

Omni said, "I see a problem with fuel valve three. Auto shut-off."

Baxter came to an instant decision. "We have to risk it. Override—now!"

She had only a moment to wonder if Jim Corey had said something similar at the AstroBug's controls....

Omni overrode the safety systems, fired the engines again. The thrusters gushed columns of exhaust, and the plasma engines ignited. The glare filled the cold night around them.

Then the AeroFox lifted off, leaving a scorch mark on the rocks. The landing gear retracted as the ship soared straight into the sky.

CHAPTER 46

U nder the ruddy sunlight, the landscape started to look familiar as Darcy approached Node 212. The high, straight-edge uplifts of the geoglyph looked like the walls of a gigantic labyrinth.

The TerraCat climbed the ridge of angular pyrite material to the top of the metallic rise. As she saw the swath of bright material like a highway across the plain, a rush of anger penetrated her fog of pain and nausea. She could only concentrate on one thing. That alien pattern was more than a message, more than an odd metallic design. Knowing its destructive intent, Darcy thought of it more like a spiderweb.

You already know what to do, Corey had told her in her vision. It didn't matter if he was a dream, a hallucination, or a manifestation of her subconscious. He was right.

She could not let Captain Faraday and the *Odyssey* down.

The rewritten node board was beside her. Once she uploaded it into the tower and sent it through the network, it would be like a powerful vaccine to drive away the deadly geoglyph infection. She realized now that the geoglyph was an invasive organism attacking the colony's systemic defenses.

"Yes, Corey, I damn well know what to do," she whispered to herself and pushed the rover onward. Time was running out.

She saw the damaged shield tower just ahead, a metal structure rising up from the geoglyph. The aeroshell containing the complex node had had the misfortune to land on the alien metal. When the protective shell had split open and the tower erected itself, it had been vulnerable.

Darcy thought the metal-lattice structure looked like the Eiffel Tower, the graceful architectural marvel of old Earth, She had never seen the real thing, of course, but her father had been proud to show her images. He had called up his personal photo library to share memories with her, and his expression showed a special kind of awe and wonder.

"Before we left Earth, your mother and I went to Paris so we could see the Eiffel Tower for ourselves. We'd just been married, so we could call it a honeymoon, although our work for the *Odyssey* consumed everything."

Sebastian had smiled as he stared at the images. The Eiffel Tower was an impressive, ethereal work of architecture, though Darcy could not understand what purpose it served.

He continued in a distant voice, "The weather was horrible that day. Black clouds, cold temperature, wet wind ... but the weather was always terrible then, and we knew it was not going to get better." The image showed a blue sky, grinning tourists, flowers. "This is just a tourist picture, not something we took ourselves. Paris didn't look at all like this when we visited, and the skies were never blue anymore."

Sebastian's gaze had an intensity that made her realize how important he considered this conversation to be. "This photo is an *aspiration*, showing what humanity can do ... what humanity can be! We can't ever forget that, even if we're light-years away. It's a miracle that we have a second chance aboard the *Odyssey*, and I can't wait to see the next miracle when I wake up from hibernation." He gripped her hand. "We can't screw it up a second time."

Sixteen-year-old Darcy felt uneasy as she looked at the image of the Tower. "I ... we won't."

Sebastian seemed convinced that he had gotten through to her. "You're right, Darcy. We won't."

Now, out on the harsh surface of Persephone, she looked at the stark shield tower. An aspiration, the means for their survival.

The *Odyssey* should be in orbit any time now. Her father was waiting in one of those hibernation pods, expecting to wake up on a new world. He would be among the thousands who would not survive if she didn't finish her job.

Another victim of the geoglyph.

Darcy had promised to be there when he was revived. Long ago, her mother had made the same promises to him. Darcy didn't plan to break her word.

But she could feel the nausea, pounding headache, blurring vision, and burning skin from the radiation exposure. The sickness would only get worse, but she vowed to upload the firewall. She had to do that before she took care of herself.

The TerraCat rushed over the dull gold metal of the geoglyph highway, finally reaching the shield tower. Nothing was going to stop her now.

The rumbling AeroFox climbed into the sky, and Baxter held on for dear life as the side thrusters and the sputtering plasma engines pushed the craft even higher. She squeezed her eyes shut, as if she could hold the ship together by sheer willpower.

The battered scout ship rose into the night, and Baxter had to trust Omni to follow the parabolic suborbital path she had plotted. She felt like Icarus, flying high, too close to the sun—an angry red dwarf in this case—and then she would fall back to the ground. Right at Node 212.

She could see the ruddy red star just peeking over the limb of Persephone. Then the plasma engines cut off. Too soon.

Baxter looked wildly around as warning klaxons sounded, building into a great cacophony. The cabin rattled until she couldn't see straight, but somehow she managed to read the graphs on the tech screens. Engine power was fading rapidly.

Omni said, "Thrust down to seventeen percent, Engineer Baxter."

"But we're not at apogee yet." She stared at the parabolic path. "Goose them, Omni—we need to squeeze out just a bit more. Burn a little longer!"

The plasma engines coughed, sputtered, and the Fox jumped up with a satisfying lurch ... and the thrust cut out again.

She scanned the parabolic trajectory, saw how far the AeroFox had gone.

"Burn complete," Omni said.

They had made it.

Once the ship reached the peak of its trajectory, Baxter found herself in a deceptive and terrifying calm. The Fox drifted, reoriented, and finally began to fall back to the planet. Through the cockpit windowport, Baxter saw the full glory of the red star. Persephone loomed below, its dayside spread out before her.

Then she gasped. Over the curve of the planet, she saw the huge dumbbell shape of the approaching arkship. "The *Odyssey* made it! Omni, try to hail them. Maybe they can send some help." She rubbed her eyes, still trying to clear her thoughts. "They've got to know what's going on."

Had Kyle's message gotten through to them?

After a pause, the AI responded, "Unfortunately, another solar flare is interrupting communications. I have not been able to hail them, but the problem appears to be more extensive than flare interference. Their comm systems seem to be inoperable, perhaps damaged."

"All the comms on the whole ship are nonfunctional? That doesn't seem likely." She stared at the enormous arkship lumbering into orbit, knowing that Faraday wanted to offload colonists right away. There was so much the captain didn't know, but surely she could see the shield network was offline. "Hail them again. Maybe they can hear us, even if they can't respond."

Omni did so, but still got no answer. "The communications array is visibly damaged. My telescopic observations indicate the ship is under considerable stress."

In the magnified image, the *Odyssey* looked as if it had been through a street brawl and lost. Gases vented from part of the central habitation ring. A stream of water sprayed out from the front of the hibernation disk like a veil of frozen diamonds. The transmitting masts and comm antennas drooped, as if they had been melted. Radiation damage marred the hull.

"There is no way to measure the severity of their situation from our current distance and low altitude," Omni said as the AeroFox continued to descend.

She felt sick again. Darcy had explained that the arkship was on its last legs, that there was no time to consider building a brand-new solution. Seeing the wreck now hammered the reality home for Baxter. This was not a theoretical exercise to debate. The popsicles had to come down, immediately. Darcy was not wrong about that.

Below, across the sunlit surface, the diminished geoglyph pattern seemed to be mocking ... or pleading.

Exterminate one species to save another?

"Our trajectory is established, Engineer Baxter," Omni said. "Prepare for retro-burn."

"Ready when you are." She closed her eyes and drew a deep breath. "See if you can read 212 from here. Has Darcy arrived yet? Do we have time?"

"Shield Node 212 remains offline, for now."

The retro-thrusters fired, reorienting the ship as it continued to fall. Baxter watched the battered *Odyssey* disappear over the horizon, still venting gases.

The AeroFox hurtled down toward the bleak surface.

CHAPTER 47

F araday looked through the viewing windows of the command bridge as the *Odyssey* approached. The planet swelled in front of them. "Fifty years ..." she whispered.

"All systems ... as good as can be expected, Captain," said First Officer Klevc. "We're going to make it."

Faraday stared at the sun-warmed hemisphere with its inland seas, the dark stains of vegetation, and the weird metallic pattern that had so fascinated young Kyle Dyson. "Let's not take a victory lap yet."

She had received Omni's message with a summary of the disasters the planetary team had suffered, as well as Kyle's compelling case for the geoglyph, his plea to consider the mission's temporary alternative plan. It had been his last message, his last request. Now, she knew that Kyle hadn't survived.

And three hundred and ninety-six hibernating colonists were dead up here.

And Jim Corey.

She drove back her own dismay and tears. But they were here.

The strange alien world did not look like any home Faraday had ever expected, but this was the finish line, no matter what. Alarm screens kept flashing on various bridge stations, but she'd grown numb to it now with so many systems failing.

They were here, and they wouldn't stop now.

"Prepare for orbital insertion, Mr. Hamelin."

"It'll take every scrap of what we have left, Captain," said the helmsman.

Faraday looked out along the axis of the huge ship. Jets of steam were gushing out from a ruptured shielding reservoir at the front of the hibernation disk.

"Trying to compensate, but it'll use the last of our maneuvering thrusters. Don't worry, I'll get us into orbit." Hamelin gripped the controls, sweating profusely. "But I can't promise it'll be a stable one."

"No choice. We knew this was going to be quick and dirty," Faraday said. "We need to start implementing the wake-up and exodus plan—right now." She hit the ship intercom, heard bursts of static as the network searched for a clear channel. "Mr. Adducci, can you hear me in the hibernation section?"

"We're here, Captain. That rupture of the water tanks didn't help any. Lights here are flickering, and temperature has dropped about twenty degrees. Some of the life-support systems have already failed."

"We'll have to run on fumes long enough to revive the first-wave colonists and start transporting the rest of the pods."

"There are ten thousand of them, Captain! It'll take—"

"It'll take what it'll take," she snapped. "And you're right, it's neither feasible nor even possible to awaken all ten thousand of them." She tightened her lips and turned around to survey the bridge. She'd been captain of this vessel for forty-two years and, dammit, she was going to bring it home. Kyle was right, and the mission's alternative plan would give them a way to keep the hibernation pods functioning and allow some breathing room in their desperate situation.

She scanned her bridge skeleton crew, decided she could do without three of them for now. "Chandra Timms, Amaka Obi, and Charley Grand, head up the axis to the hibernation section and assist Mr. Adducci. We will continue a massive, full-scale awakening operation. But the three of you ..."

She saw their expectant expressions, knew that they were confident their captain would find a solution to the crisis. "Prepare the rest of the hibernation pods for direct transport to the surface. We just need sustainable power units to keep those colonists frozen until we can be sure the colony is functional. They'll have to sleep a little longer—but they can't stay here." She swallowed hard, visualizing the enormity of the effort.

"We have almost fifty AstroBugs for the mass exodus, and we need to load them up fast. The Bugs can act as shuttles, up and down, as many trips as they need to take." She couldn't guarantee that the *Odyssey* would last more than a few orbits.

Faraday sent a message to Brian Adducci, who panicked upon hearing the sudden change of plans, but he quickly came to the conclusion it was the only choice. "I agree, Captain. It's our best option—out of a bunch of bad ones. All those banks of colony generators can serve the purpose." His voice wavered.

"Commander Kleve, do we have any comms yet?" Faraday asked. "Can we contact Astronaut Clarke or Engineer Baxter? We need to know what's happening on the surface."

"We're trying to rig up an alternative with tin cans and strings. It won't have much power, but if Darcy's listening ..."

"Of course she'll be listening," Faraday said. Unless she and Baxter were dead, like the other two ...

Another shower of sparks burst from an unmanned console, and a harried bridge crewman rushed over to shut down and reroute. He groaned in dismay. "We have no more temperature-control units on the lower half of the habitation ring. It'll get real cold down there in an hour or two."

"In an hour or two we'll be in a whole different situation," Faraday said. "For now, shut off those sections and keep everybody out. Every single able-bodied crew member has to make repairs faster than new failures occur. Hamelin, can you work with the maneuvering jets?"

"It's like trying to drive a giant truck with a flat tire," the helmsman said.

The *Odyssey* came around the night side of the planet. "Keep sending messages to the surface. I need to hear back from somebody."

As the arkship headed around the planet, the captain felt as if they would just keep falling toward it. The dark hemisphere looked like a black hole.

Then to her shock, down at the terminator line, she saw the jets of a spacecraft burning plasma engines toward the top of the atmosphere.

"That's the AeroFox!" Faraday said. "What are they doing? Can you raise them?"

"I don't have communications, Captain!"

"We're in stable orbit, Captain." Hamelin sounded surprised. "At least for some definition of 'stable.'"

The *Odyssey* crossed the terminator line and soared high above the bright sunlit landscape. "Ready or not, here we come," Faraday whispered.

Kleve's voice was leaden. "They're not ready for us. The shield isn't operational. The nodes remain down."

Captain Faraday continued to feel as if she had fallen into a crushing gravity well. Their temporary solution would have to work, or else. "That's one more option off the table. Plan B it is."

CHAPTER 48

The TerraCat stopped at the base of the damaged tower. Darcy felt disturbed, jumpy, and she wondered if radiation sickness was making her paranoid. But there was nothing paranoid about her concern. The geoglyph infestation had attacked them last time. If she had not broken the wheels free of the malicious pyrite grip, she and Tanya Baxter would have been trapped out in the deadly flare storm. The geoglyph would have killed them, just like it had killed Jim Corey!

Darcy was careful to park the rover directly on the flat aeroshell, not on the metallic material itself. The alien presence couldn't know what she intended to do, and it certainly couldn't *think*. It was just a reactive life form that basked in radiation storms.

After she locked down the TerraCat, she just sat in the driver's seat, steeling herself. Her insides felt as turbulent as the terminator storm. If she had stayed back at the AeroFox, she could have been treated by the X-Doc, but she had chosen to do this, to complete her mission for the *Odyssey* and all those people ... for the opposite reasons that Kyle had thrown away his life to protect the geoglyph. He had made the wrong decision, but she would not.

A fog of dizziness crackled around her vision. Time was up. In the back of her mind, she felt Corey watching her.

She detached the reprogrammed node board from the drive deck, grabbed her oxygen mask, and exited the rover. All she had to do was insert the board into the tower operating module, and it would rewrite the shield network. Then her people would be safe at last.

Like a barely controlled meteor, the AeroFox hurtled toward the surface, glowing with the superheated air of reentry.

Baxter could not change their trajectory or soften the descent. The scout ship rattled, buffeted by fierce air currents. Through gritted teeth, she said, "Isn't this fun, Omni?"

"I do not understand how you are defining 'fun,' Engineer Baxter. I thought I had a better grasp of the concept."

"Also lacking a grasp of sarcasm. Please verify that at least we're on course?"

"Heading directly for the designated target." The AI sounded pleased.

Baxter saw the surface coming up at them fast.

Darcy took two steps away from the rover, lost her balance, swayed, but trudged on. She was really feeling the effects of the radiation now.

She carried the node board under her arm as she walked on the aeroshell. The protruding geoglyph growth looked like a cancerous tumor, metallic and insidious as it penetrated and wrapped around the tower.

In disgust, she turned away from the encrustation and headed to the main terminal. She felt a wash of relief to see the green lights that indicated the operating system was still functional.

Her gloved hands shook uncontrollably as she held the board. All she had to do was install it, and the rest would be automated. The firewall would let the shield network function again. The AR goggles focused and refocused as they tried to assist her.

She saw the slot for the replacement board, and she tried to align the contacts ... missed, and finally used both hands to guide the end into the narrow slot. When she pushed the board into place and made the contact, she felt as if she had finished running a marathon. She shoved harder, seating it properly.

The system lit up, and the green lights flickered as the startup routine began.

She was ready to collapse, and she wanted to cry. The firewall was uploading.

On the verge of losing consciousness, Darcy looked up into the coppery sky, hoping she might see the *Odyssey* up there with Captain Faraday transmitting congratulations, giving her permission to rest now. As soon as the shield rebooted, the survivors of humanity could come down and take refuge in the hab modules. Her father would be one of the first out of the hibernation pods. Before long, the colonists would start working the algae ponds, set up greenhouses, build cities, turn Persephone into a new home....

But she didn't see the *Odyssey* up in the sky. Instead, she heard a sonic boom resounding through the air and spotted the flare of some spacecraft hurtling like a missile toward the tower node.

The AeroFox.

Inside a cocoon of heated air, the AeroFox plunged toward the target. Against all instincts, Baxter refused to squeeze her eyes shut, and she could see the geoglyph design, the tower node—and the TerraCat parked near the base.

It was all happening too fast to make out details.

Omni blurted out, "Holy shit! Astronaut Clarke is rebooting the system."

"Language, Omni!" The cockpit was shaking so much she couldn't see the screen clearly, but the image of the shield node begin to change. "How long until the firewall propagates?"

"Thirty seconds. She has already installed the node board."

Before the scout ship hit the ground, the soft-landing retrorockets fired, slowing them. The noise inside the pilot deck increased to a roar, and she could feel the braking jets guiding them in. Omni used the retrorockets to maneuver them toward a landing zone a few meters from the TerraCat.

But they wouldn't be in time to stop Darcy, and once the firewall began spreading across the network, it would be too late.

Baxter made a split-second decision. She realigned the landing target and aimed for the tower itself.

The AI voice was filled with alarm. "What are you doing?"

Baxter didn't waver. "Stopping her."

The node board lit up as it installed the new firewall software, and Darcy was filled with fatalistic triumph.

Then she saw the AeroFox shift its trajectory. The scout craft came directly toward her like a looming fist. Then its retrorockets sputtered out, and the AeroFox simply dropped from the sky.

With a yelp, Darcy ripped the node board from its socket and ran for her life.

The Fox crashed into the node tower and clipped off the top of the structure. Sparks showered out.

Darcy tripped on the aeroshell. Cradling the board against her, she rolled on the flat debris, then looked up in horror.

With a groan of twisting metal, the damaged shield tower collapsed like a big swatting hand. It crashed to the ground with a sound like an angry gong.

The AeroFox hit near the geoglyph line, slewed, and tore up

rocks and dirt. Finally, it came to a halt, canted at a steep angle. Fire and smoke flickered from beneath the hull.

CHAPTER 49

The jolt of impact threw Baxter against the restraining straps. After the scout craft ground to a halt, she groaned and blinked her eyes. She found herself hanging at an angle inside the ship; only the restraints kept her from dropping to the deck.

At least the AeroFox hadn't exploded, but sparks gushed up from blown circuits across the control panel. The cockpit screens were dull and blank, but Baxter would never fly the ship again.

She winced as she twisted around, trying to get free. She remembered where she was and how little time she had. "Omni, you still with me? Can you read the tower? What happened?"

She was glad to hear the reassuring AI voice. "Engineer Baxter, I am happy to report that Node 212 is officially offline, since we smashed into it."

"And where's Astronaut Clarke?" Her stomach suddenly twisted with dread. "She was standing right at the base of the tower. Is she harmed?"

One of the monitor screens flickered to life and showed external images dully lit by reddish sunlight. The details remained blurry as the cameras adjusted. Some of the lenses had been covered with dust, others cracked.

Finally, one sharp image showed Darcy Clarke sprawled on the ground—but she *moved*, picked herself up onto her hands and knees. She seemed dazed as she adjusted the oxygen mask, rubbed a sleeve across her AR goggles, then she looked around. Darcy spotted the node board that had fallen on the tower's aeroshell covering. In pain and desperation, she hauled herself toward it.

Inside the AeroFox, Baxter struggled to disengage the safety harness, which was like a straitjacket around her. "Omni, what is she doing?"

"The TerraCat is still intact. If the node board is undamaged, then Astronaut Clarke could simply drive to the next shield node and eventually achieve the same result. There are hundreds of towers, and any individual unit could upload the firewall to the entire network."

Finally releasing the buckle, Baxter tumbled out of her seat to the deck. She picked herself up, tried to keep her balance. "If she heads away from here, we'd have no way to stop her. The AeroFox sure as hell isn't going anywhere!"

"Correct, Engineer Baxter. This craft will not fly again."

She pushed her way across the slanted deck. "Cycle me through the airlock! I've got to get to her!"

When she grabbed the node board, Darcy saw that it was intact. That gave her a jolt of victory. She rocked on her hands and knees, then levered herself to her feet. Her ears were ringing, but at least she had the board.

Now to do something with it.

The AeroFox was nearby, still smoking after the crash. Darcy had been only moments away from restoring the whole shield network—and exterminating the damned geoglyph.

Then Baxter had crashed a ship into it!

The impact had wrecked not only the tower, but also damaged the alien pyrite growths, smashing the shiny metal around the site. Darcy wished the blow had been enough to kill the thing.

She recoiled and retreated onto the protection of the aeroshell as she watched the golden fragments move, melt, and slither together, congealing like blobs of quicksilver. The fragments pulled back to form a larger portion of geoglyph material, fresh and raw.

If she couldn't get to the TerraCat, she would never get out of here. The radiation exposure was already killing her, and she didn't know how much longer she would be able to function. But if she could get to another, uncontaminated shield node, she might be able to complete her mission.

Gaining strength and resolve, Darcy ran across the aeroshell surface. Carrying the node board, she dodged the eerily moving metal bits, afraid that some steely tentacle would burst through the aeroshell and grab her. She heaved great breaths in her airmask as she ran.

The AeroFox's airlock burst open, and Tanya Baxter emerged, half balanced in the tilted doorway. She swung down the ladder and dropped to the ground, yelling into the comm implant. "Darcy, stop!"

As she kept running toward the rover, huffing loudly in her facemask, Darcy's legs could barely hold her up.

Baxter bounded after her and grabbed Darcy by the shoulder, turning her around. "Not so fast, kid!"

Darcy snarled, "Get your hands off me!" Lifting a gloved hand, she shaded her eyes, as if she could hide the crashed scout ship, the wrecked tower, the crawling pieces of geoglyph. "Look what you did—you're insane! So was Kyle!"

Baxter refused to release her iron-hard grip. "Maybe I am, and maybe he was. But this is over now. You can't go on anymore, and you'll be dead if you don't get rad treatment right away. You're done!"

Darcy wrenched herself free. "No, I am *not* done!" She staggered away, clutching the node board. "I'm just getting started. The *Odyssey* is depending on us! The captain, all those people ..."

But Baxter was faster, stronger, and tore the node board out of her hands. Darcy screamed, but the engineer brought the vital board down hard on her knee, snapping it in half. She dropped the broken pieces to the ground.

Seeing red, Darcy charged into Baxter, knocking her flat onto the hard aeroshell. The two wrestled, sliding up against the base of the tower.

Baxter used the strut for leverage and pushed back against her weakening opponent, pinning Darcy against the base. "Goddamn it, stop! There's nothing you can—"

Suddenly the ground beneath them trembled with convulsions, as if one of the nearby volcanoes had erupted. Both women sprawled flat. Darcy tried to regain her footing, but the convulsions grew more extreme.

The geoglyph substrate buckled around the edge of the hard aeroshell material, like shards of crystal in a frantic growth state. Planes of shining pyrite rose up, swelling toward the nearby AeroFox as if with a deliberate purpose. A grinding, rushing sound filled the air.

Darcy and Baxter both retreated against the tower, forgetting their struggle as rock shards rose up like an ocean wave, raising the wrecked scout craft in a giant metallic hand.

Abruptly, the alien quicksilver material came to a frozen halt, leaving only the sound of the wind. The frenetic geoglyph growth solidified, holding the AeroFox like segments of amber shimmering under Persephone's sunlight.

Baxter rose to her feet and stared. She touched the comm implant. "Omni, are you there? Omni?" Distracted, she reached down and offered her hand to Darcy, who reluctantly took it. They both stared at the elaborate new metal formation that had grown over the damaged ship.

Darcy felt wrung out and broken. "It's destroying the AeroFox!"

Baxter touched her comm again. "Omni, please answer me. Come in."

Darcy felt an awed chill when she realized that the horrific growth was more than just a blob of metal. The formation covering the AeroFox had an organic, yet mathematical order to it, like the continent-wide patterns seen from orbit. It had a *shape*.

The AI voice finally responded, surprising them. "I am here, Engineer Baxter. That was ... most unusual. It is what I hoped for, actually. You said that I should figure it out, so ... I figured it out."

With her skin crawling, Darcy started to retreat back to the waiting TerraCat, anxious to get away from the alien metal. What if another geoglyph blob reached out to seize her and Baxter?

But the engineer kept facing the wrecked ship. "What did you do, Omni? What do you mean that you figured it out?"

"After analyzing the original EMP that struck the AstroBug—the pulse that overloaded me and caused us to crash—I decided to send an EMP of my own. I hoped that would get the geoglyph's attention."

"You poked it," Baxter said.

"Yes, and this formation is the result. Not quite the reaction I was looking for, but unquestionably a direct response to my overture. It opens the lines of communication."

Darcy just stared in horror.

Clearly fascinated, Baxter walked along the edge of the aeroshell, looking at the churned dirt and fresh new lines of geoglyph metal that extended to the AeroFox. "Does that mean you can talk to it?"

The AI voice hesitated. "Not per se. I do, however, detect a pattern in the energy signal from the geoglyph. It remains indecipherable, yet appears to have complex organization. Obviously, it is not just a series of random glitches." Then Omni sounded more excited. "I have an idea. Astronaut Clarke, I know you are afraid, but will you come approach the AeroFox? I don't believe there's any danger to you."

Darcy froze. "Me? I've been trying to eliminate that thing!"

"So I have observed. It's time to face your fears." When she hesitated, Omni pressed, "Please trust me—as you have always trusted me. I ask you to come over here to me, to the ship."

Baxter nodded encouragement. "Please, Darcy—we need to find a way out of this. The *Odyssey* is already here in orbit—I saw it during the Fox's brief flight, and it looked in pretty bad shape. We've got to figure this out, and now."

Hesitant and defeated, Darcy looked toward the geoglyph encrustation. Even if she did make it to the TerraCat, she no longer had the node board and the firewall. Where would she go?

Taking a leap of faith, she stepped off the hard shell material to the open ground where the Fox had crashed. She walked toward the monstrous fresh growth that rose like armor around the scout ship. Darcy couldn't think straight, and she still felt very afraid. "What do you want me to do, Omni?"

The AI had a plan that would have matched Kyle's most bizarre ideas. "The geoglyph knows that *I* exist because we share a fundamental similarity in our base silicon structure. Now, I need to make it understand that you exist as well. I think there might be a way."

Darcy stared at the towering, angular structure. With its forceful growth, it had shifted the crashed scout ship and raised it up on thick pyrite columns. The looming presence scared the hell out of her. The geoglyph had been trying to kill them all along.

In the eerie quiet, she heard crunching footsteps, and Baxter came to stand next to her. "Now what, Omni?"

"Step closer. I'm going to send a series of more complex pulses. Maybe I can evoke another response."

Darcy looked at the ominous growth, then down at her boots and the exposed alien metal. "I'm not sure I want to see any more response than this."

Without warning, a chunk of the geoglyph thrust upward, a waist-high wall of metallic rock that grew toward Darcy—but it stopped there.

She stared at it in horror. "What's it doing?"

"Don't worry," Omni said, even though she could think of a hundred things to worry about. "Now ... extend your hand."

She found the idea repulsive, making her recall all the terrible things this sentient metal monster had done, but she felt compelled. She slowly extended her left hand toward the mass in front of her.

Her gloved fingers sank into the geoglyph metal as if it were no more than water. Her entire hand went in, and she was on the edge of hyperventilating. But her hand felt intact.

A grinding rumble emanated from the metallic structure around the AeroFox. The pillar of pyrite shifted until it exactly mimicked an extended arm and a human hand. *Her* hand! Darcy yanked her hand away, and the alien metal retreated.

Then the entire mound of extruded geoglyph material reshaped itself, forging into a new shape that rose into a towering humanoid form—a titanic statue made of the ruddy polished pyrite, smooth and curved, with soft angular edges. The strange colossus cast a long shadow in the red-orange sunlight.

Darcy stared, speechless. She couldn't believe what she was seeing.

"It's you!" Baxter cried.

The massive replica of Darcy Clarke mirrored her exact stance. The planes and angles added details, but there was no question it had copied her in every way.

"It's a ... a Darcy glyph," Baxter said. "Omni, how big is that thing?"

"Twenty-one meters high."

The screeching, grinding sound ended, and the metallic sculpture stopped growing, frozen in place. Its perfectly formed left hand was extended, just as Darcy's had been. The mammoth pyrite figure appeared to be reaching for them.

Frightened but also awed, Darcy looked up at the enormous statue. "Why ... why is it doing that?"

Baxter gave her a stern look. "Maybe it's saying, 'Stop trying to kill me ...'"

Omni said, "I believe the manifestation is part of its analysis of *you*, Astronaut Clarke. A way of understanding your existence within its own context."

Frowning, she stared at the gleaming figure. "How does it even know I'm here? It can't see or hear anything."

"All living things have an electromagnetic signature. I simply made the geoglyph aware of yours. This is what it ... sees."

Baxter said in a whisper, "This is its way of smiling at you, kid."

The looming colossus made Darcy uneasy. "Or threatening me. Omni, if the geoglyph can make something this massive in the blink of an eye, why didn't it just crush all of our shield towers?"

"That is not how it thinks. I have been trying to develop a shared context. The geoglyph has been alone on Persephone for billions of years. When the *Forerunner* deposited our shield network, the geoglyph was trying to gather information to ascertain what was happening, why it was starving."

Baxter didn't take her eyes from the Darcy glyph. "Now do you believe what Kyle was saying? He saw it before either of us did."

Darcy could barely stand as her mind connected the dots. The realization overwhelmed her, but then another wave of nausea washed over her, and her knees buckled. "I ... I don't feel so good."

Baxter rushed to catch her before she sprawled on the ground. She scanned the deep-red dosimeter patch and the suite of medical indicators on the young woman's envirosuit. Everything had turned red.

CHAPTER 50

B efore the motionless giant glyph, Baxter wrapped one of
Darcy's arms over her shoulder and hauled her to her feet.
The young woman groaned, entirely wrung out.

"Kid, you're a mess. We've got to get you that rad-treatment
from the X-Doc." She realized with dismay that the pyrite metal
growth had shoved the AeroFox up at a precarious angle and
wrapped around the hull. The airlock remained uncovered, but it
was high off the ground. Baxter could never climb up there
carrying Darcy.

Omni's voice spoke in the comm. "I've accessed Astronaut
Clarke's bio-signs. It may be too late for effective treatment, given
the limitations of the X-Doc."

"We've got to try." Darcy moaned in her arms, on the verge of
unconsciousness. "The *Odyssey* is up there, and they have much
more sophisticated medical facilities. Have communications
cleared?"

The red sunlight beat down on them, and Baxter waited an
interminable moment. "I attempted another transmission and
received a brief response, then only static as it cut out. We saw
how much damage the *Odyssey* suffered, but they are likely
working on an interim solution."

"They know we're down here. Faraday will manage it if

anyone can." Baxter looked at the half-encased AeroFox. "Meanwhile, I need to get into the cabin. Even if the X-Doc can't cure all the radiation damage, it'll keep the kid alive." She began to drag Darcy closer to the spacecraft.

"Oh, there is one other problematic element, Engineer Baxter," Omni said. "Sorry, I almost forgot to mention it."

Baxter groaned. "Now what?"

"I detect turbulence on Proxima Centauri. Another flare storm appears to be imminent." The AI sounded apologetic.

Baxter wheezed an exhausted sigh. "Oh, for—" She looked at the ruddy star low on the horizon. "Shit. The AeroFox has shielding. How bad was the hull compromised in the crash?"

"It will not provide sufficient shelter for either of you. Sorry, Engineer Baxter."

Darcy would have pointed out that if she'd succeeded in installing the firewall, the shield network would protect them now.

She looked back toward the night side. "I'm getting us back to that crater. It provided enough shelter before."

"I approve of that idea. Meanwhile, I will keep attempting to contact the *Odyssey*."

"Don't *attempt* it, Omni—make it happen! Use Satellite-A as a relay. The boost may be enough to get through to the *Odyssey*, if they've jury-rigged some of their comms."

Baxter turned and struggled toward the rover vehicle instead. Darcy weakly attempted to help, but was mostly just dead weight. She finally wrestled the groaning young woman to the open hatch of the TerraCat. "Stay with me, kid!"

Darcy slumped in the seat. Her face was slack behind the half-mask, the eyes closed beneath the AR goggles. Baxter took a breath, forced calm on herself, even though she didn't know whether her companion could hear or understand anything. She made up her mind. "I'm going to grab the X-Doc from the Fox and let the unit work on you while I'm driving us out of here."

Darcy managed a rattling whisper. "Knock yourself out."

Baxter sprinted across the ground, which was even more uneven now that the geoglyph material had flowed and formed its bizarre Darcy avatar. But the scout ship's airlock was still far out of reach, thrust up off the ground by the geoglyph encrustations.

"Omni, could you ask your new friend to make me some stairs? Or even just a stepstool?"

"That's beyond my current ability to communicate, Engineer Baxter."

She mumbled under her breath. "Figures."

She jogged around the jagged pyrite structures, looking for a way up. The crystalline planes of amber metal offered ledges and flat zones, and Baxter was able to grab one at shoulder height. She pulled herself up, found a foothold, and climbed closer to the airlock. "And I got out of hibernation for this ..."

When she finally made it the rest of the way, Omni opened the external airlock hatch for her.

Once she'd returned with the X-Doc and hooked it up to Darcy, the TerraCat rolled out, spitting dust and gravel beneath its large tires. Baxter didn't even attempt to activate the auto-drive. Retrieving the medical unit had taken longer than expected, and the next round of flares was imminent.

She set course back toward the line of mountains and the lip of the large crater several kilometers away. She would never be able to make it to the terminator storms or the safety of the dark side in time, but the deep crater would offer shelter, as before.

As the rover raced away from the titanic Darcy glyph, the human face of burnished pyrite seemed to be watching them.

With the vehicle's cabin pressurized again, Baxter removed her oxygen mask, still breathing hard in the hot, dusty air. Sprawled in the back seat, Darcy lay groggy. Baxter had peeled off the young woman's mask and goggles, but only after installing the X-Doc. The medical device wrapped around her, administering

KEVIN J. ANDERSON & JEFFREY MORRIS

diagnostic-and-repair nanomachines. They were going to have to work overtime just to keep her alive.

Before Darcy fell completely unconscious, Baxter bent over her. "I brought you something, kid. Thought you'd like to have it as you're undergoing treatment." The young woman blinked her dark eyes, confused. Baxter extended the photograph of her family. "I took this from the AeroFox."

Darcy looked at the photo and somehow managed a smile before her expression fell again. "Couldn't save them ..." Her fingers clutched the picture as she slumped back, then dropped into deep sleep as the X-Doc continued to work.

"You need to learn the difference between *the* solution and *a* solution, kid."

Baxter drove at top speed along the smooth geoglyph highway. Omni delivered the grim news that more flares had indeed erupted, and the subsequent radiation storm was on the way.

"One damn thing after another," she grumbled.

In a cheerful voice, Omni said, "Good news, Engineer Baxter —I did make contact with the *Odyssey*. They have rigged up a temporary communications system, but no visuals. I gave them a full briefing of our current situation. I also gave them a detailed summary of the sentient geoglyph and its attempts to ... communicate using the Darcy glyph."

She wondered how the captain, and the rest of the awake crew, had reacted to the news that the huge alien sentience had rendered the protective shield inoperable. And what would happen when they learned that Baxter—and Kyle—had also prevented it from being fixed? With the arkship falling apart in orbit, and ten thousand frozen colonists at stake, Baxter doubted they would take it well. Her eyes burned with tears. She had gambled everything....

"And what is the outlook for the *Odyssey*?"

"It appears they are preparing the fleet of AstroBugs to transport hibernation pods, colony generator units, and temporary base equipment to a suitable area just inside the terminator line.

256

Captain Faraday says we can use forty or so of the AstroBugs as temporary habitation units for quite some time, provided the majority of the colonists remain frozen."

Baxter felt a wash of relief. "So, Kyle must have been convincing."

"The alternative plan was already in the mission logs. The *Odyssey* needed a viable and immediate solution. The crew is in the midst of a full-scale effort to revive the hibernating colonists before more systems fail. Fortunately, the *Odyssey* will be behind the night side of the planet when the flares hit."

"Yeah, fortunately," Baxter said. "And can they send assistance for Darcy?"

"The captain was concerned about Astronaut Clarke's condition. She is sending a med-evac team to rendezvous with you in the crater, once you have taken shelter."

She realized she was trembling with relief. "Good work, Omni." If this had gone differently ...

Baxter could see the lip of the crater up ahead, which would offer safety in the heavy shadows below the rim. Also down there, the smaller version from the metal samples, the "junior glyph," must still be growing in the harsh sunlight.

"They'll have plenty to see when they get here." Baxter kept driving. The reddish sky around them seemed threatening, even though the flares hadn't arrived yet. "When it's time, I'll bring the team back to Node 212 and show them everything."

Omni sounded hesitant. "Engineer, please don't be offended, but I am looking forward to working with actual scientists on this."

She laughed. "No offense taken. I get it, and I've done my bit." The TerraCat toiled up the slope that led to the steep plunge into the crater.

"While we wait for them, I will continue my conversation with the geoglyph." The simulated voice sounded eager. "This is the greatest discovery in the history of science. I intend to learn all I can and, uh, 'do my bit,' as you say."

Baxter smiled. "Omni, I envy you the opportunity."

"Thank you, Engineer Baxter. This could have been a disaster if you hadn't been so determined."

She let out a sad sigh. "My husband always called it being pig-headed."

It could also have been a disaster if the arkship was not in a condition to implement the alternative offloading plan.

A deep bump in the road made Darcy stir in the back seat. She struggled to lift her head and touched the X-Doc unit, disoriented. She fought to speak. "Tanya ..."

Baxter was glad to see the patient at least partly conscious. "What is it, kid?"

The young woman's expression was wracked with guilt and shame as much as pain. Her deep brown eyes filled with tears. "Sorry I punched you."

Baxter snorted. "Just don't do it again. Next time, I'll punch back."

Darcy slumped, but still remained awake. "I was trying to save everybody.... Are you positive we shouldn't just kill that thing?"

"The easiest solutions are never the best ones—I learned that in engineering school. And in life."

Darcy passed out again as the TerraCat rolled over the crater rim and down into the shelter of shadows.

CHAPTER 51

Huddled in the darkness at the bottom of the large crater, Darcy lay unconscious in an induced coma. The X-Doc remained in place, keeping her alive until the *Odyssey* medics could arrive.

The sun never moved near the horizon, the line of black shadow never changed, and the area of bright light did not grow or shrink.

Baxter sat inside the TerraCat, exhausted, lost in thought. She felt she could use another decade or two of hibernation. She stared through the windshield to the patch of sunshine. Bathed in the coppery light, the metallic mound of the junior-sized glyph was all straight lines, sharp angles, pyrite planes—a motionless, shimmering enigma, full of potential.

An unexpected voice spoke in her comm. "Engineer Baxter, this is the rescue AstroBug from the *Odyssey*. We have your coordinates, approaching the crater now."

Baxter touched the implant. "I'm here, ready and waiting." And waiting ...

"The flares have calmed, and we're coming down."

Baxter looked at the wedge of sunlight on the crater floor. "Just don't squash the baby geoglyph. The TerraCat is here in the shade."

Before long, she heard the roar of rocket engines and looked up to see a familiar saucer-shaped vessel, marked with red stripes as a medical rescue vessel.

Baxter could gauge the pilot's skill by the ease with which the large spacecraft glided along the crater wall and settled among the boulders and rubble. Landing struts extended, then adjusted to stabilize the AstroBug. A bay door on the side of the hull dropped open, and a wide ramp extended.

"Drive right aboard, TerraCat," said the voice in her ear. "Our med crews are standing by."

Baxter had the rover's engines powered up. "You don't need to tell me twice." She glanced at Darcy's motionless form wrapped in the medical device. "Just hang on, kid."

Baxter guided the vehicle up the ramp and into the wide hangar like a fish swimming into the gullet of a whale. The planet's gravity felt lighter now as hope built up inside her again. When the rover was safely in the bay, the ramp retracted, and the bay door sealed again.

As soon as the pressurization indicators switched from amber to green, Baxter opened the rover's hatch. Five *Odyssey* crew members bounded in with a stretcher to help extricate Darcy's limp form. The X-Doc still gripped her in an embrace, as if unwilling to relinquish her to the med techs.

The lead doctor came up, bending down next to Darcy. He had dark curly hair, heavy eyebrows, and a warm, concerned expression. "I'm Doctor Nathan Davieau, head of the medical team. We'll do what we can—trust me, she's in good hands."

"Were you on the skeleton crew?" Baxter asked. "You weren't part of the team that revived me."

He let out a tired sigh. "I was revived with the first batch five hours ago, barely got on my feet. Captain Faraday is waking up as many medical personnel as possible. I didn't expect to be thrown into my duties headfirst, but … we're alive, and we made it here. Can't complain."

"Find an Autobrew and make yourself some coffee," Baxter suggested, then hardened her voice. "Just don't let Darcy die."

"The X-Doc kept her alive." Dr. Davieau sounded relieved. "Now let's get her into the full med chamber."

Darcy roused herself enough to look over at Baxter, and the two shared a look of understanding.

More crew members entered the AstroBug's pressurized bay. Captain Faraday was among them, looking ragged and worn, but exhibiting a new kind of energy. Baxter couldn't believe she was here. "Captain, you came on the rescue mission yourself! But, the *Odyssey*—"

Faraday smiled at her as Dr. Davieau led the med techs out of the rover with the stretcher. "I didn't want to trust any of my other pilots. Darcy is like one of my kids. We've ... we've already lost Kyle and Corey." Her voice cracked.

"Newborns," Baxter said. When the captain gave her a questioning look, she answered, "Just a teasing name I made up for them. I never got to use it for Corey or Kyle."

Faraday stepped up to the stretcher, where Darcy blinked up at her as if she were an apparition. "Captain?" she said in a hoarse voice. "You're here? What about the ship? Is everyone okay? Did we save—?"

Faraday's weathered hand squeezed hers. "The arkship had a rough ride getting into orbit, I won't kid you. We suffered some damage, some loss of hibernating colonists, but most everyone is fine. Scared, but fine—especially with the major last-minute change of plans." Her brows furrowed. "We're waking up the first wave, and our fleet of AstroBugs will be shipping thousands of operational hibernation pods down to the surface. We're implementing Plan B as fast as we can."

On the stretcher, Darcy's expression fell, and her eyes glistened with moisture. "Sorry we didn't finish the job. Corey and Kyle ... they did their best."

"I know that." Faraday nodded, but obviously still full of questions.

"And we found a way to save the colonists without killing the geoglyph," Baxter said. "But Darcy was trying to save us, too."

The young woman looked queasy, beyond the radiation sickness. "I didn't want to risk anything but the obvious solution, but I almost ... I almost ..." She looked as if the weight was crushing her.

Faraday said, "Personally, I am getting sick of impossible choices. Darcy, I'm just sorry your first mission to Proxima b had to end like this."

"Persephone," Darcy whispered. "Kyle's name for it ... Call this planet Persephone."

Baxter nodded. "We agree. That's what Kyle wanted."

The captain considered, then nodded. "All right, as captain of the *Odyssey*, I get to name things. Persephone, it is." She placed her palm on Darcy's sweaty forehead. "See you soon."

"I'll be here...."

The med techs hurried the stretcher to the elevator hatch.

Together, Baxter and Captain Faraday turned to the dusty rover sitting in the middle of the bay. Outside, across the crater, the exotic junior glyph basked in the sun.

Faraday crossed her arms over her chest. "I received Omni's summary report, Engineer, but I'm staying down here so I can have a look around myself. You still owe me plenty of answers." She paused, looking wistful for a moment. "And you and I have a lot of brainstorming to do."

Though the X-Doc had been working on her for hours in the TerraCat, Darcy still just wanted to collapse. The finish line must be somewhere up ahead. It still didn't seem real that they had been rescued, that the *Odyssey* had arrived, that the captain herself had come down here. It felt like a delirious dream.

But the colonists were going to survive, even if they had to live in the dark. Maybe they could find some way to coexist with the geoglyph. She still didn't understand, and the sickness and confusion did not let her think straight. She had her orders and was so fixed on the *Odyssey*'s needs. She had seen the geoglyph as an absolute obstacle that needed to be obliterated. She hadn't even considered it might not be necessary. What if she'd killed the ... the soul of Persephone?

Above her, Dr. Davieau looked intent, but reassuring. The med techs jostled her stretcher, and she managed to raise her head as the elevator door whisked open to take her to the main deck of the AstroBug.

A man stood there wearing a joyful expression. She recognized him instantly. "Dad!"

Sebastian Clarke strode forward, wobbling a little on his feet. "Peanut!"

A female med tech accompanied him, supporting her father. He wore a tight stimsuit like the one Tanya Baxter had needed after awakening, but his grin was so large that it alone seemed to buoy him up. "I just got out of the pod, and I'm still getting my legs under me—but no way was I going to miss seeing you. Captain Faraday didn't dare leave me behind."

The med tech helped him forward, but Sebastian only had eyes for his daughter. Darcy pawed at the X-Doc as she struggled to sit up on the stretcher. She wanted to throw herself into his arms, but she couldn't manage that. The best she could do was squirm to the side, reaching out to embrace him.

Since both were equally weak and shaky, the two just rocked back and forth, holding each other. Tears streamed down Darcy's cheeks. "I didn't know if I would ever see you again, Dad. I missed you so much."

He buried his face in her short hair, kissed the top of her head. "When I woke up, I asked where you were. All I could remember was that the last time I came out of hibernation, I learned about what happened to your mother ... But you're here—*we're* here, on the planet at last after such a long voyage!"

"I'm glad you came down. I was ... about at the end of what I could do here. And I didn't *know* what to do!" Her ragged voice hitched. "I almost made some very big mistakes. Persephone isn't what we thought it would be. We weren't ready for it."

Sebastian held her shoulders so he could just look at her face. "We'll have some serious challenges ahead, no doubt about it. And it sure isn't what we planned for. Now we'll need to reconfigure the whole colony setup, live in the AstroBugs on the night side for a while ..."

She pressed her face against his chest, tried to stop herself from crying. "But you're awake now, Dad. You're with me." She reached to her breast pocket, fumbled with the battered picture of her family that Baxter had retrieved for her. "We'll still make a home here, me and you together. All I care about is facing the challenges with you."

The med techs helped them to their feet, and Dr. Davieau tried to hurry them along. Both patients walked on wobbly legs into the elevator, arm in arm. Sebastian said, "We will, Peanut. We will."

As the elevator carried them up to the medical bay, Darcy could feel the vibration as the AstroBug's plasma engines fired. She held onto the elevator wall, and also her father, as the ship flew out of the crater and headed toward the sky, where the *Odyssey* waited in orbit.

The TerraCat rolled up and over the crater rim and then set off across the new world.

Baxter and Captain Faraday watched the rescue AstroBug take off behind them. Faraday nodded to herself. "They'll patch Darcy up. She'll be fine ... or as fine as she can be after what she's been through." She sighed. "Jim Corey was a part of her ... and so was Kyle. They were part of me, too."

"It's a new world, Captain, with plenty of challenges. We came here at quite a cost, but staying on Earth would have cost us even more." Baxter followed the clear tread marks the rover had left on its previous travels. She drove across the untouched terrain with all the freedom she could imagine. She doubted she would use the auto-drive again.

"We're going to take a lot of crap for the unexpected complications this geoglyph thing has caused," Faraday said. "Ten thousand people had already accepted all the hardships they were going to face, but we did promise them a certain type of colony. Your shield was supposed to make this a new Earth."

Baxter scoffed. "Persephone was never going to be another Earth, and we were always going to make compromises and changes. Look at how much you had to adapt just during the voyage of the *Odyssey*."

Faraday looked wistfully out the rover's window. "Yes, three babies born on the way ... that wasn't part of the plan. Neither was having much of our airmoss die off, or the greenhouse solar lights fail, or the communications array die. Every day, it was like running uphill in a hurricane. But I got us here." She nodded to herself. "And now we're damn well going to pull it off."

As Baxter drove along in the direction of the giant geoglyph, Faraday rattled off ideas that she must have been considering for some time. "Each AstroBug can support twenty to twenty-five people living aboard. The settlers will just learn to live in crowded quarters."

Baxter ran calculations in her mind. "Even if we use forty-five Bugs as dwelling structures, they'll still only hold about a thousand colonists. That leaves nine thousand in cold storage. That can't last forever."

The captain nodded. "As long as we get them off the *Odyssey* and hook them up to generators, those hibernation pods can last another decade." She shrugged. "Maybe longer. It'll give us time to get on our feet, build more permanent shelters on the night side. Maybe even enough time to work out some solution with the geoglyph."

Baxter stared ahead. "Adapt or die, Captain. The basic rule of Nature."

On the way toward the shield node, they passed expansive ponds simmering with genetically tailored algae. Spiderlike agricultural tenders swung over the pools, stirring the greenish-brown sludge.

Baxter mused, "I know people aren't going to be happy, Captain. They planned on living in their hab modules on their own fresh homesteads, but the night side isn't really a harder survival challenge. Sure, it's cold and dark, but at least you don't have to worry about solar flares all day long."

Faraday stared out at clumps of spiny black inkweed, the bare rocks, and the arid terrain under thick orange sunlight. "Well, this side isn't a vacation resort either."

Ahead, the burnished geoglyph mound extended like a wall toward the horizon. Baxter drove up the rubble slope to reach the top of the dull metal expanse, then increased speed.

Faraday said, "You'll have to convince me, and a lot of restless colonists, that this geoglyph thing is worth upending all of our plans. We could see the pattern from orbit, and we know how vast it is, but ... I still don't understand."

"Just wait and see." Baxter kept driving until they finally reached the rise overlooking Node 212, the tower, and the remarkable amber colossus. "I've got something to show you, Captain. Something amazing."

They rolled toward the titanic, enigmatic Darcy glyph.

CHAPTER 52
THREE MONTHS LATER

I n orbit over Persephone, the battered and weary *Odyssey* kept circling. By now, the arkship was mostly abandoned, but many of the habitation ring systems had been patched up and repaired. Although the colony vessel would not fly anywhere again, Captain Faraday refused to abandon it entirely.

Faraday had returned aboard along with a handful of people who stayed by choice, rather than desperation. She remained here and felt oddly satisfied, even content. Each orbit of Persephone seemed like a victory lap. She lounged in her command chair and stared out the broad windows, marveling at the bright expanse of the planet below.

"It's not really the retirement home I expected," she mused.

She crossed her arms over her chest and drew a long breath of the ship's recycled air—healthy enough air, now that the oxygen scrubbers had been restored. The sunlight from Proxima was enough for them to grow real crops in the greenhouses again.

"But the operative word is *retirement*." She smiled over at her first officer. "But you're too young to retire, Mr. Kleve."

"I am still very much on duty, Captain. After all this time, I don't think that settling on a planet is really my thing."

Down below, the bright hemisphere showed the prominent geoglyph pattern, intricate lines and angles in an incomprehensible message. The metallic alien sentience had regrown, undeterred now that the shield was entirely offline. The structure could thrive, as it had done for billions of years.

"The geoglyph certainly prefers the situation," Faraday said.

"While our people are still stuck in the dark, crowded on AstroBugs ..." her first officer replied with a frown.

"Who knows what the geoglyph thinks?" Ron Purvis interrupted. The bridge officer had opted to stay aboard, for a while.

"We've got teams trying to figure that out—just give the experts time to work," Faraday said. "Omni is starting to decipher the patterns and the EMPs. Sooner or later those two will be singing a duet."

"Singing a duet?" Purvis said with a sour frown. "We flew half a century to get here. We were looking for homesteads, a new start. I'd rather we worked out some kind of compromise."

"Our settlers are in a stable enough situation, Mr. Purvis. I'm willing to invest some time. We're not going anywhere." She lowered her voice to a whisper. "We owe it to Kyle."

When the arkship's communication array had finally been repaired, Captain Faraday had dispatched a lengthy triumphant message burst toward the silent Earth. She needed to tell anyone still listening that the *Odyssey* had arrived at the new world.

She straightened in her seat. "Now that Governor Koffi is awake, the colony is his problem to handle." She watched the *Odyssey* orbiting over the spectacular alien design below. "Did I mention that I was retired?"

At Node 212, Tanya Baxter planted her hands on her hips as she looked up at the damaged shield tower. She decided it did look a little like the Eiffel Tower, as Darcy Clarke had once suggested to her.

The science team had set up recording apparatus to take

complete surveys of the local geoglyph section. Clad in envirosuits and half facemasks, the team members spent regular shifts trying to solve the mystery, ducking into emergency "storm shelters" when necessary. They had been at their work for the past month and a half.

Some of them scanned the metallic intrusion that had engulfed part of the tower, while other specialists obtained analytical samples, though the exotic pyrite material still defied any kind of chemical or mineralogical analysis. Baxter found it amusing that they would bother with such tiny fragments, when they could just study the massive Darcy glyph that loomed over them like a titan.

Looking at the eerie formation, she half expected the sculpture to shift its angular face and smile back at her. Even though Omni had spent a great deal of time attempting to convey rudimentary concepts to it, the geoglyph was far from being able to understand human expressions. The immense metallic statue had not moved an inch after forming itself.

Baxter spoke aloud to the giant glyph. "We'll figure you out someday. We have to learn to coexist." She turned away from the straight metallic lines that extended to the horizon to see the mechanical activity nearby, necessary colony work that continued on the dayside even if humans couldn't live full-time over here—not yet.

An array of shallow farming pools glistened in the perpetual sun, filled with algae that thrived under the red light. Agricultural specialists continued to test and modify the strains for hardiness as well as flavor. Baxter thought it all tasted like crap mixed with dirt, even if the protein score was high.

Dayside workers drove tankers up to the farming pools, extended tubes into the water and vacuumed up the thick, greenish sludge. Some of the algae was a bright emerald green, while other pools were black or brown, like oil slicks. Smaller rovers attached themselves to the enormous tanker and began to pull the vessel across the desert landscape like a mule train.

They headed toward the distant mountains and the terminator line.

"*Bon appetit,*" Baxter muttered as the algae tanker trundled away. She would stay here with the science team and eat preserved rations. With a few small greenhouse domes now up and functional, sooner or later she might even be able to have strawberries.

Just another day in paradise.

Back on the nightside, a small city clustered along the ancient frozen lake near the AeroFox crash site. Forty-five landed and locked-down AstroBugs had become a makeshift colony town. Since the spaceships had landed in a precise array, the settlement looked planned, efficient, and modern.

Kyle's grave felt like an anchor point, and Darcy had insisted on naming the settlement Port Dyson. The lake, of course, was named after Corey....

Streets and pathways wound between the illuminated AstroBugs, that were now repurposed for habitation. With a snort, Baxter had once suggested the settlement looked like an old trailer park, but Darcy didn't know what that meant. Her father told her that daily life in the compound was not much worse than a deep winter in Alaska ... another reference for which Darcy had no context.

Each AstroBug held several awakened popsicle families, while thousands of the hibernation pods remained powered up and in storage on the surface, most of the refugees sleeping away until the city could provide all their life-support needs. Even so, Darcy was around more people now than ever before in her life.

TerraCats bustled back and forth on regular supply runs, delivering resources, extracting water, distributing algae and yeast cakes, shuttling people to work sites back on the dayside. Other colonists in envirosuits and masks chose to walk around town, touring the neighborhood. Darcy watched two rovers returning from an expedition to the active volcanoes in the nearby mountains.

Two AstroBugs remained available for use as heavy spacecraft, but the smaller AeroFoxes served as regular shuttles for resource survey missions over the landscape or up to orbit.

Born on the immense arkship, she had spent her life with nothing to see outside but the black vacuum of space. Now that she was here and used to the idea, even the cold nightside of Persephone didn't seem all that bad. After the ordeals and tragedies they had gone through to get here, she felt little sympathy for the scattered complaints. The colonists were not so much angry as disappointed that this new home wasn't what they had been led to expect.

But the Earth was dead, and half a century behind them. And they were alive, and the AstroBug habitats could sustain them for quite some time.

Standing outside, Darcy felt the cold air on her exposed cheeks. It had taken her a while to realize she'd been looking at the crisis all wrong. Instead of exterminating the strange alien life form so they could have a more convenient settlement, they needed to change the plan and consider the entire problem. Humans could be ingenious and resourceful, rather than just destructive.

That was what Kyle and Baxter had insisted on, but she had been too focused on only one solution.

Right now, regular work crews were able to harvest enough food from the dayside, while the population made their homes in the sheltered dark, away from the frequent solar flares. Yes, they were comfortable enough. The colony had geothermal heat, liquid water, and more than a dozen greenhouse domes. Governor Koffi had already announced construction plans for larger, permanent structures.

The colonists gradually came to realize that even this was a far more amenable environment than living on the Mars colony, which had failed so spectacularly. Or in one of the lunar redoubts. Or an asteroid-belt complex ...

Darcy looked up as three AeroFoxes streaked overhead, leaving yellow vapor trails like scratches on the starry sky. They were heading deeper into the dark hemisphere on an extended surveillance mission. She wondered what they might find; there was so much left to explore.

She met her father just outside the AstroBug they shared with several other families. He stretched his arms, then gave her a hug, squeezing hard so she could feel him through her insulated suit. She glanced at the Bug. "It's a lot more cramped in there than our quarters aboard the *Odyssey*."

He took her arm and they walked off, headed toward the new launch complex on the far shore. "Yes, Peanut, but it's much more spacious than a hibernation pod."

"Can't argue with that."

Together, she and her father walked along the excavated streets. They waved at other suited colonists moving about, and the others waved back. Sebastian continued, and she listened to his muffled voice through the facemask. "Humans can get used to anything. Someday this will feel like home. We'll *make* it our permanent home."

"Yes, we will," she said, then looked up into the sky. "Unless there's something better at Alpha Centauri A or B." *Always more places to explore ...*

She could see the sparkle in his eyes. "Depending on what the Alpha probe will tell us in a few years. Someday, maybe in your lifetime, we'll stretch our legs and check out the neighborhood. We aren't done being audacious yet."

Standing at the edge of the ice of Corey's lake, they watched the nearby launchpad, checking the countdown on their wrist monitors. Exactly on time, a bright flare of rocket exhaust illuminated the night.

Long ago, back in the Earth orbital construction yards, some wildly imaginative dreamers had loaded the ready-made Alpha probe onto the arkship, an astronomy crew who didn't think Proxima b needed to be the end point for humanity. Rather, it could be a stepping stone.

Always looking for glimmers of hope, Captain Faraday had scheduled the probe launch as soon as the temporary colony was established. Alpha would take years to reach its destination, the adjacent binary star a quarter of a light-year away. They already knew that Alpha Centauri A had at least one other planet in the habitable zone.

Maybe that would be a next step for humanity.

Someday.

Never stop dreaming.

Together, Darcy and her father watched the automated probe vehicle ascend. "I'm going to pilot that mission, if we ever go there," she mused.

"You might at that, Peanut. But in the meantime ... one planet at a time."

Darcy felt a rising hope as she watched the ascending rocket dwindle into a bright flare. It was on its way. After finding the geoglyph here, she couldn't even imagine what might be waiting for them at Alpha Centauri A.

Darcy kept looking toward the future, but she also made sure that she would never forget the past. For now, humanity had found a new home around an unfamiliar star, on another planet.

Persephone.

EPILOGUE

Out in space, still far beyond the fringe of the Proxima system, a gigantic arkship cruised toward the small red star. The dumbbell-shaped vessel was adorned with towers and angles, as well as blocky gun emplacements. The design did not need to be aerodynamic in interstellar space.

The nonreflective hull metal made the ship look like a black club hurtling between the stars. Far forward of the bridge, heavy banks of blue-white engines flared bright with deceleration thrust. The journey had been long, but the ship was intact, well-maintained, and ready for imminent arrival.

It had been built along the same basic design as the *Odyssey*, with great engines on one end and an enormous hibernation disk on the other, connected by a long axis. At the center was a rotating habitation ring. After decades of space travel, its bright lights were like a triumphant shout to the universe.

The *Valkyrie* had nearly reached its destination.

Inside his armored bottle suit, John Rivera cruised along the length of the great vessel, inspecting with a critical eye. The ship's name was emblazoned in huge letters to remind and reassure all the brave people aboard who had survived so much.

Rivera jetted along the magnetic railguns affixed to the hull, implacable cannons that could rip apart any threat. Also mounted and ready for immediate deployment were dozens of disk-shaped SkyWolf attack fighters, fully armed with missiles.

Rivera shone his inspection lights, ensuring that all armaments were ready—as he knew they would be. He tweaked his control stick, guiding the bottle suit along, and toggled the comm. "Captain Sakamoto, this is Rivera. I just completed a survey of our weaponry. Everything looks nominal. The crew can begin the final phase of their training at your discretion."

The captain's calm, hard voice responded immediately. "Excellent, Mr. Rivera. We still have two years before we reach Proxima Centauri, and we will use the time to prepare."

Inside the bottle suit, Rivera gave a confident nod. "Yes, sir." He rotated his bottle suit and jetted farther along the spine of the enormous vessel. He looked at the brightest star in the tapestry of dots against the black emptiness, one burning red ember. "When we reach Proxima b, *Valkyrie* will be at peak strength."

As he looked at the red dwarf, he pondered the peaceful stillness of space around him, confident that no one knew they were coming.

APPENDIX

Partial list of first-wave colonists on Persephone
Noted on celebratory plaque outside Port Dyson

Peter Bauer
Shawna Biggs
Binky Bowberg
Erwin Bush
James Doom
Paige Minerva Fernandes
Barry Galbraith
Craig Griffith
Tara Henderson
Luke Herstedt
Gary Tevix Iber
Mark David Mandell
Michael L. Mandell
Sean Maxwell
Peter McQuillan
Ian Morris
Patricia Olver
Titina Koliva Paxinos
Amber Reeves

Hannah Sheldon
Holly Smith
Mary Turzillo
Robert Vitas
Khen Van Vuu
Anderson Wilder
Arill Wiltker

ABOUT THE AUTHORS

Kevin J. Anderson has published more than 180 books, 58 of which have been national or international bestsellers. He has 24 million copies in print in 34 languages.

He has written numerous novels in the Star Wars, X-Files, and Dune universes, as well as the unique Clockwork Angels steampunk trilogy with legendary Rush drummer Neil Peart. His original works include the Saga of Seven Suns series, the Wake the Dragon and Terra Incognita fantasy trilogies, the humorous Dan Shamble, Zombie P.I. series and The Dragon Business series.

He has edited numerous anthologies, written comics and games, and the lyrics to two rock CDs as companions to his Terra Incognita trilogy.

Anderson is the director of the graduate program in Publishing at Western Colorado University, and he and his wife Rebecca Moesta are the publishers of WordFire Press.

He worked on the recent films *Dune Part One* and *Dune Part Two* from Legendary Entertainment, as well as the forthcoming Dune TV series from MAX, and other films in development, including *Persephone* and *Karousel*.

His most recent novels are *Bats in the Belfry*, *Skeleton in the Closet*, *Persephone*, and *Princess of Dune* (with Brian Herbert).

Jeffrey Morris is a writer, director, and production designer focused primarily on the creation of hard science-fiction films. His projects include the forthcoming deep-space adventure *Persephone* and the animated techno-fantasy *Parallel Man*. He also serves as the co-writer, narrator, and director of the new documentary *The Eagle Has Landed*, which explores the legendary spacecraft showcased in the classic sci-fi series *Space: 1999*.

Morris has directed short films, commercials, music videos, and documentaries. Additionally, he has published graphic novels and award-winning science curricula. For nearly a decade, as founder of the former nonprofit Project Universe, Morris brought Hollywood-style storytelling and visuals to educational initiatives at NASA's Jet Propulsion Laboratory, Lockheed Martin, and the International Space University.

As a lifelong science-fiction enthusiast, Morris has built a career that unifies his interests in futurism, art, education, and entrepreneurship. His role models include undersea explorer Jacques Cousteau, astronomer Carl Sagan, TV creator Gene Roddenberry, and futurist film designer Syd Mead. Early in his career, Morris worked with the musician Prince as a dancer/choreographer and eventually moved on to directing and producing for Paisley Park Studios.

Jeffrey established the "FutureDude" monicker in 2012. It began as the name of his highly successful science blog which morphed into the dba for his production company, Morris FutureWorks. Today, FutureDude Entertainment is focused on an approach that is rooted in intelligent, optimistic action and adventure stories—each with a sensibility not seen since the golden age of science-fiction cinema in the 1960s and 70s.

Visit futuredude.com for more details.